VIRGIL

created by
STEVE ORLANDO
J.D. FAITH

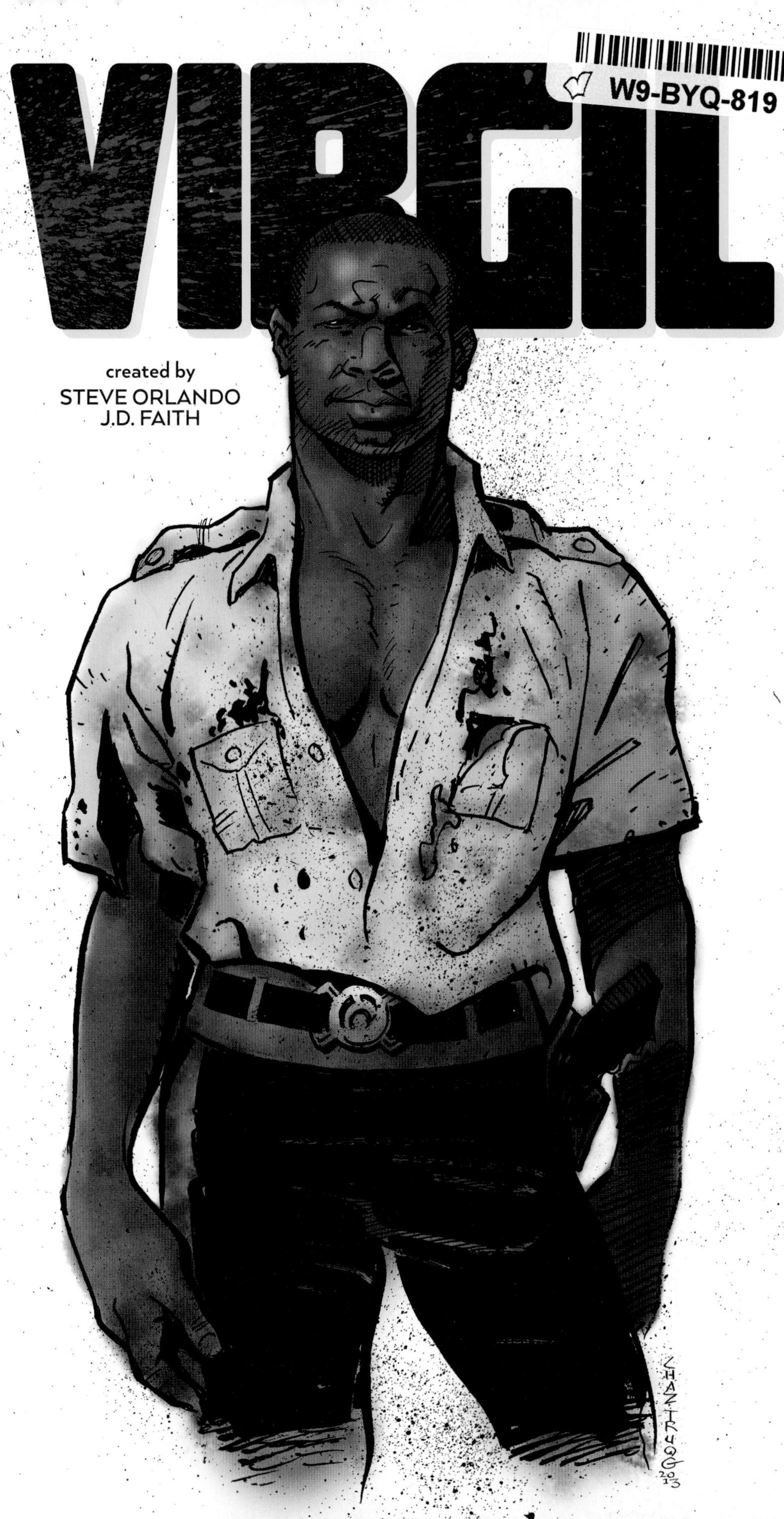
CHAZ TRUOG 2013

Image Comics, Inc.

Robert Kirkman — Chief Operating Officer
Erik Larsen — Chief Financial Officer
Todd McFarlane — President
Marc Silvestri — Chief Executive Officer
Jim Valentino — Vice President

Eric Stephenson — Publisher
Corey Murphey — Director of Sales
Jeremy Sullivan — Director of Digital Sales
Kat Salazar — Director of PR & Marketing
Emily Miller — Director of Operations
Branwyn Bigglestone — Senior Accounts Manager
Sarah Mello — Accounts Manager
Drew Gill — Art Director
Jonathan Chan — Production Manager
Meredith Wallace — Print Manager
Randy Okamura — Marketing Production Designer
David Brothers — Branding Manager
Ally Power — Content Manager
Addison Duke — Production Artist
Vincent Kukua — Production Artist
Sasha Head — Production Artist
Tricia Ramos — Production Artist
Emilio Bautista — Sales Assistant
Chloe Ramos-Peterson — Administrative Assistant

www.imagecomics.com

VIRGIL
ISBN: 978-1-63215-439-2
First Printing

For information regarding the CPSIA on this
printed material call: 203-595-3636 and provide
reference #RICH-636393.

For international rights, contact:
foreignlicensing@imagecomics.com.

story
STEVE ORLANDO

art
J.D. FAITH

colors
CHRIS BECKETT

letters & design
THOMAS MAUER

cover art
ARTYOM TRAKHANOV

title page art
CHAZ TRUOG

Steve Orlando asked me to check out his graphic novel *Virgil* with little by way of description. He did, however, tell me that *Virgil* was "queersploitation"—although that particular bit of information struck me as some sort of disclaimer more than a description.

My mind immediately envisioned some kind of comic book version of Gregg Araki's *The Living End* crossed with a slightly less hardcore helping of a Joe Gage flick. And if that's all Steve and artist J.D. Faith managed to deliver with *Virgil*, I would've been happy. Don't get me wrong...because the book you hold in your hand is in fact, for lack of a better term, unabashed and unapologetic queersploitation. But to be clear, there is something more going on here—something that elevates *Virgil* above the enticing, yet simplified label that can be used to describe it.

At its heart and soul, *Virgil* is a good old-fashioned revenge fantasy, set against the backdrop of corruption and injustice in Jamaica. The setting of *Virgil* invites comparisons to director Perry Henzell's 1972 classic film *The Harder They Come*, starring Jimmy Cliff. Both take place in Jamaica, and both deal with one man settling scores with those who crossed him, and on these points alone, the comparisons are inevitable. However, the similarities between *Virgil* and *The Harder They Come* run much deeper, venturing into a realm where the seemingly salacious and exploitative rise above the trappings of sex and violence, and enter into the area of deeper meaning and resonance.

As a revenge thriller, *Virgil* serves its genre well, delivering the requisite levels of violence that have come to define similar tales told in other mediums. It's important to note that the success of this particular story doesn't come from the violence and vengeance (although those help), because violence in and of itself is not what makes a story work. At their core, the best revenge fantasies are driven by raw humanity. In order for these stories to work, we have to feel for the person who has been wronged. We must feel their loss and pain. We have to want to see them get their vengeance. This is what keeps us engaged.

Steve Orlando and J.D. Faith have taken the conventions of the revenge thriller, mixed them in with elements of queersploitation, and managed to deliver a graphic novel that is entertaining, relevant, and politicized. More than the sum of its parts, *Virgil* is a story of liberation and transformation, love and loss, corruption and redemption. It is, quite simply, a great graphic novel.

—David F. Walker (*Shaft, Cyborg*)

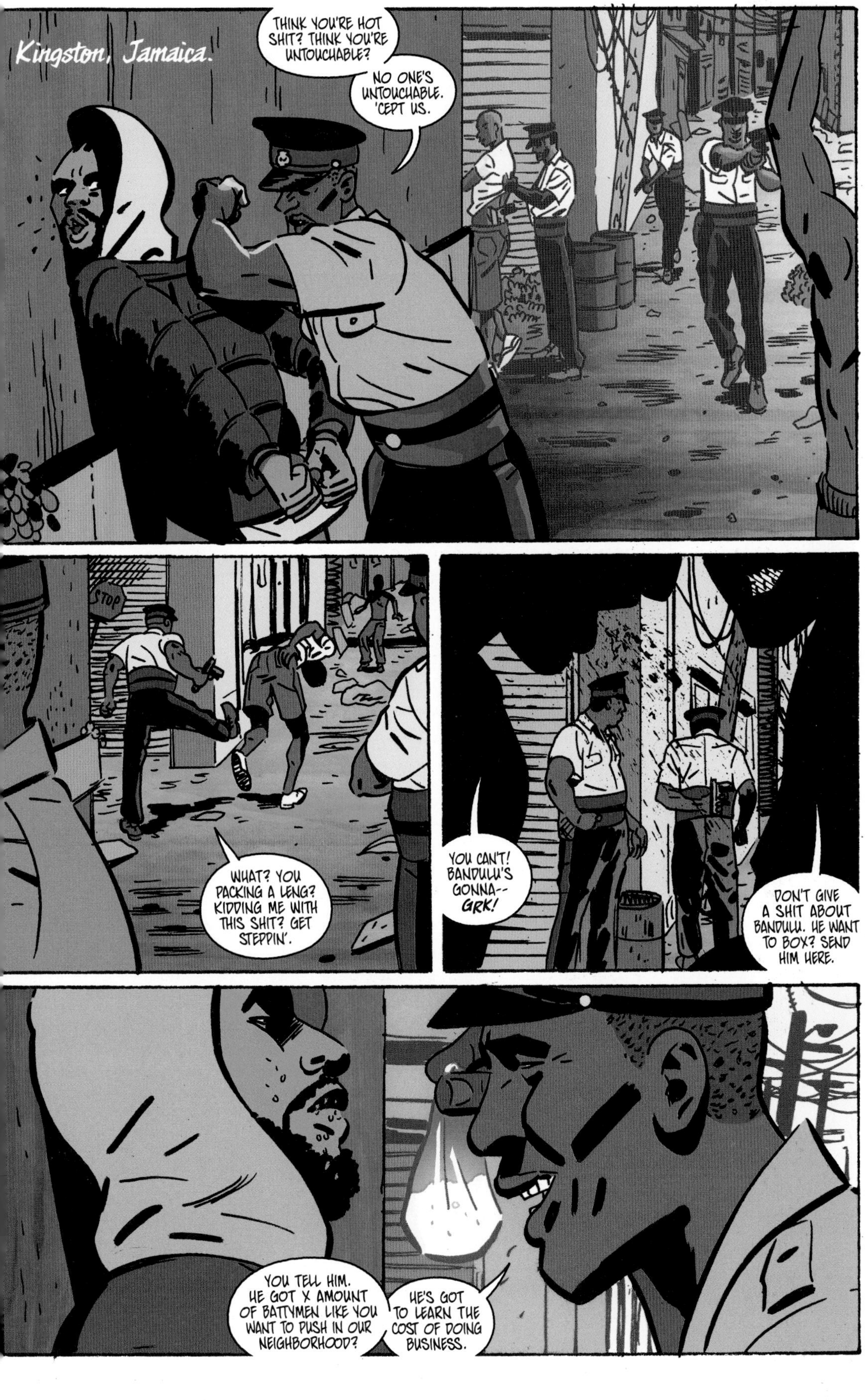
Kingston, Jamaica.
THINK YOU'RE HOT SHIT? THINK YOU'RE UNTOUCHABLE?
NO ONE'S UNTOUCHABLE. 'CEPT US.
WHAT? YOU PACKING A LENG? KIDDING ME WITH THIS SHIT? GET STEPPIN'.
STOP
YOU CAN'T! BANDULU'S GONNA-- GRK!
DON'T GIVE A SHIT ABOUT BANDULU. HE WANT TO BOX? SEND HIM HERE.
YOU TELL HIM. HE GOT X AMOUNT OF BATTYMEN LIKE YOU WANT TO PUSH IN OUR NEIGHBORHOOD?
HE'S GOT TO LEARN THE COST OF DOING BUSINESS.

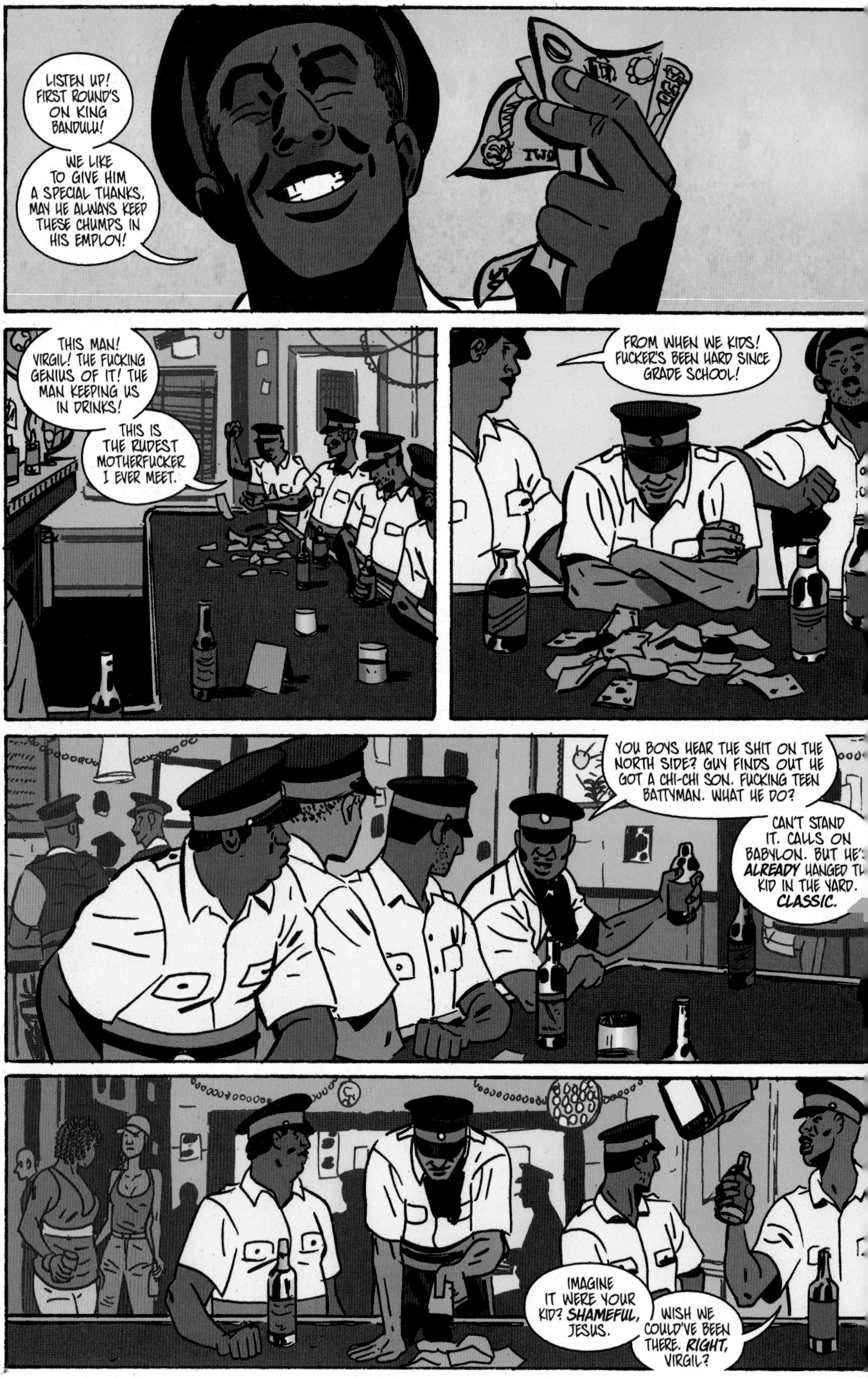
LISTEN UP! FIRST ROUND'S ON KING BANDULU!
WE LIKE TO GIVE HIM A SPECIAL THANKS, MAY HE ALWAYS KEEP THESE CHUMPS IN HIS EMPLOY!
THIS MAN! VIRGIL! THE FUCKING GENIUS OF IT! THE MAN KEEPING US IN DRINKS!
THIS IS THE RUDEST MOTHERFUCKER I EVER MEET.
FROM WHEN WE KIDS! FUCKER'S BEEN HARD SINCE GRADE SCHOOL!
YOU BOYS HEAR THE SHIT ON THE NORTH SIDE? GUY FINDS OUT HE GOT A CHI-CHI SON. FUCKING TEEN BATTYMAN. WHAT HE DO?
CAN'T STAND IT. CALLS ON BABYLON. BUT HE'S **ALREADY** HANGED THE KID IN THE YARD. **CLASSIC.**
IMAGINE IT WERE YOUR KID? **SHAMEFUL,** JESUS.
WISH WE COULD'VE BEEN THERE. **RIGHT,** VIRGIL?

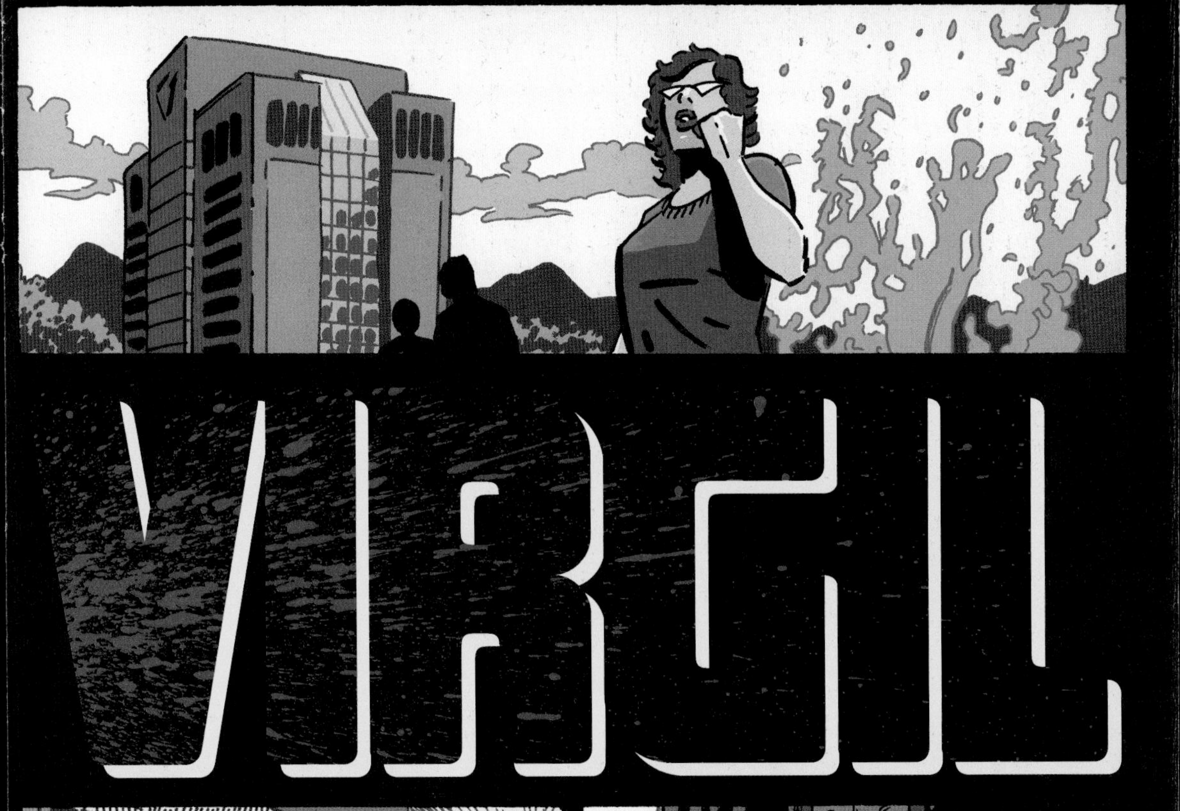

VIRGIL

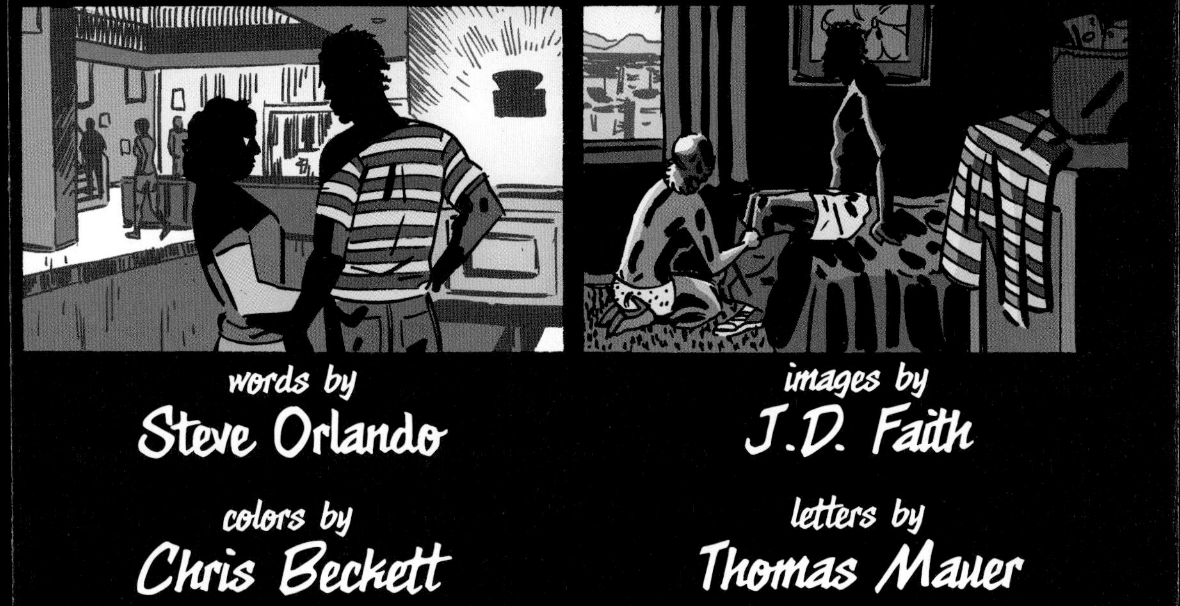

words by
Steve Orlando

images by
J.D. Faith

colors by
Chris Beckett

letters by
Thomas Mauer

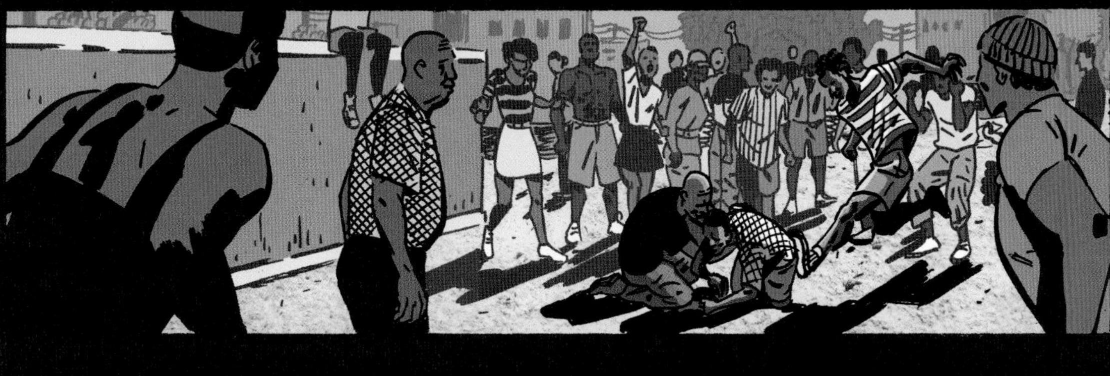

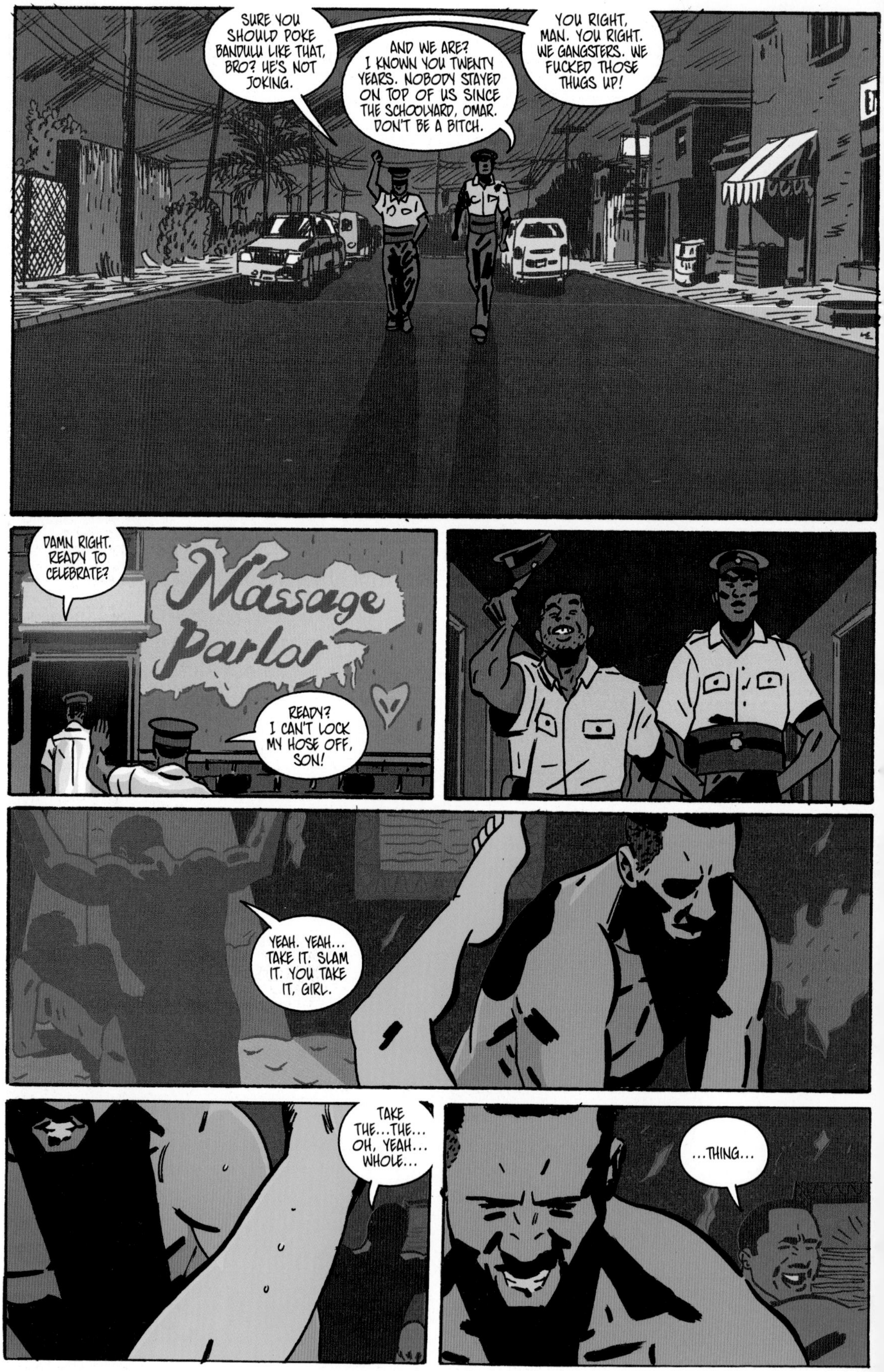
SURE YOU SHOULD POKE BANDULU LIKE THAT, BRO? HE'S NOT JOKING.
AND WE ARE? I KNOWN YOU TWENTY YEARS. NOBODY STAYED ON TOP OF US SINCE THE SCHOOLYARD, OMAR. DON'T BE A BITCH.
YOU RIGHT, MAN. YOU RIGHT. WE GANGSTERS. WE FUCKED THOSE THUGS UP!
DAMN RIGHT. READY TO CELEBRATE?
Massage parlor
READY? I CAN'T LOCK MY HOSE OFF, SON!
YEAH. YEAH... TAKE IT. SLAM IT. YOU TAKE IT, GIRL.
TAKE THE...THE... OH, YEAH... WHOLE...
...THING...

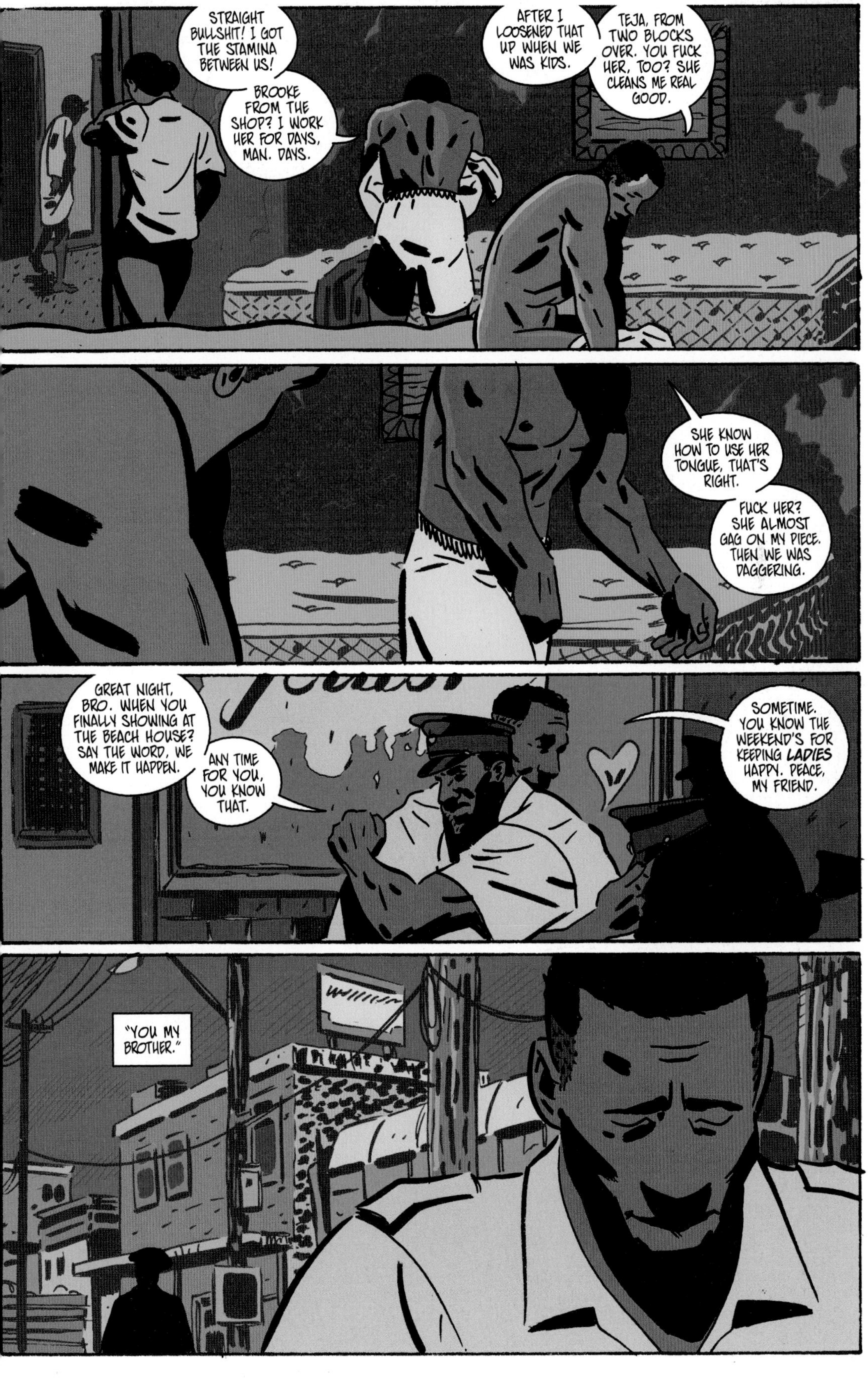
STRAIGHT BULLSHIT! I GOT THE STAMINA BETWEEN US!
BROOKE FROM THE SHOP? I WORK HER FOR DAYS, MAN. DAYS.
AFTER I LOOSENED THAT UP WHEN WE WAS KIDS.
TEJA, FROM TWO BLOCKS OVER. YOU FUCK HER, TOO? SHE CLEANS ME REAL GOOD.
SHE KNOW HOW TO USE HER TONGUE, THAT'S RIGHT.
FUCK HER? SHE ALMOST GAG ON MY PIECE. THEN WE WAS DAGGERING.
GREAT NIGHT, BRO. WHEN YOU FINALLY SHOWING AT THE BEACH HOUSE? SAY THE WORD, WE MAKE IT HAPPEN.
ANY TIME FOR YOU, YOU KNOW THAT.
SOMETIME. YOU KNOW THE WEEKEND'S FOR KEEPING LADIES HAPPY. PEACE, MY FRIEND.
"YOU MY BROTHER."

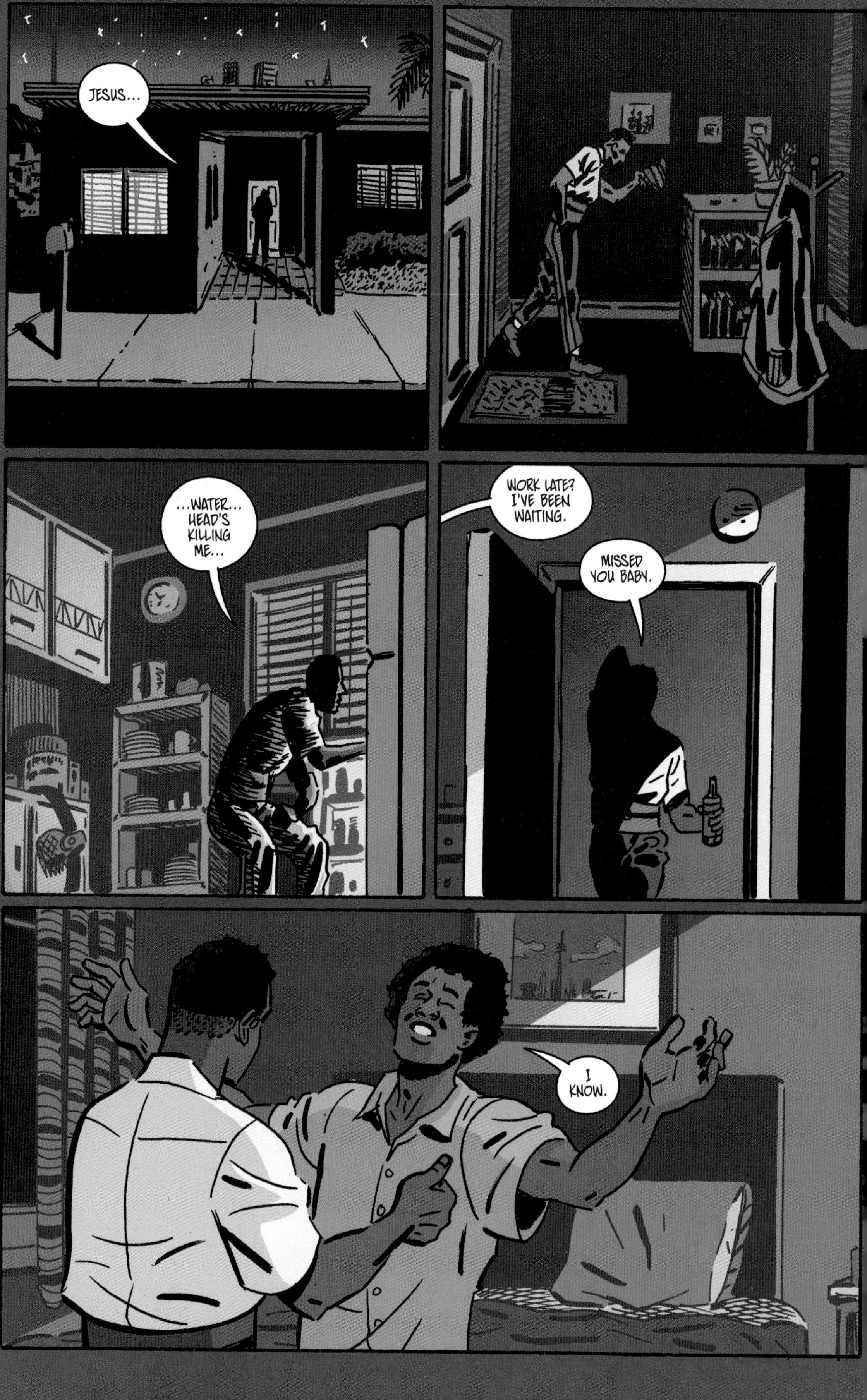

JESUS...
...WATER... HEAD'S KILLING ME...
WORK LATE? I'VE BEEN WAITING.
MISSED YOU BABY.
I KNOW.

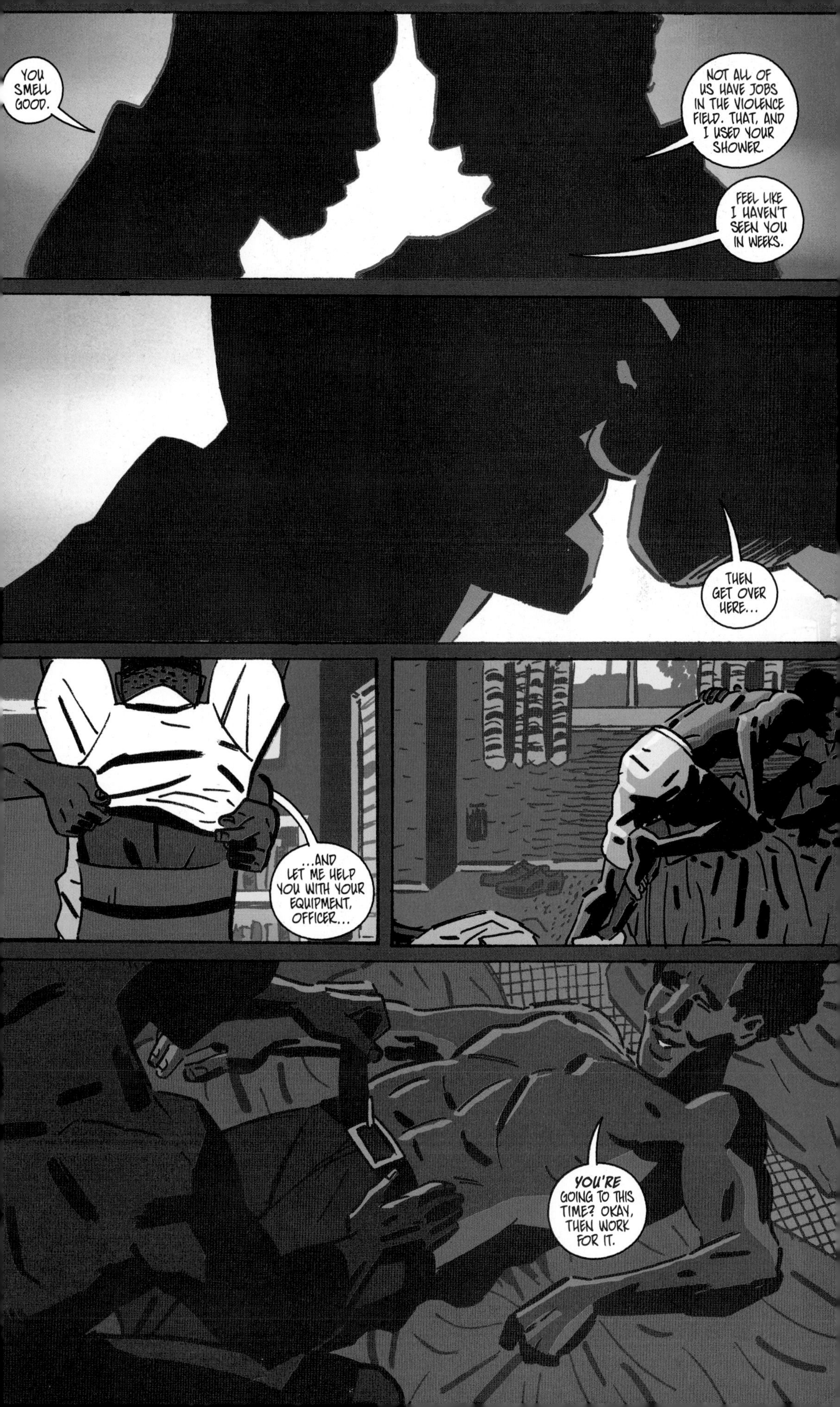
YOU SMELL GOOD.
NOT ALL OF US HAVE JOBS IN THE VIOLENCE FIELD. THAT, AND I USED YOUR SHOWER.
FEEL LIKE I HAVEN'T SEEN YOU IN WEEKS.
THEN GET OVER HERE...
...AND LET ME HELP YOU WITH YOUR EQUIPMENT, OFFICER...
YOU'RE GOING TO THIS TIME? OKAY, THEN WORK FOR IT.

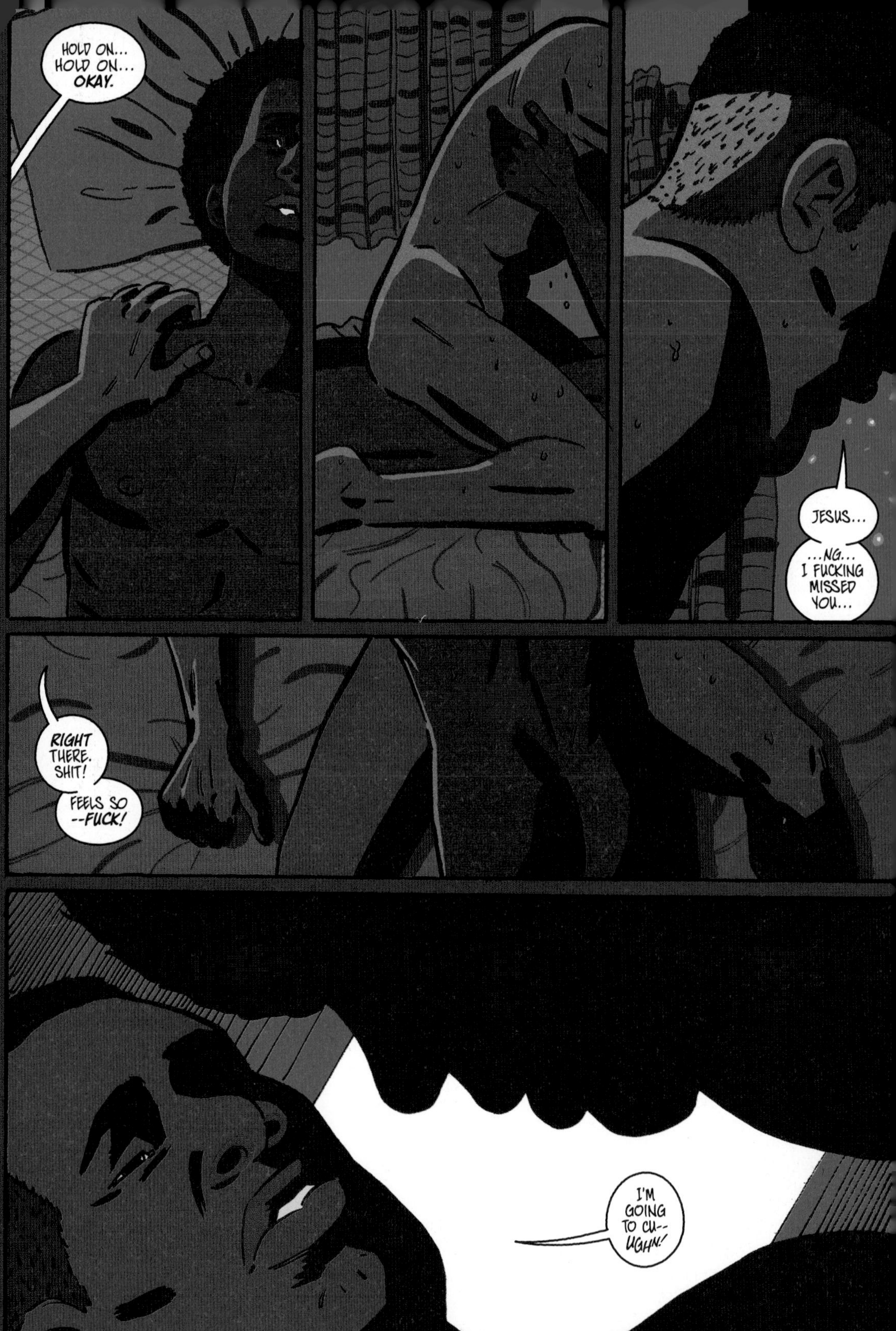
HOLD ON... HOLD ON... OKAY.
JESUS...
...NG... I FUCKING MISSED YOU...
RIGHT THERE. SHIT!
FEELS SO --FUCK!
I'M GOING TO CU-- UGHN!

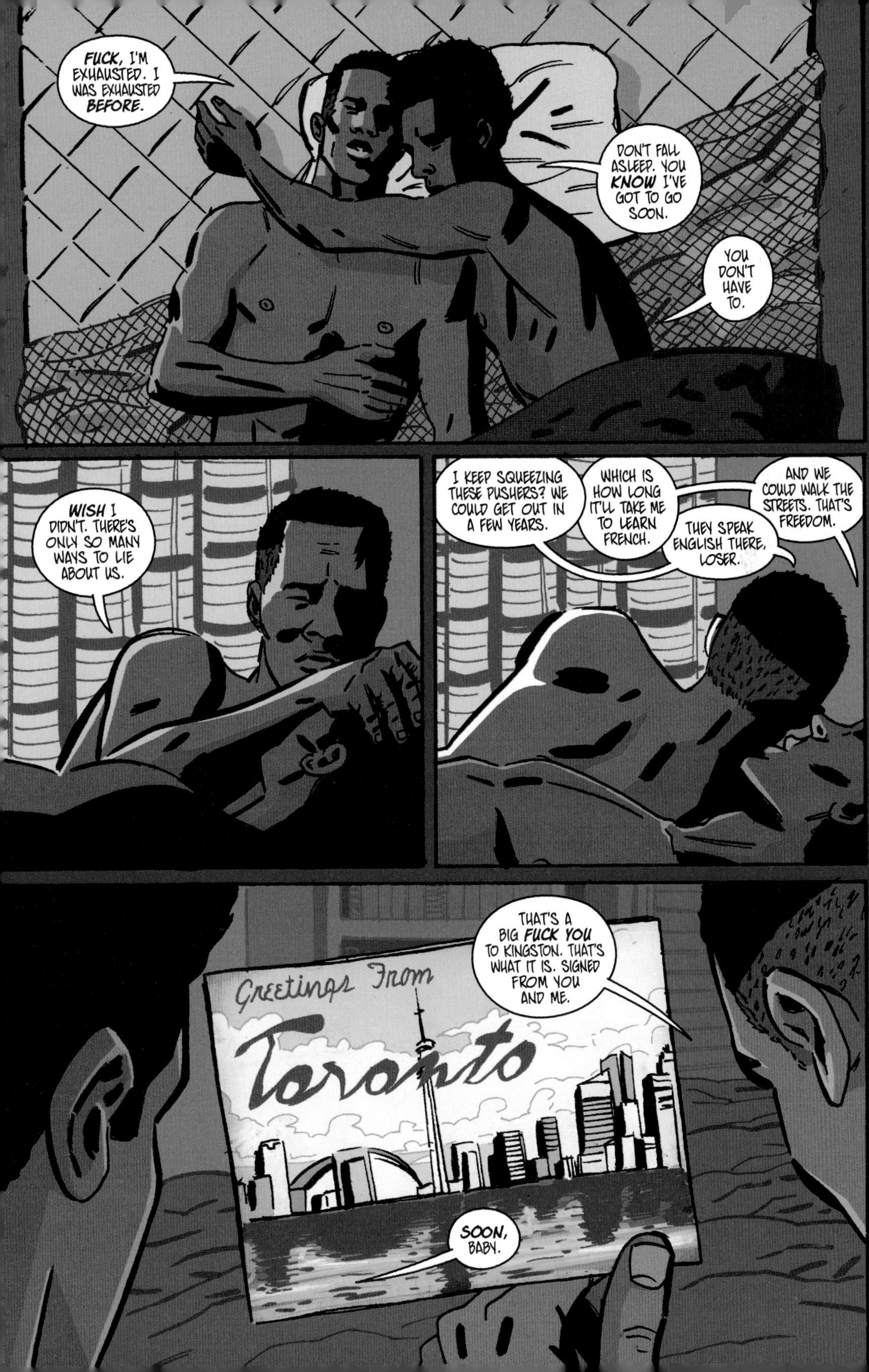
FUCK, I'M EXHAUSTED. I WAS EXHAUSTED BEFORE.
DON'T FALL ASLEEP. YOU KNOW I'VE GOT TO GO SOON.
YOU DON'T HAVE TO.
WISH I DIDN'T. THERE'S ONLY SO MANY WAYS TO LIE ABOUT US.
I KEEP SQUEEZING THESE PUSHERS? WE COULD GET OUT IN A FEW YEARS.
WHICH IS HOW LONG IT'LL TAKE ME TO LEARN FRENCH.
THEY SPEAK ENGLISH THERE, LOSER.
AND WE COULD WALK THE STREETS. THAT'S FREEDOM.
Greetings From
Toronto
THAT'S A BIG FUCK YOU TO KINGSTON. THAT'S WHAT IT IS. SIGNED FROM YOU AND ME.
SOON, BABY.

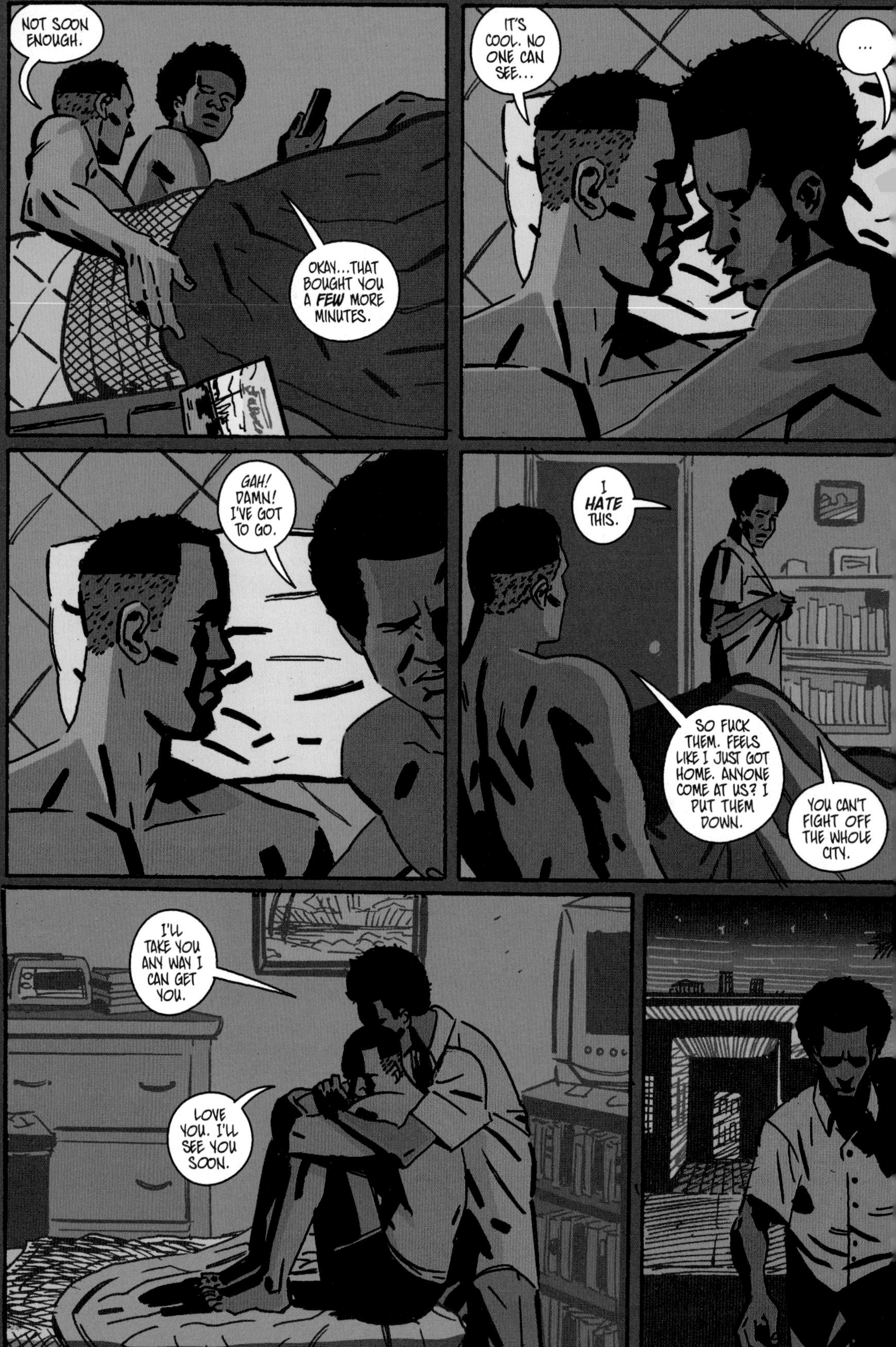
NOT SOON ENOUGH.
OKAY...THAT BOUGHT YOU A FEW MORE MINUTES.
IT'S COOL. NO ONE CAN SEE...
...
GAH! DAMN! I'VE GOT TO GO.
I HATE THIS.
SO FUCK THEM. FEELS LIKE I JUST GOT HOME. ANYONE COME AT US? I PUT THEM DOWN.
YOU CAN'T FIGHT OFF THE WHOLE CITY.
I'LL TAKE YOU ANY WAY I CAN GET YOU.
LOVE YOU. I'LL SEE YOU SOON.

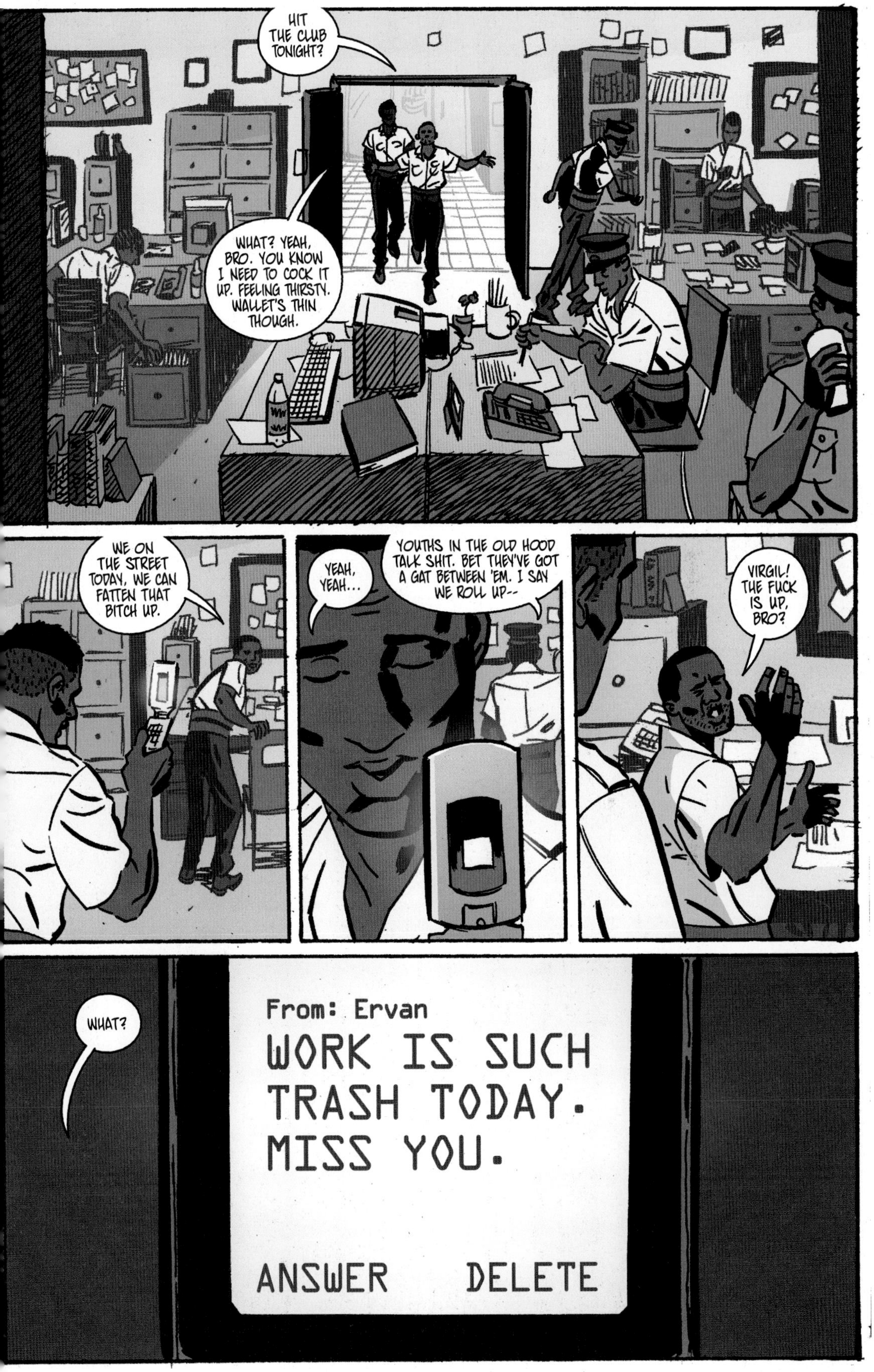
HIT THE CLUB TONIGHT?
WHAT? YEAH, BRO. YOU KNOW I NEED TO COCK IT UP. FEELING THIRSTY. WALLET'S THIN THOUGH.
WE ON THE STREET TODAY, WE CAN FATTEN THAT BITCH UP.
YEAH, YEAH...
YOUTHS IN THE OLD HOOD TALK SHIT. BET THEY'VE GOT A GAT BETWEEN 'EM. I SAY WE ROLL UP--
VIRGIL! THE FUCK IS UP, BRO?
WHAT?
From: Ervan
WORK IS SUCH TRASH TODAY. MISS YOU.
ANSWER DELETE

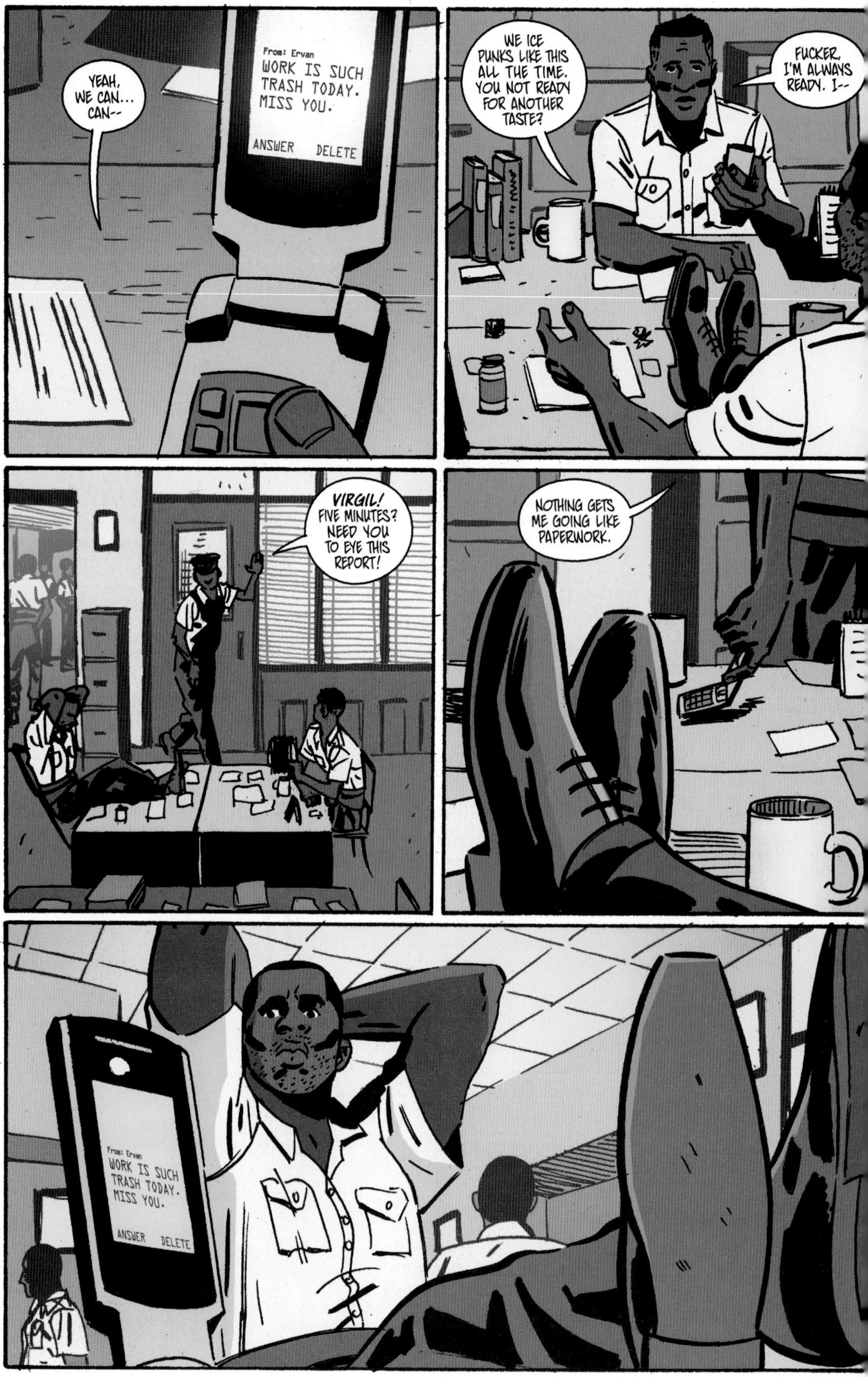
From: Ervan
WORK IS SUCH TRASH TODAY. MISS YOU.
ANSWER DELETE
YEAH, WE CAN... CAN--
WE ICE PUNKS LIKE THIS ALL THE TIME. YOU NOT READY FOR ANOTHER TASTE?
FUCKER, I'M ALWAYS READY. I--
VIRGIL! FIVE MINUTES? NEED YOU TO EYE THIS REPORT!
NOTHING GETS ME GOING LIKE PAPERWORK.
From: Ervan
WORK IS SUCH TRASH TODAY. MISS YOU.
ANSWER DELETE

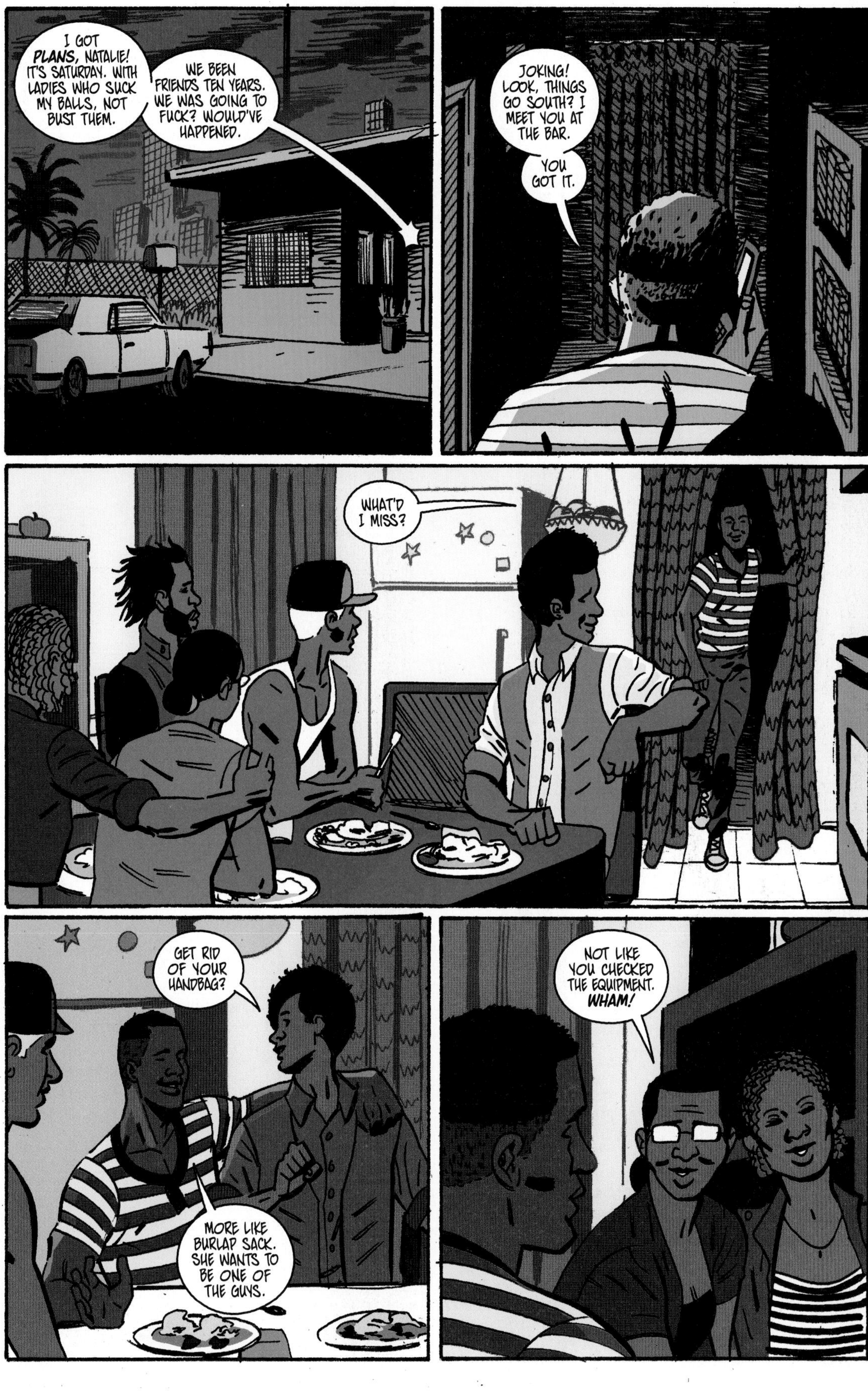
I GOT PLANS, NATALIE! IT'S SATURDAY. WITH LADIES WHO SUCK MY BALLS, NOT BUST THEM.
WE BEEN FRIENDS TEN YEARS. WE WAS GOING TO FUCK? WOULD'VE HAPPENED.
JOKING! LOOK, THINGS GO SOUTH? I MEET YOU AT THE BAR.
YOU GOT IT.
WHAT'D I MISS?
GET RID OF YOUR HANDBAG?
MORE LIKE BURLAP SACK. SHE WANTS TO BE ONE OF THE GUYS.
NOT LIKE YOU CHECKED THE EQUIPMENT. WHAM!

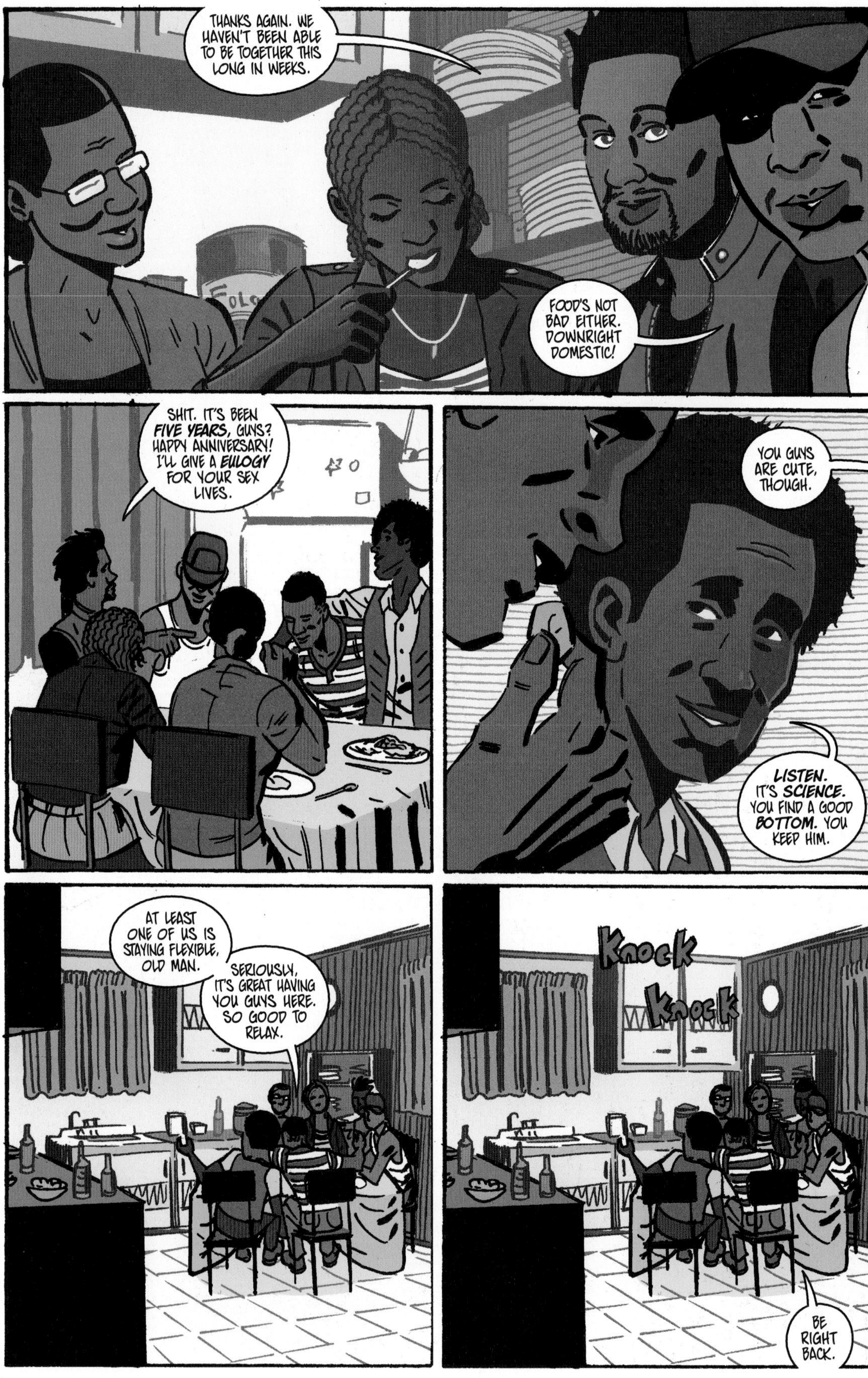
THANKS AGAIN. WE HAVEN'T BEEN ABLE TO BE TOGETHER THIS LONG IN WEEKS.
FOOD'S NOT BAD EITHER. DOWNRIGHT DOMESTIC!
SHIT. IT'S BEEN FIVE YEARS, GUYS? HAPPY ANNIVERSARY! I'LL GIVE A EULOGY FOR YOUR SEX LIVES.
YOU GUYS ARE CUTE, THOUGH.
LISTEN. IT'S SCIENCE. YOU FIND A GOOD BOTTOM. YOU KEEP HIM.
AT LEAST ONE OF US IS STAYING FLEXIBLE, OLD MAN.
SERIOUSLY, IT'S GREAT HAVING YOU GUYS HERE. SO GOOD TO RELAX.
KNOCK
KNOCK
BE RIGHT BACK.

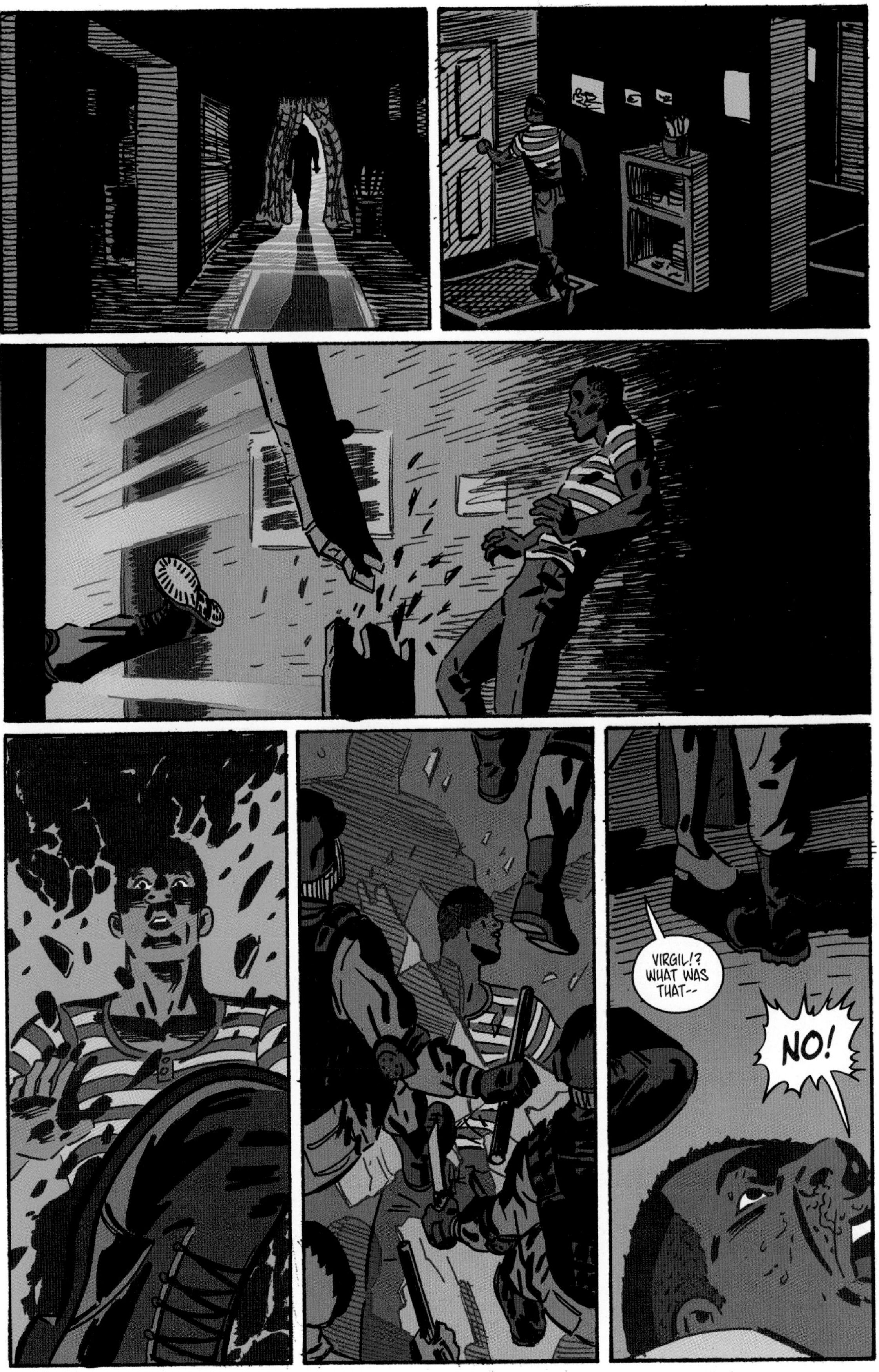
VIRGIL!? WHAT WAS THAT--
NO!

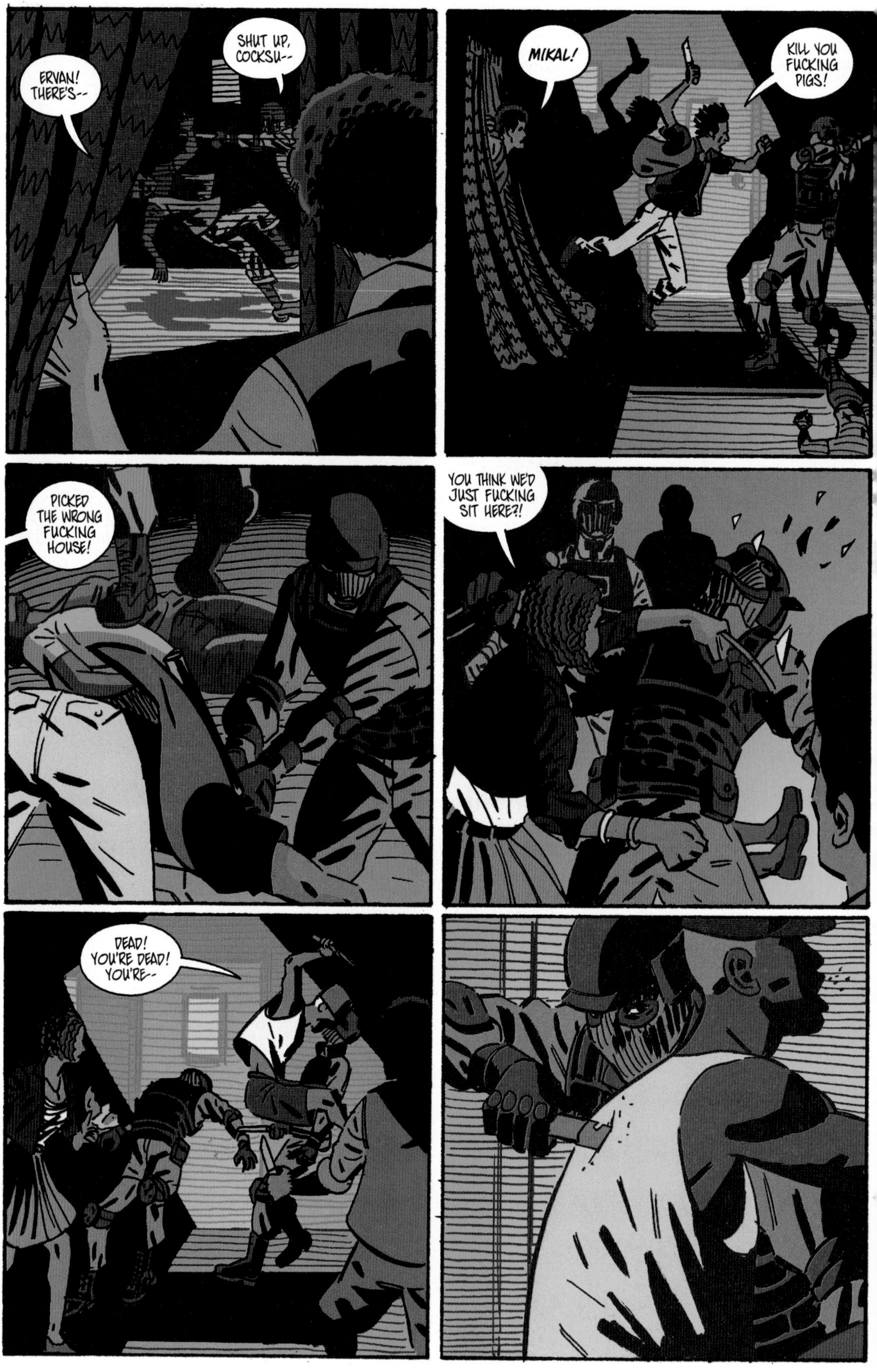
ERVAN! THERE'S--
SHUT UP, COCKSU--
MIKAL!
KILL YOU FUCKING PIGS!
PICKED THE WRONG FUCKING HOUSE!
YOU THINK WE'D JUST FUCKING SIT HERE?!
DEAD! YOU'RE DEAD! YOU'RE-

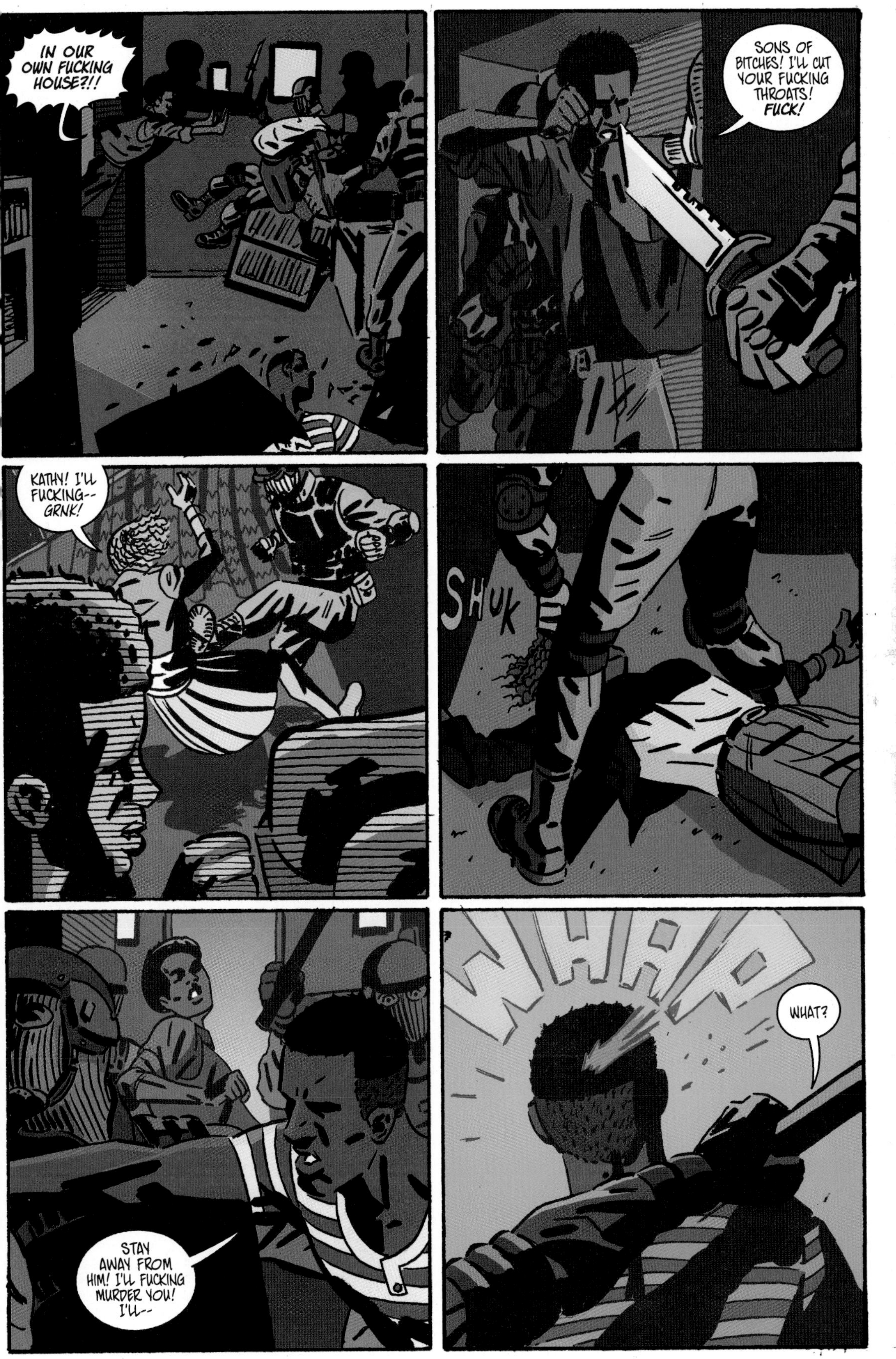
IN OUR OWN FUCKING HOUSE?!!
SONS OF BITCHES! I'LL CUT YOUR FUCKING THROATS! FUCK!
KATHY! I'LL FUCKING-- GRNK!
SHUK
STAY AWAY FROM HIM! I'LL FUCKING MURDER YOU! I'LL--
WHAP
WHAT?

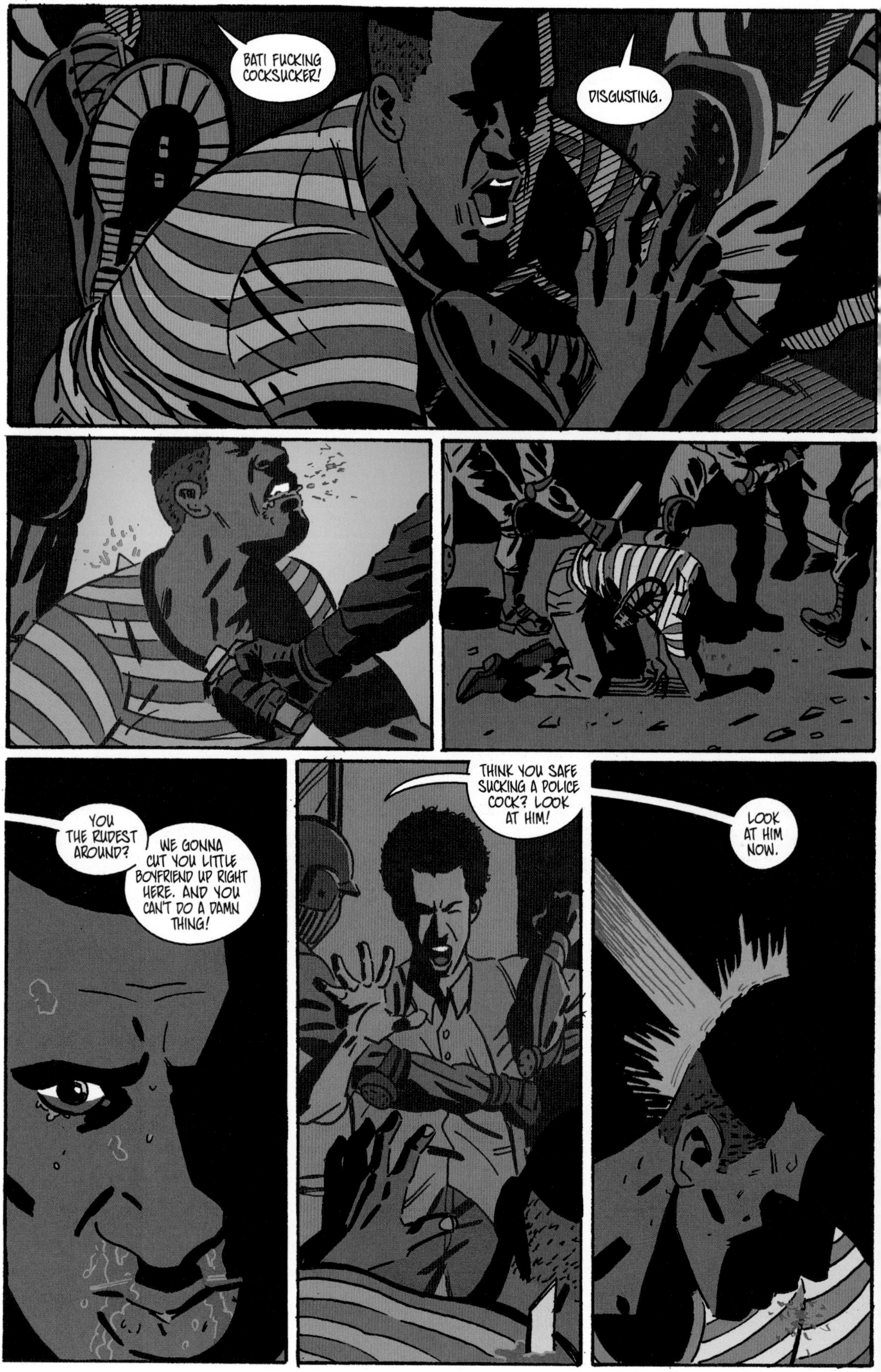
BATI FUCKING COCKSUCKER!
DISGUSTING.
YOU THE RUDEST AROUND?
WE GONNA CUT YOU LITTLE BOYFRIEND UP RIGHT HERE. AND YOU CAN'T DO A DAMN THING!
THINK YOU SAFE SUCKING A POLICE COCK? LOOK AT HIM!
LOOK AT HIM NOW.

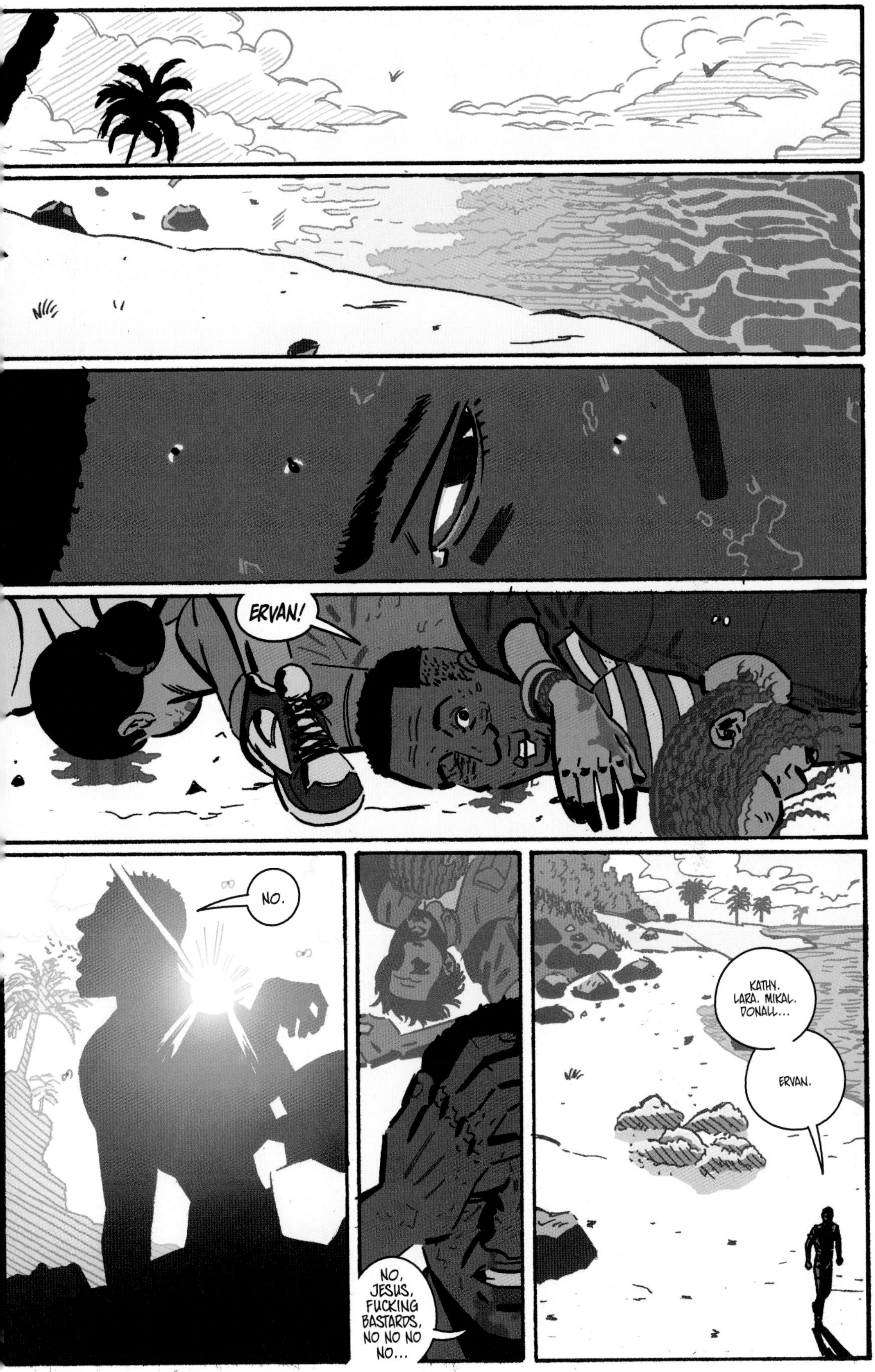
ERVAN!
NO.
NO, JESUS, FUCKING BASTARDS, NO NO NO NO...
KATHY. LARA. MIKAL. DONALL...
ERVAN.

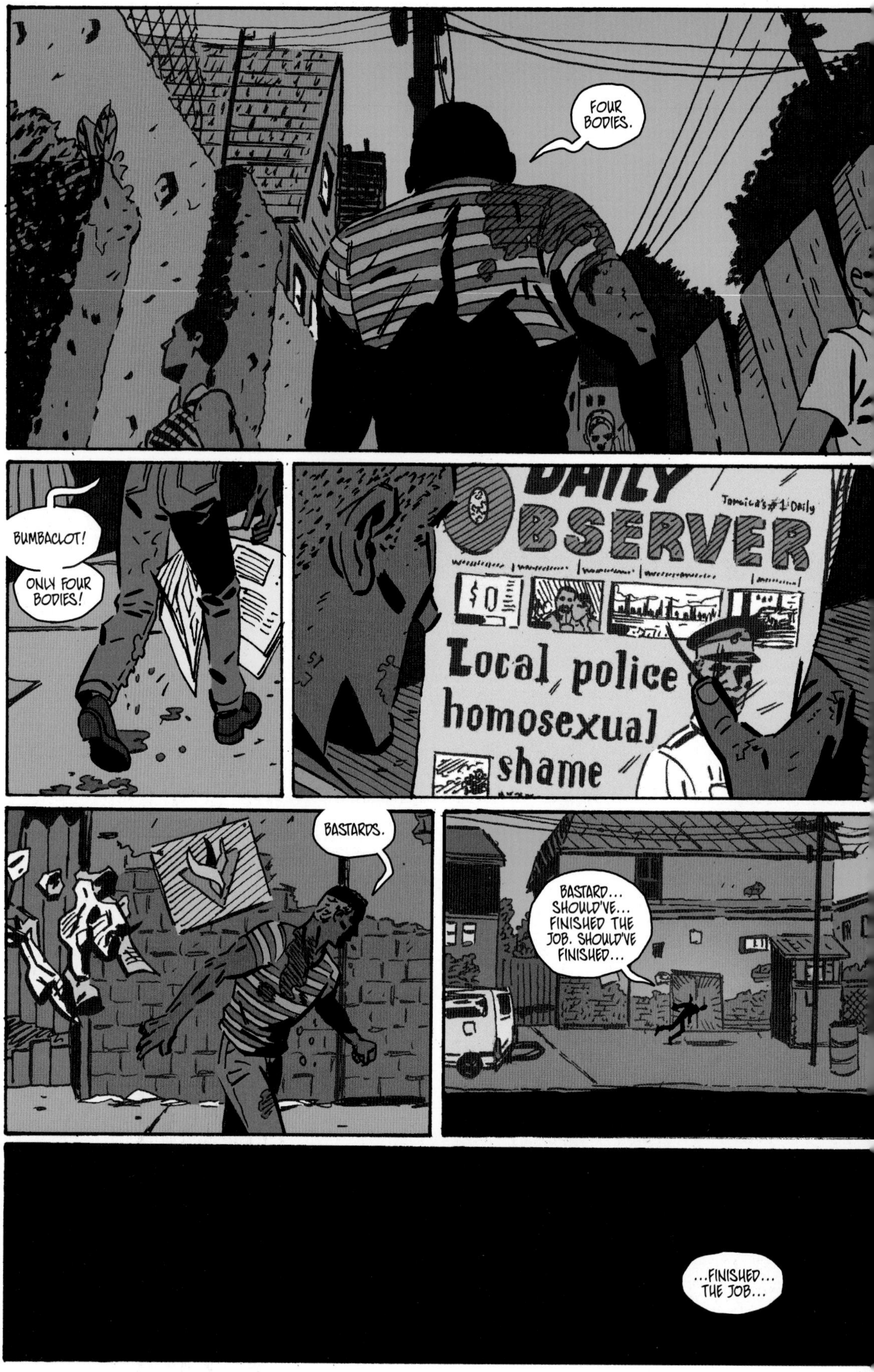
FOUR BODIES.
BUMBACLOT!
ONLY FOUR BODIES!
DAILY OBSERVER
Jamaica's #1 Daily
Local police homosexual shame
BASTARDS.
BASTARD... SHOULD'VE... FINISHED THE JOB. SHOULD'VE FINISHED...
...FINISHED... THE JOB...

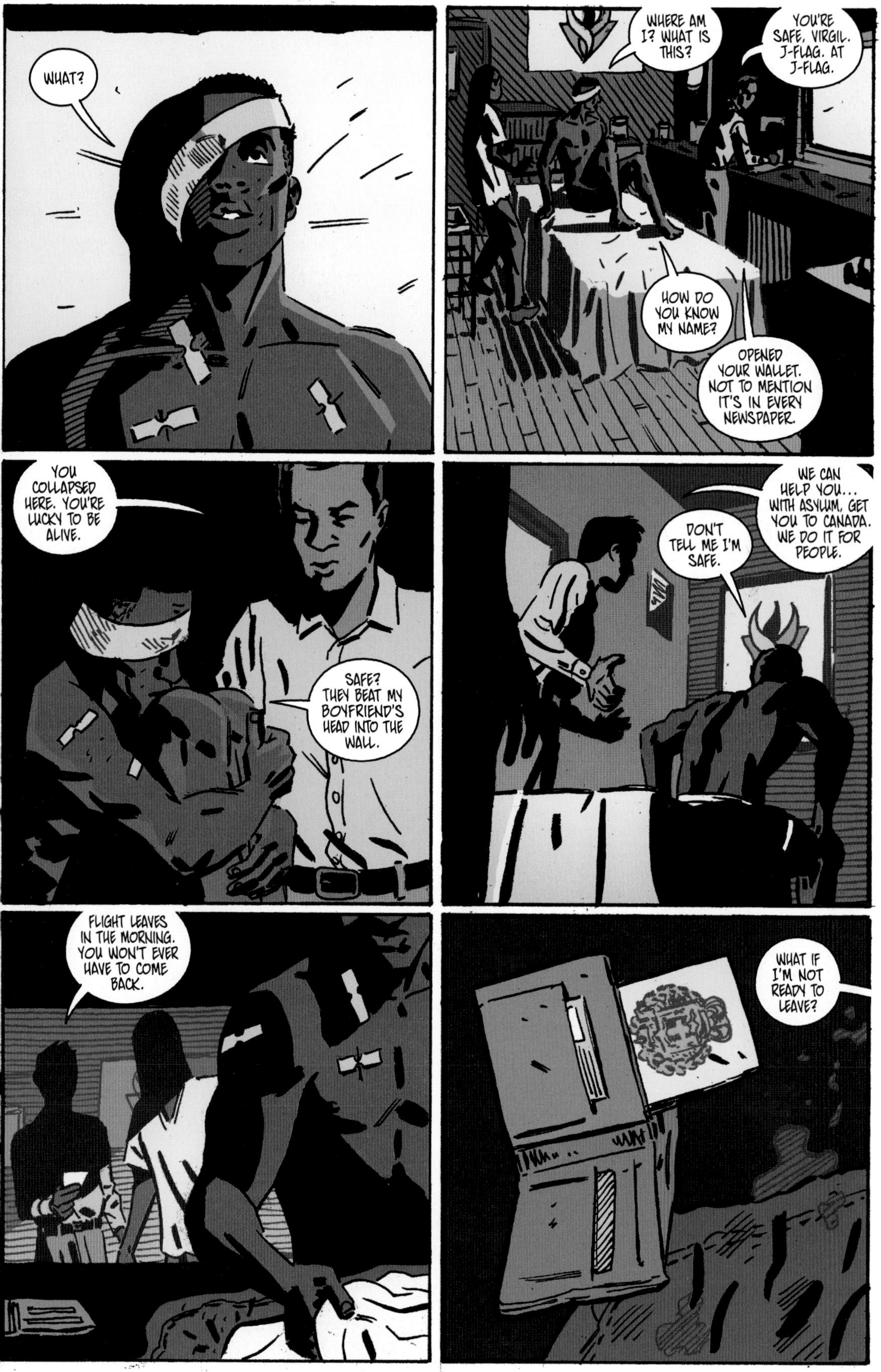
WHAT?
WHERE AM I? WHAT IS THIS?
YOU'RE SAFE, VIRGIL. J-FLAG. AT J-FLAG.
HOW DO YOU KNOW MY NAME?
OPENED YOUR WALLET. NOT TO MENTION IT'S IN EVERY NEWSPAPER.
YOU COLLAPSED HERE. YOU'RE LUCKY TO BE ALIVE.
SAFE? THEY BEAT MY BOYFRIEND'S HEAD INTO THE WALL.
WE CAN HELP YOU... WITH ASYLUM, GET YOU TO CANADA. WE DO IT FOR PEOPLE.
DON'T TELL ME I'M SAFE.
FLIGHT LEAVES IN THE MORNING. YOU WON'T EVER HAVE TO COME BACK.
WHAT IF I'M NOT READY TO LEAVE?

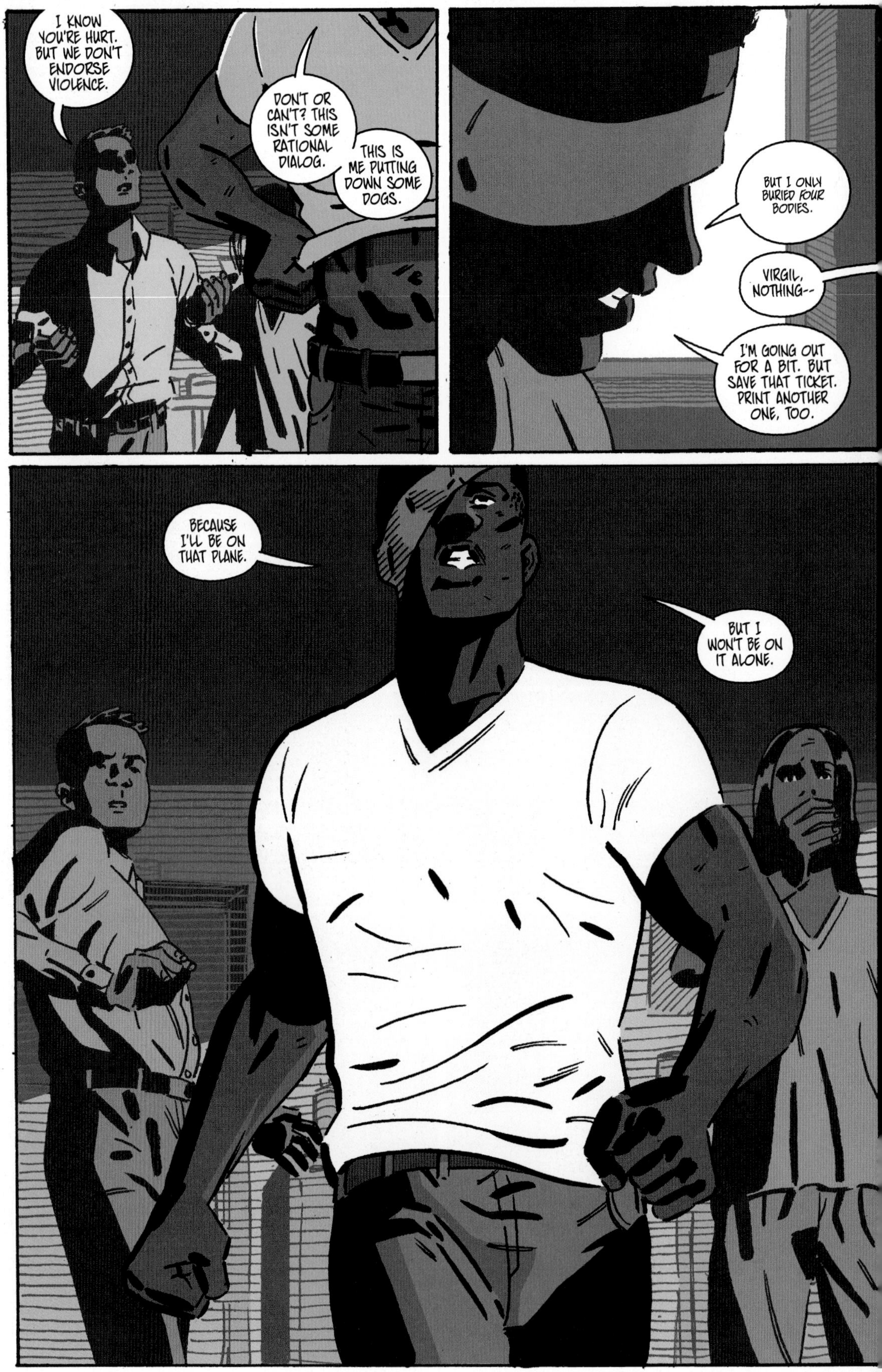
I KNOW YOU'RE HURT. BUT WE DON'T ENDORSE VIOLENCE.
DON'T OR CAN'T? THIS ISN'T SOME RATIONAL DIALOG.
THIS IS ME PUTTING DOWN SOME DOGS.
BUT I ONLY BURIED FOUR BODIES.
VIRGIL, NOTHING--
I'M GOING OUT FOR A BIT. BUT SAVE THAT TICKET. PRINT ANOTHER ONE, TOO.
BECAUSE I'LL BE ON THAT PLANE.
BUT I WON'T BE ON IT ALONE.

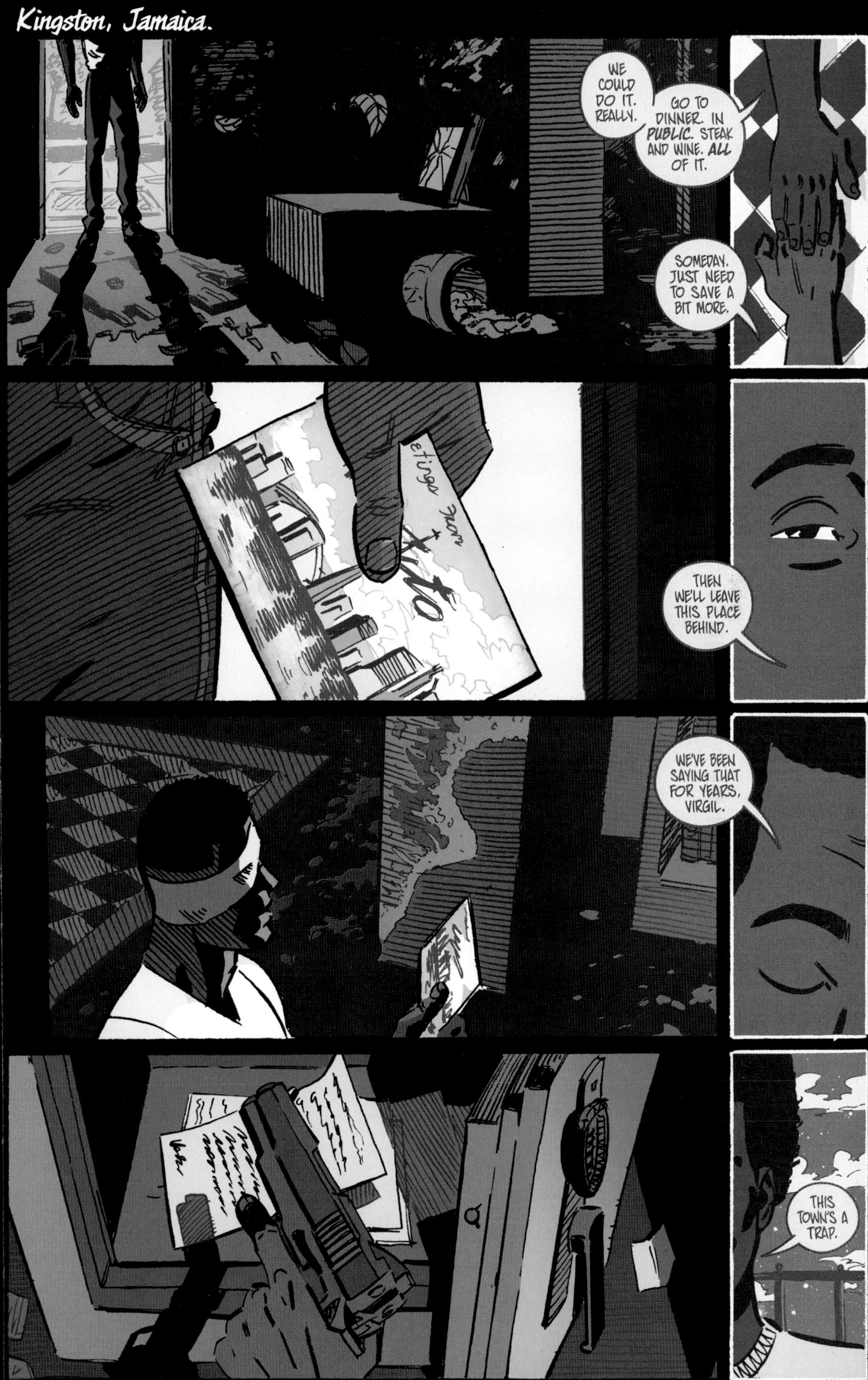
Kingston, Jamaica.
WE COULD DO IT. REALLY.
GO TO DINNER. IN PUBLIC. STEAK AND WINE. ALL OF IT.
SOMEDAY. JUST NEED TO SAVE A BIT MORE.
THEN WE'LL LEAVE THIS PLACE BEHIND.
WE'VE BEEN SAYING THAT FOR YEARS, VIRGIL.
THIS TOWN'S A TRAP.

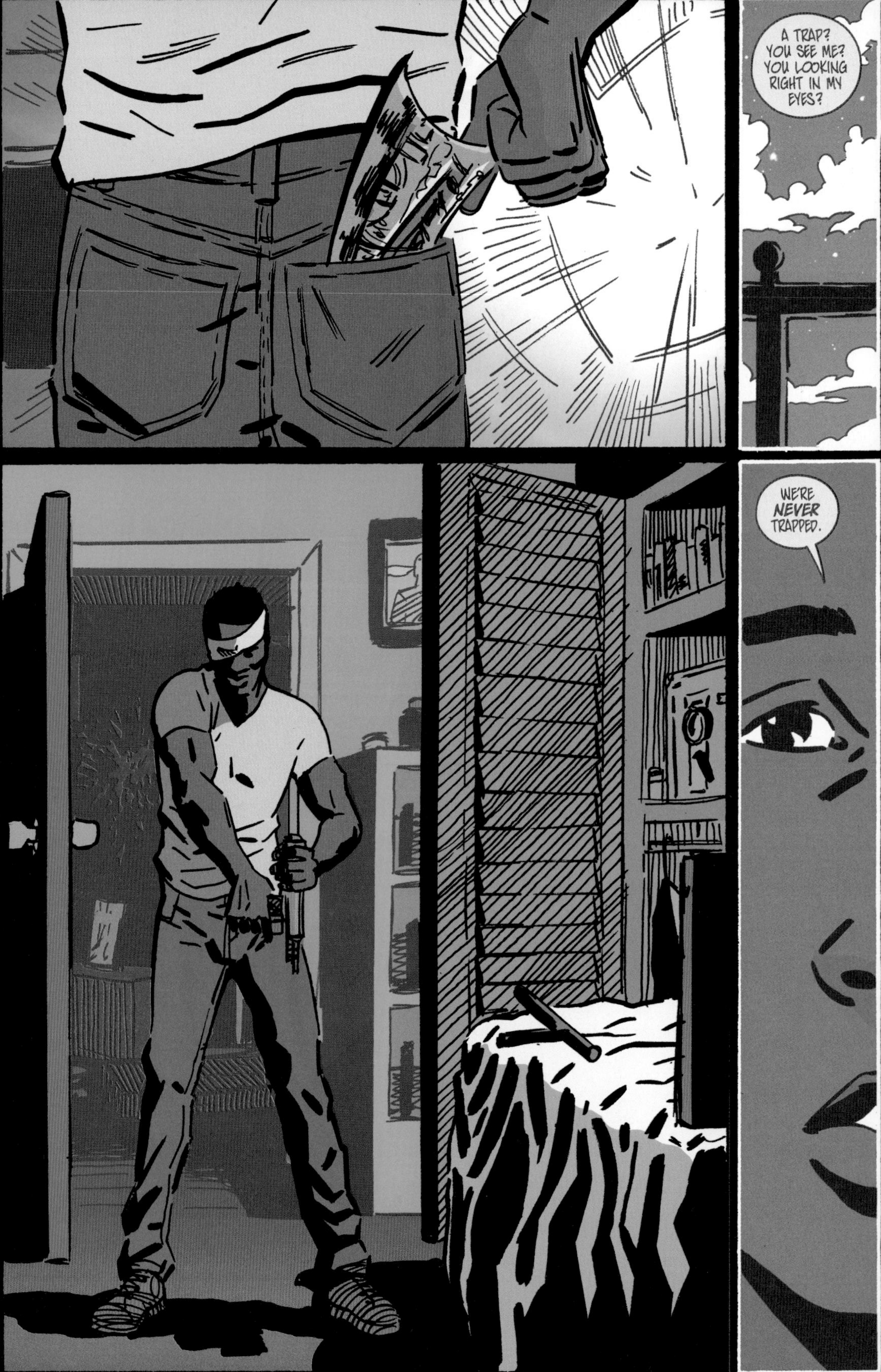
A TRAP? YOU SEE ME? YOU LOOKING RIGHT IN MY EYES?
WE'RE *NEVER* TRAPPED.

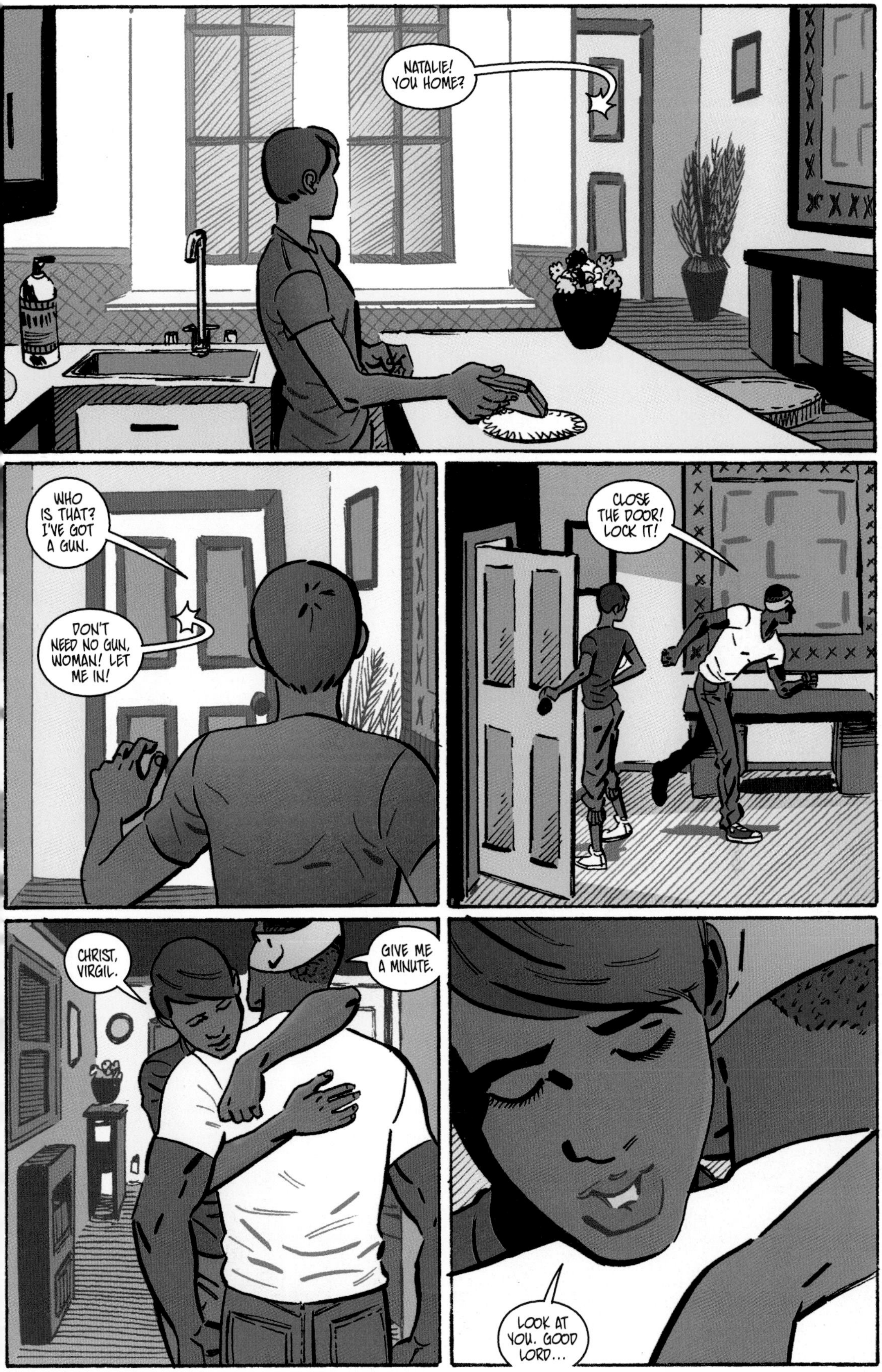
NATALIE! YOU HOME?
WHO IS THAT? I'VE GOT A GUN.
DON'T NEED NO GUN, WOMAN! LET ME IN!
CLOSE THE DOOR! LOCK IT!
CHRIST, VIRGIL.
GIVE ME A MINUTE.
LOOK AT YOU. GOOD LORD...

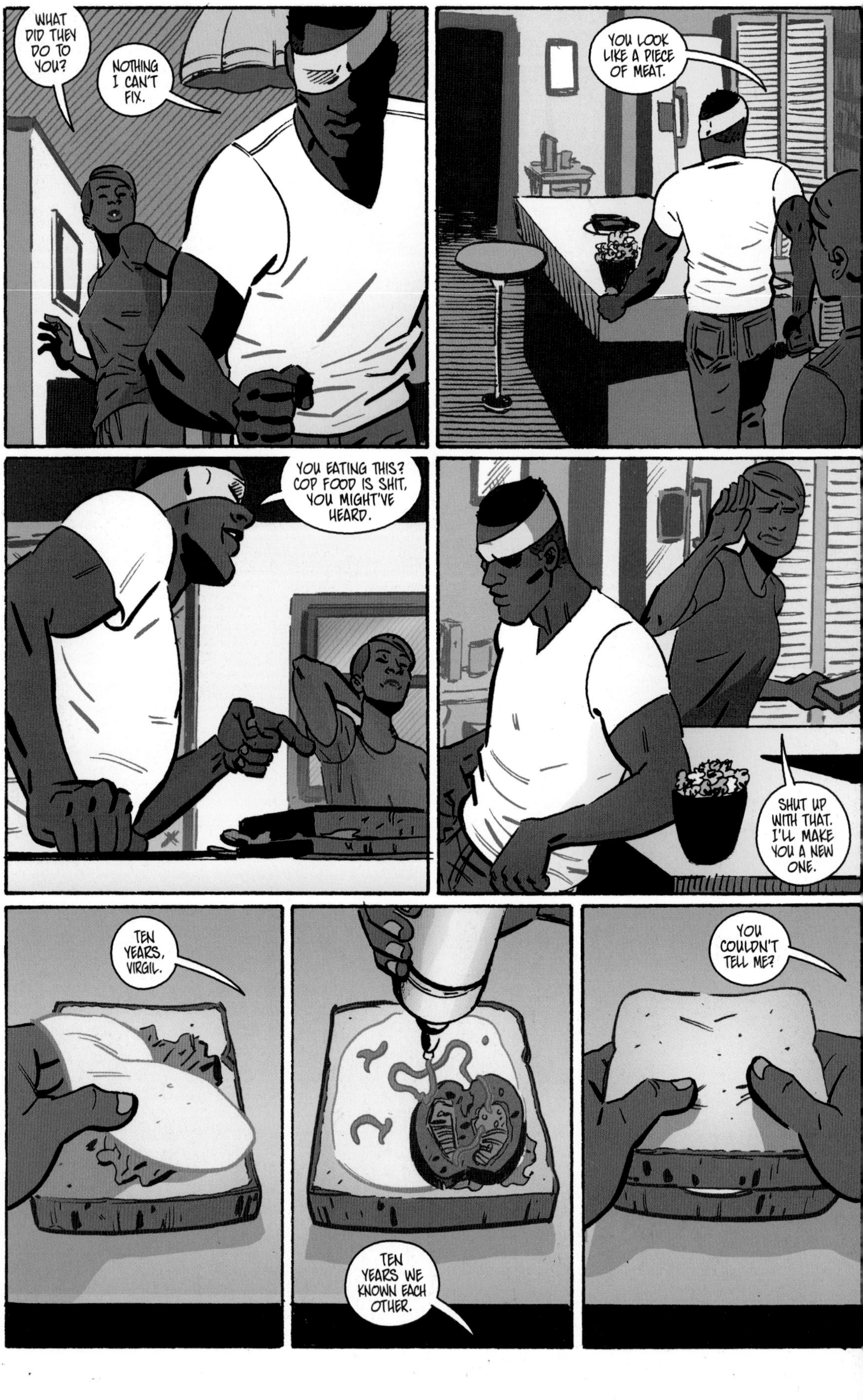
WHAT DID THEY DO TO YOU?
NOTHING I CAN'T FIX.
YOU LOOK LIKE A PIECE OF MEAT.
YOU EATING THIS? COP FOOD IS SHIT, YOU MIGHT'VE HEARD.
SHUT UP WITH THAT. I'LL MAKE YOU A NEW ONE.
TEN YEARS, VIRGIL.
TEN YEARS WE KNOWN EACH OTHER.
YOU COULDN'T TELL ME?

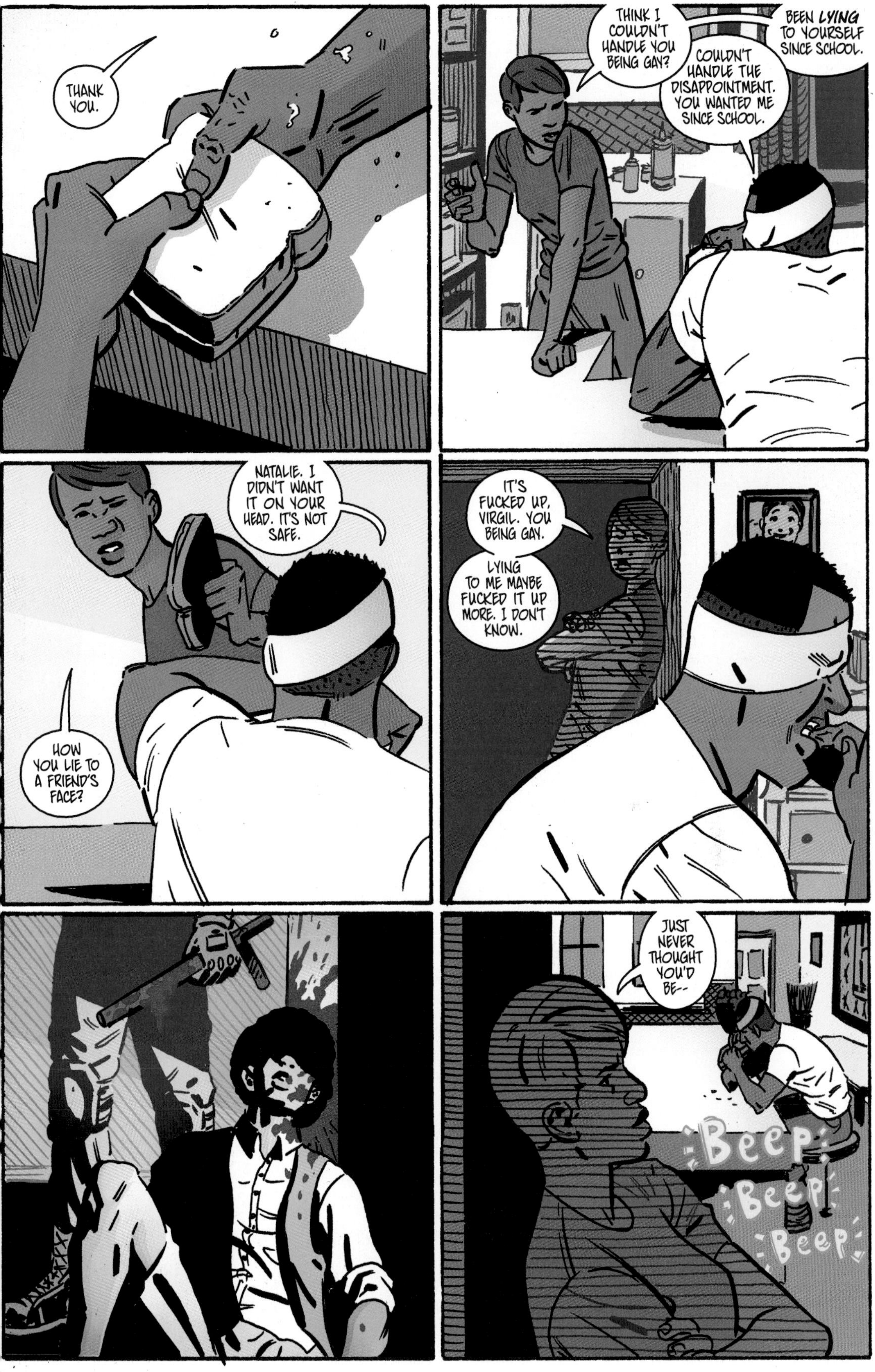
THANK YOU.
THINK I COULDN'T HANDLE YOU BEING GAY?
COULDN'T HANDLE THE DISAPPOINTMENT. YOU WANTED ME SINCE SCHOOL.
BEEN LYING TO YOURSELF SINCE SCHOOL.
NATALIE. I DIDN'T WANT IT ON YOUR HEAD. IT'S NOT SAFE.
HOW YOU LIE TO A FRIEND'S FACE?
IT'S FUCKED UP, VIRGIL. YOU BEING GAY.
LYING TO ME MAYBE FUCKED IT UP MORE. I DON'T KNOW.
JUST NEVER THOUGHT YOU'D BE-
Beep
Beep
Beep

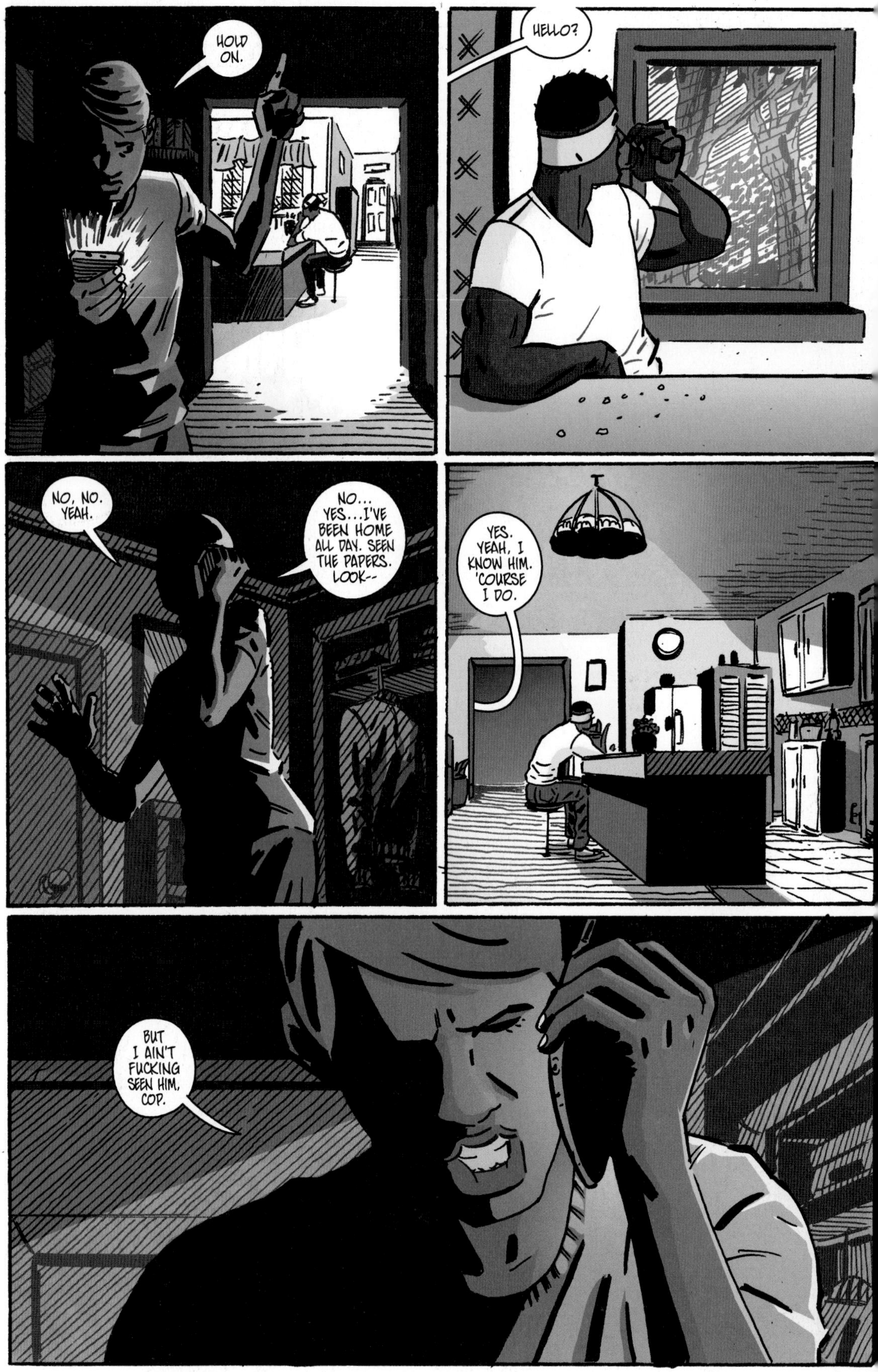
HOLD ON.
HELLO?
NO, NO. YEAH.
NO... YES...I'VE BEEN HOME ALL DAY. SEEN THE PAPERS. LOOK--
YES. YEAH, I KNOW HIM. 'COURSE I DO.
BUT I AIN'T FUCKING SEEN HIM, COP.

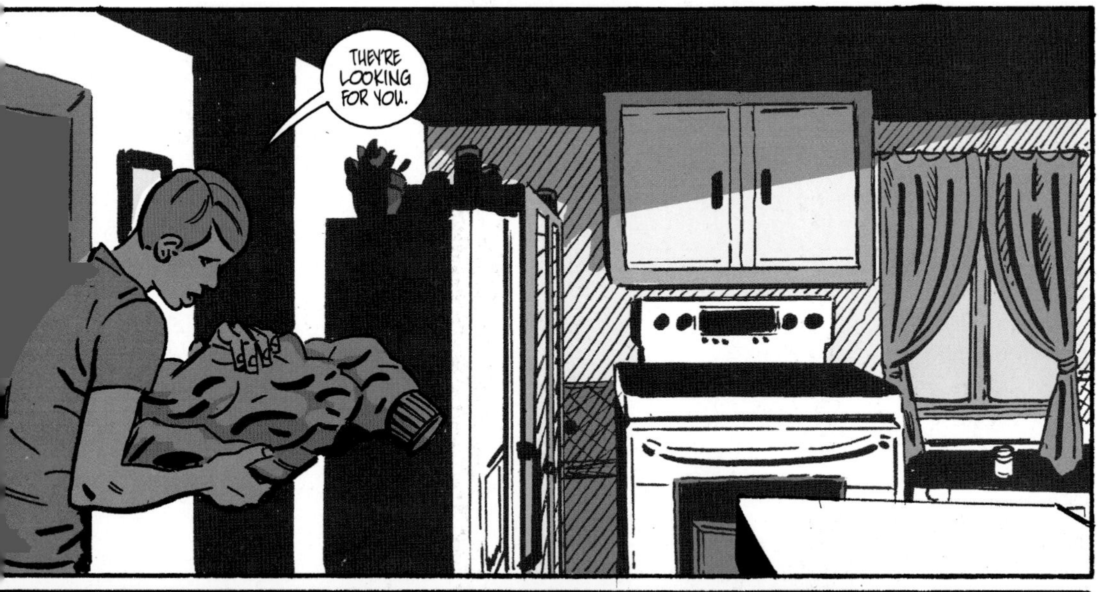
THEY'RE LOOKING FOR YOU.

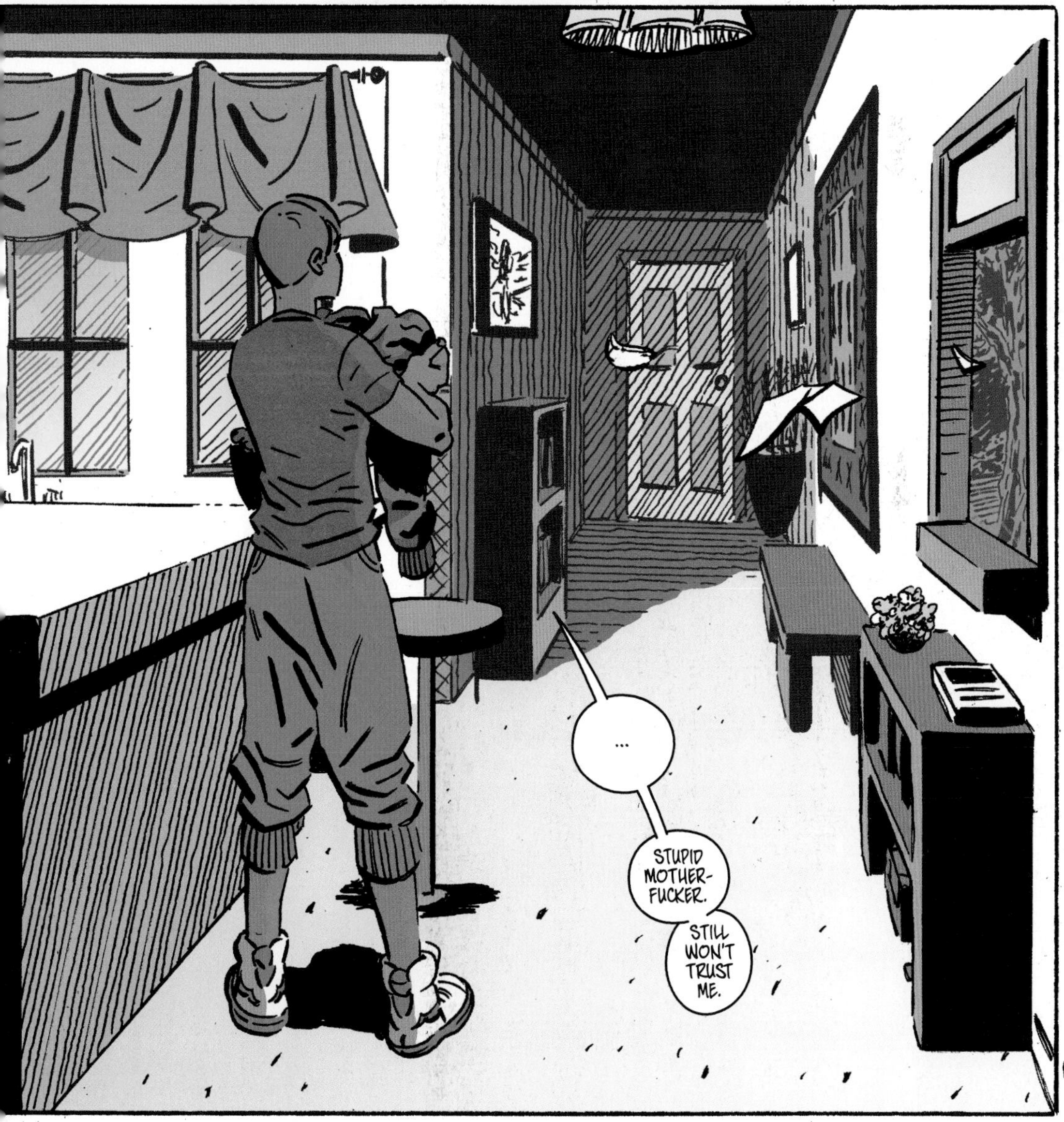
...
STUPID MOTHER-FUCKER.
STILL WON'T TRUST ME.

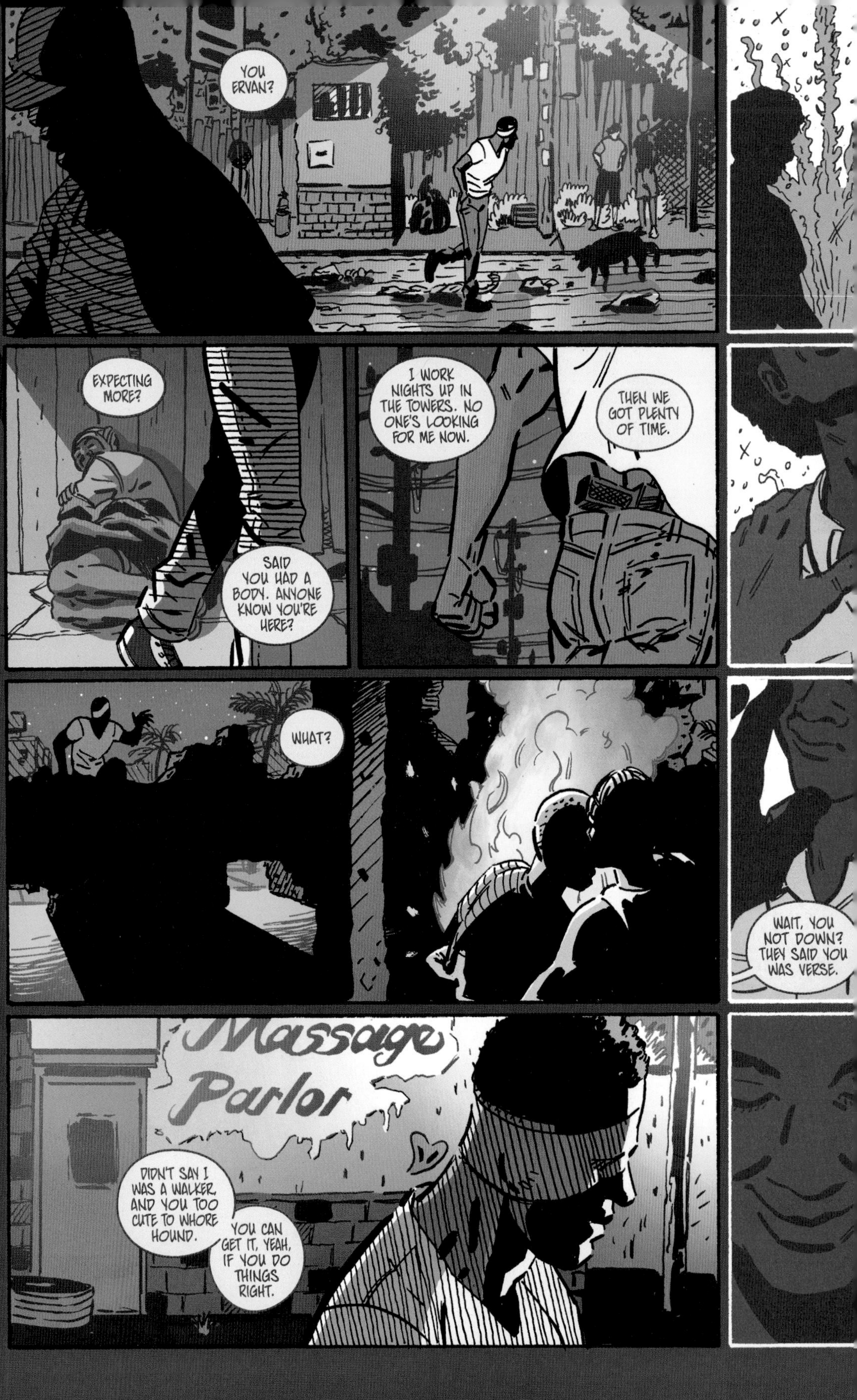
YOU ERVAN?
EXPECTING MORE?
SAID YOU HAD A BODY. ANYONE KNOW YOU'RE HERE?
I WORK NIGHTS UP IN THE TOWERS. NO ONE'S LOOKING FOR ME NOW.
THEN WE GOT PLENTY OF TIME.
WHAT?
Massage Parlor
DIDN'T SAY I WAS A WALKER, AND YOU TOO CUTE TO WHORE HOUND.
YOU CAN GET IT, YEAH, IF YOU DO THINGS RIGHT.
WAIT, YOU NOT DOWN? THEY SAID YOU WAS VERSE.

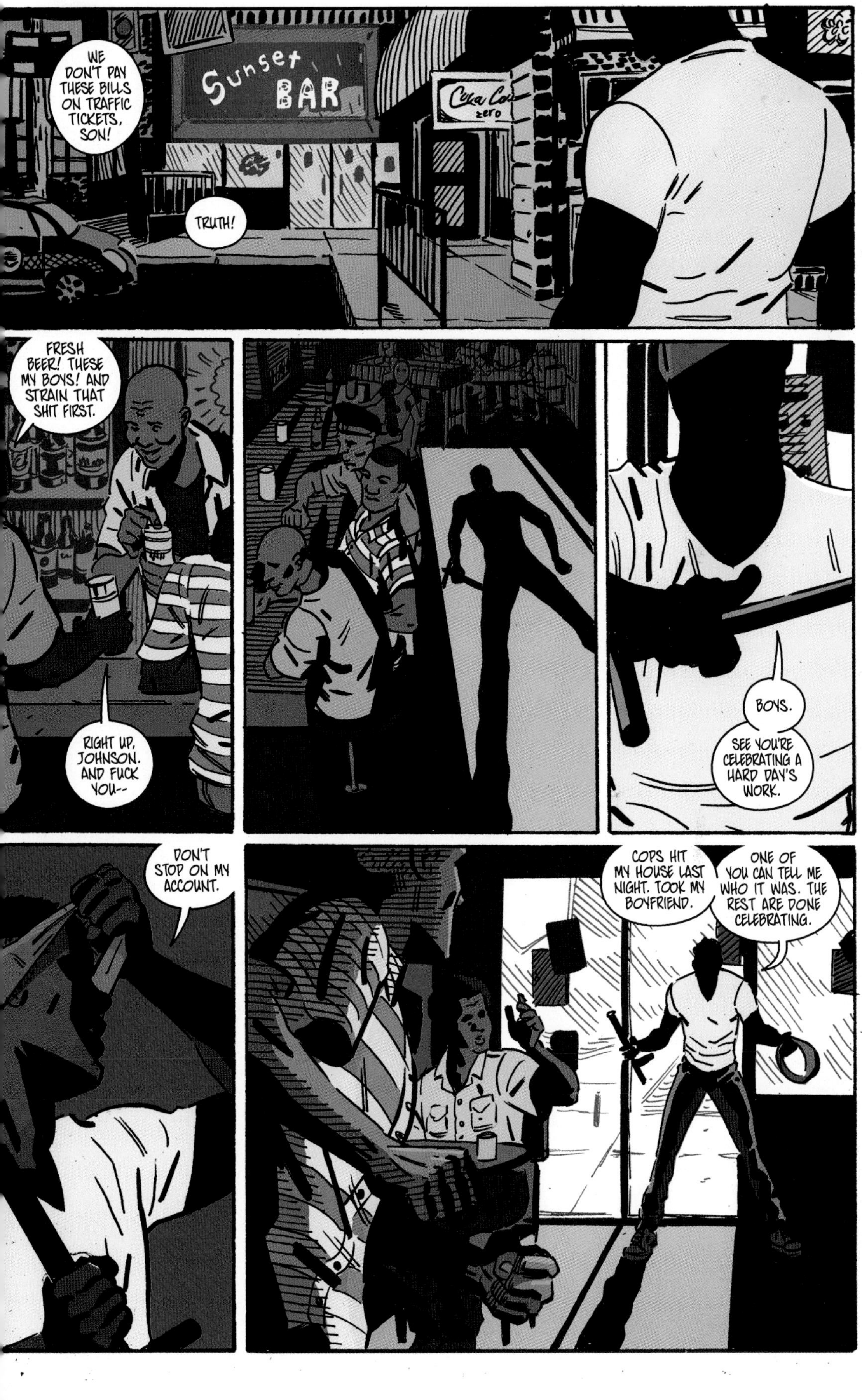
Sunset BAR
Coca Cola zero
WE DON'T PAY THESE BILLS ON TRAFFIC TICKETS, SON!
TRUTH!
FRESH BEER! THESE MY BOYS! AND STRAIN THAT SHIT FIRST.
RIGHT UP, JOHNSON. AND FUCK YOU--
BOYS.
SEE YOU'RE CELEBRATING A HARD DAY'S WORK.
DON'T STOP ON MY ACCOUNT.
COPS HIT MY HOUSE LAST NIGHT. TOOK MY BOYFRIEND.
ONE OF YOU CAN TELL ME WHO IT WAS. THE REST ARE DONE CELEBRATING.

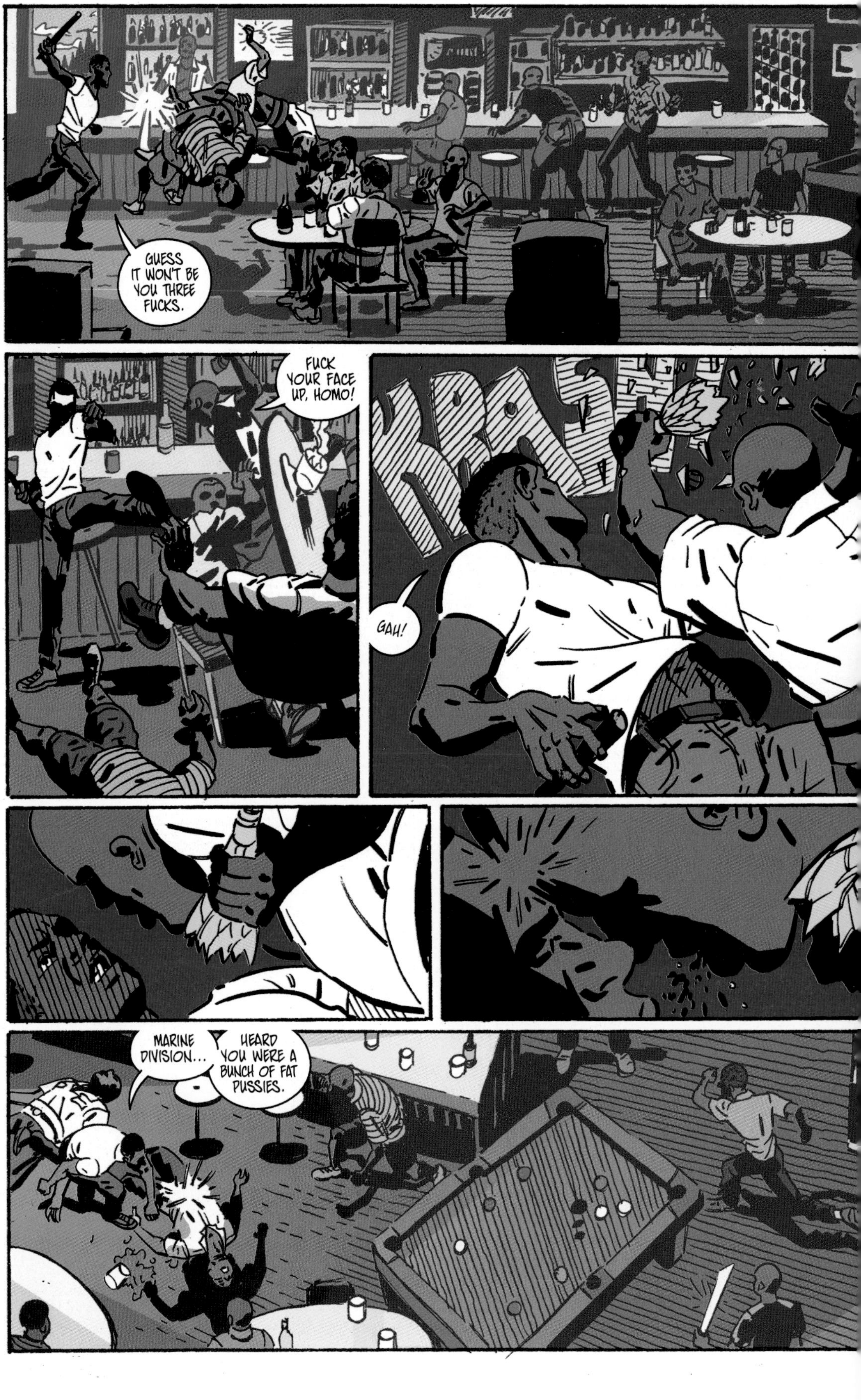
GUESS IT WON'T BE YOU THREE FUCKS.
FUCK YOUR FACE UP, HOMO!
GAH!
MARINE DIVISION...
HEARD YOU WERE A BUNCH OF FAT PUSSIES.

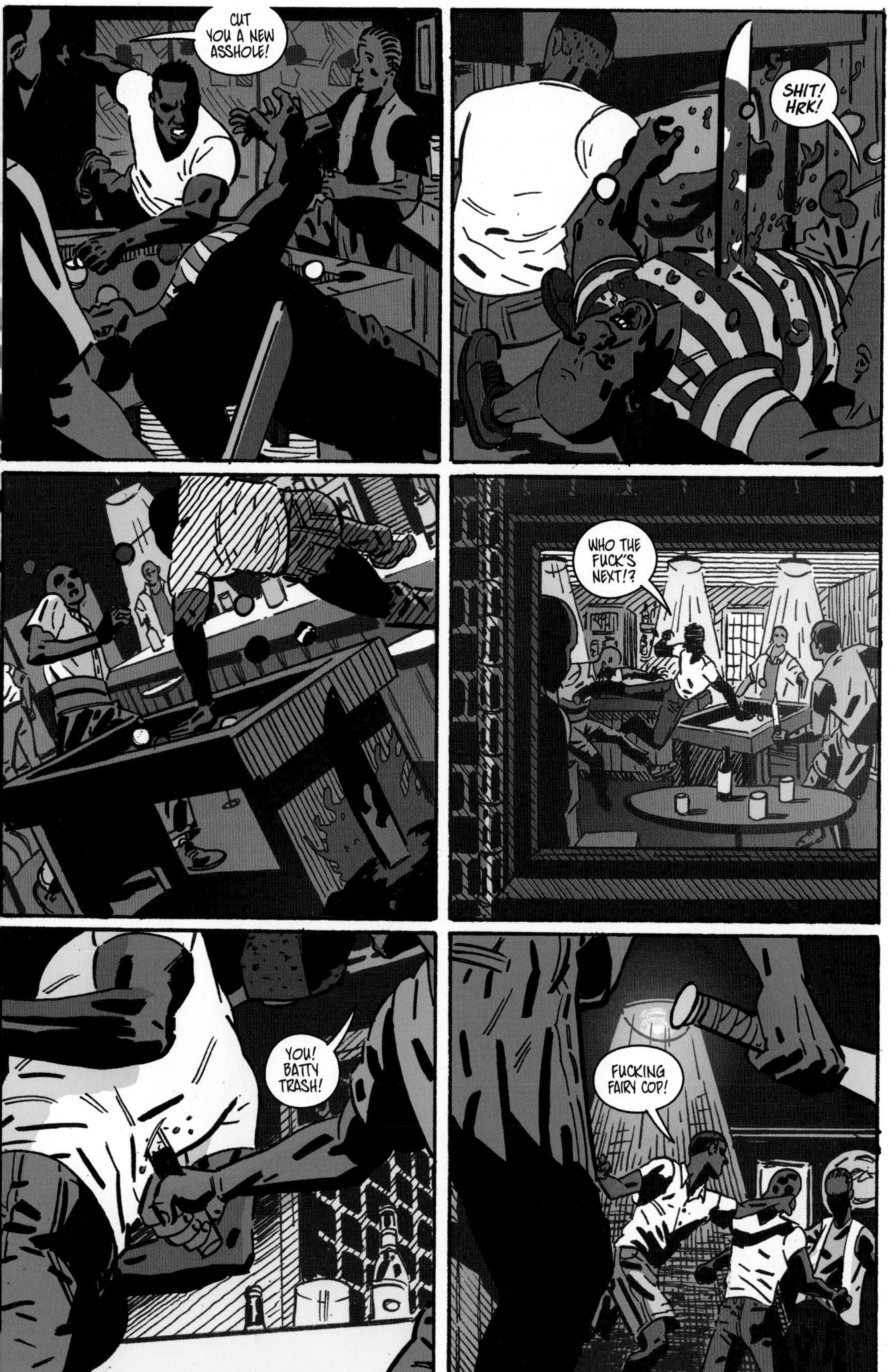
CUT YOU A NEW ASSHOLE!
SHIT! HRK!
WHO THE FUCK'S NEXT!?
YOU! BATTY TRASH!
FUCKING FAIRY COP!

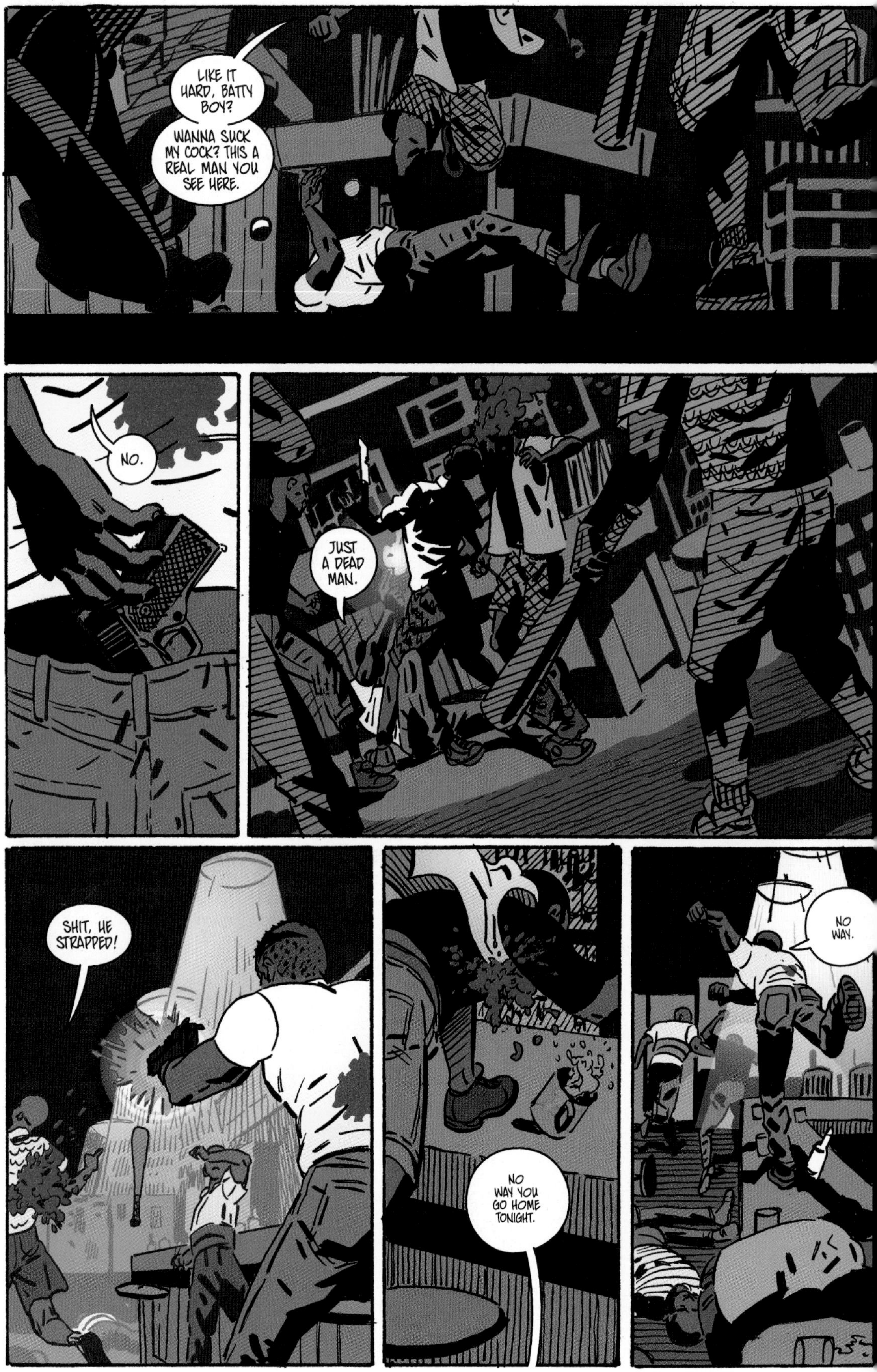
LIKE IT HARD, BATTY BOY?
WANNA SUCK MY COCK? THIS A REAL MAN YOU SEE HERE.
NO.
JUST A DEAD MAN.
SHIT, HE STRAPPED!
NO WAY YOU GO HOME TONIGHT.
NO WAY.

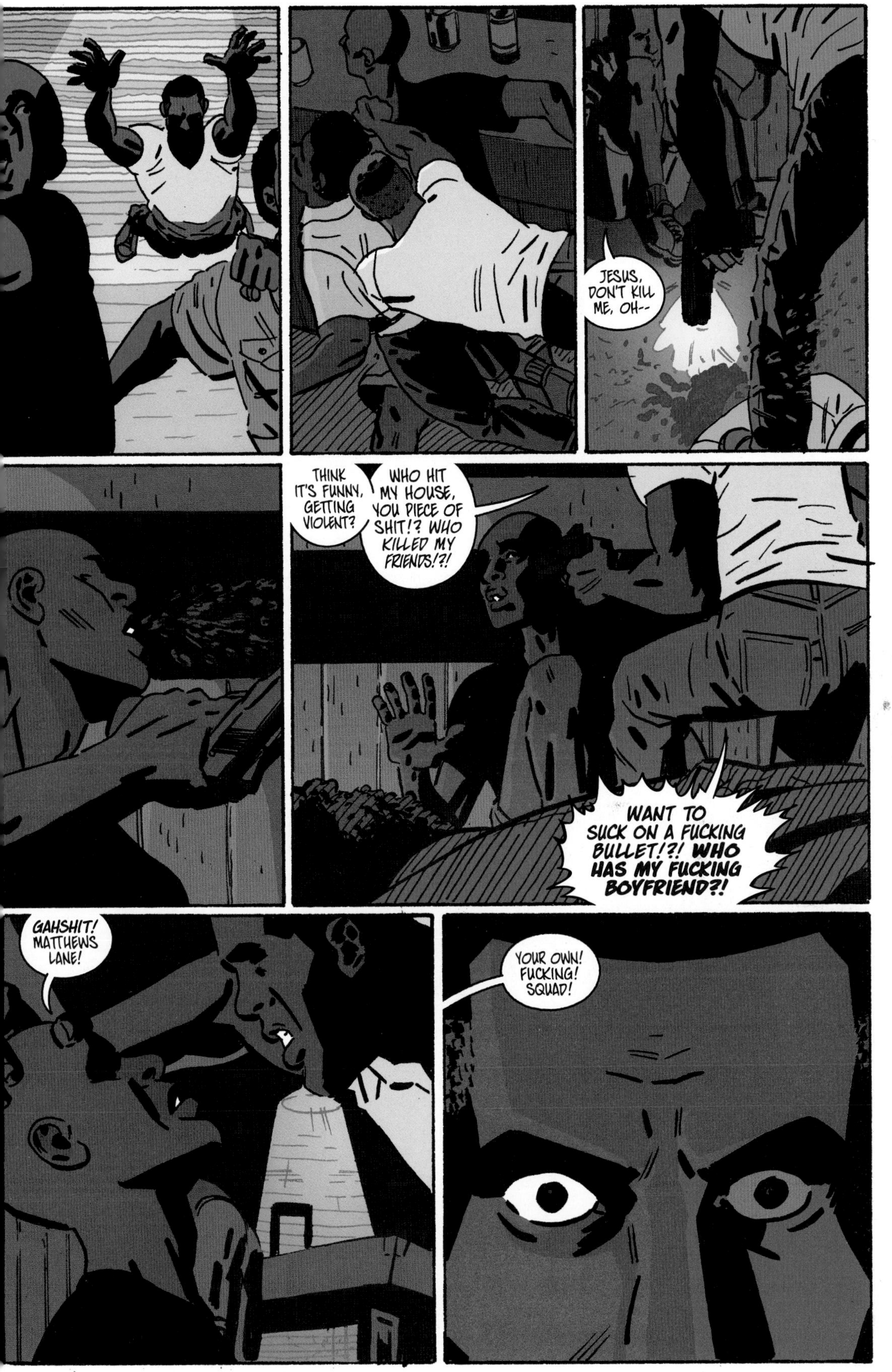
JESUS, DON'T KILL ME, OH--
THINK IT'S FUNNY, GETTING VIOLENT?
WHO HIT MY HOUSE, YOU PIECE OF SHIT!? WHO KILLED MY FRIENDS!?!
WANT TO SUCK ON A FUCKING BULLET!?! WHO HAS MY FUCKING BOYFRIEND?!
GAHSHIT! MATTHEWS LANE!
YOUR OWN! FUCKING! SQUAD!

Before.

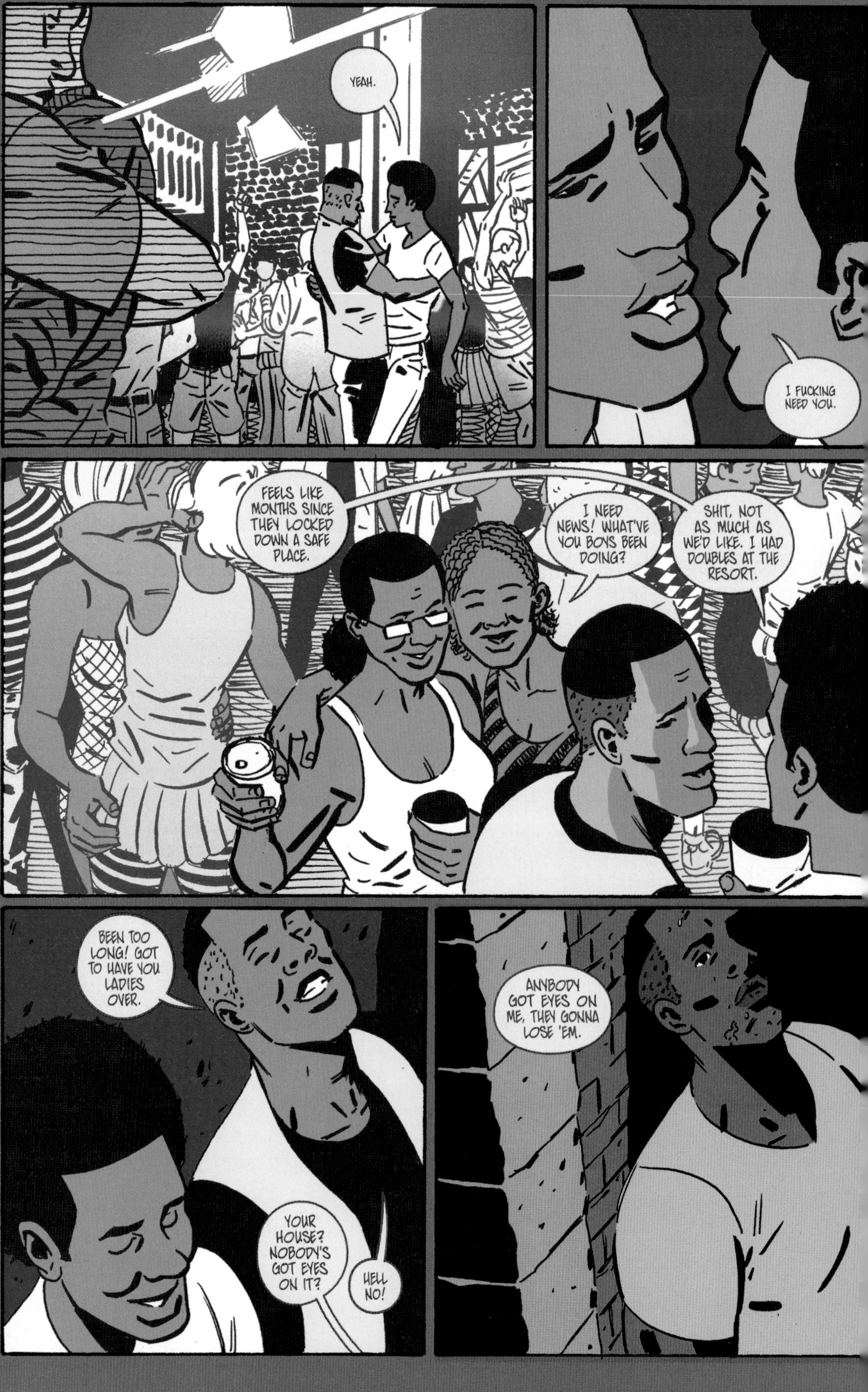
YEAH.
I FUCKING NEED YOU.
FEELS LIKE MONTHS SINCE THEY LOCKED DOWN A SAFE PLACE.
I NEED NEWS! WHAT'VE YOU BOYS BEEN DOING?
SHIT, NOT AS MUCH AS WE'D LIKE. I HAD DOUBLES AT THE RESORT.
BEEN TOO LONG! GOT TO HAVE YOU LADIES OVER.
YOUR HOUSE? NOBODY'S GOT EYES ON IT?
HELL NO!
ANYBODY GOT EYES ON ME, THEY GONNA LOSE 'EM.

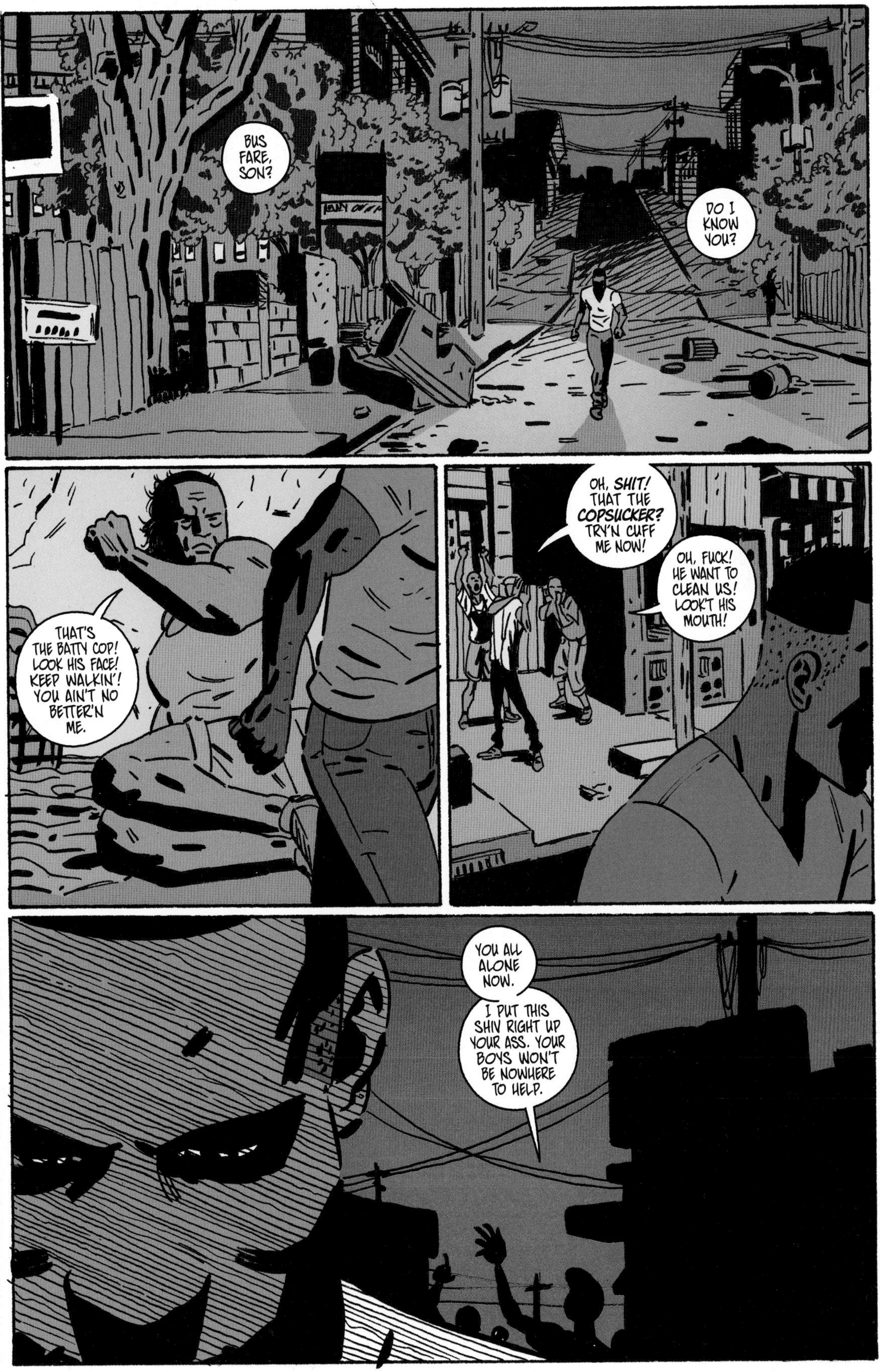

BUS FARE, SON?
DO I KNOW YOU?
THAT'S THE BATTY COP! LOOK HIS FACE! KEEP WALKIN'! YOU AIN'T NO BETTER'N ME.
OH, SHIT! THAT THE COPSUCKER? TRY'N CUFF ME NOW!
OH, FUCK! HE WANT TO CLEAN US! LOOK'T HIS MOUTH!
YOU ALL ALONE NOW.
I PUT THIS SHIV RIGHT UP YOUR ASS. YOUR BOYS WON'T BE NOWHERE TO HELP.

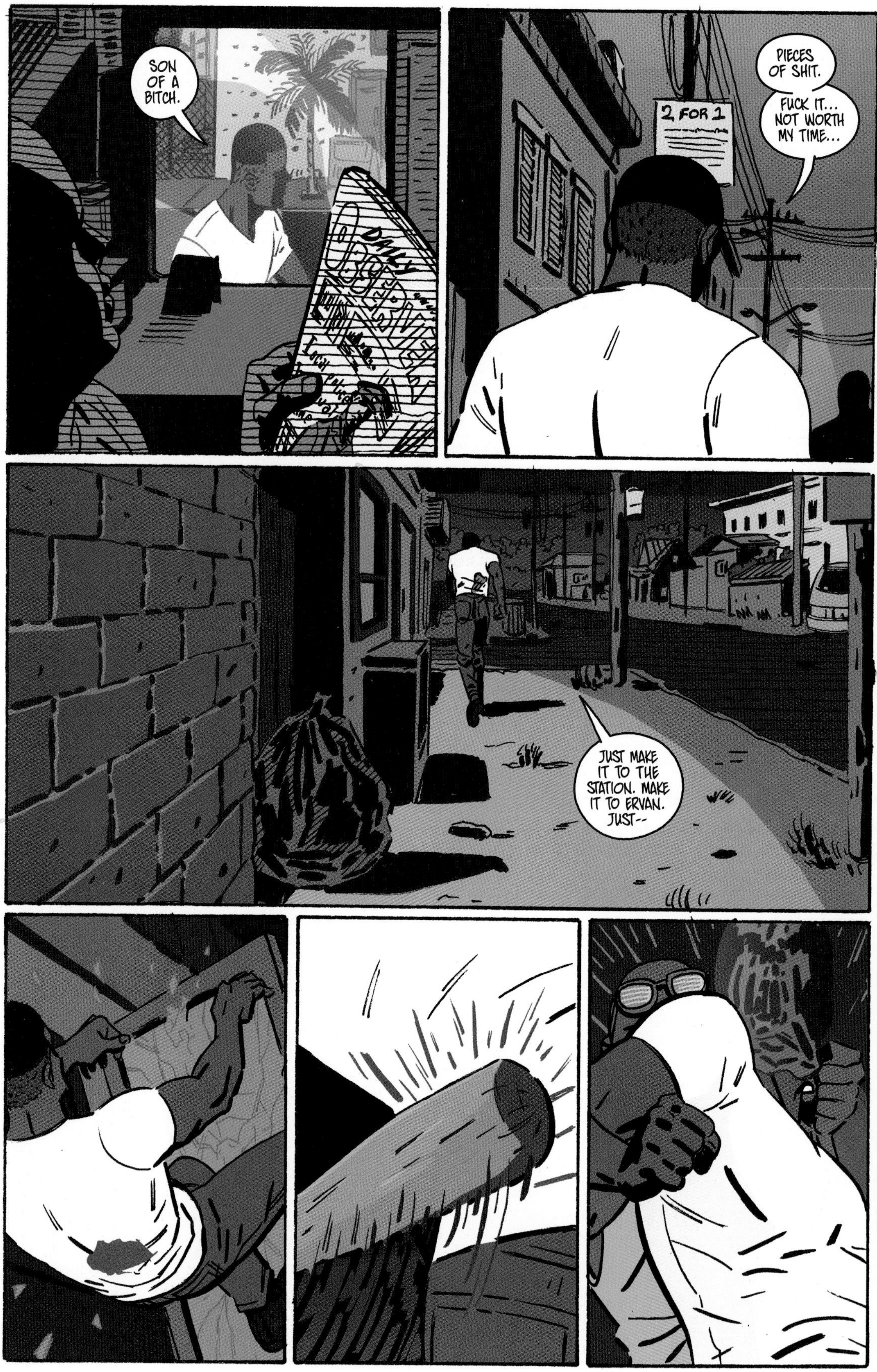
SON OF A BITCH.
PIECES OF SHIT.
FUCK IT... NOT WORTH MY TIME...
2 FOR 1
JUST MAKE IT TO THE STATION. MAKE IT TO ERVAN. JUST--

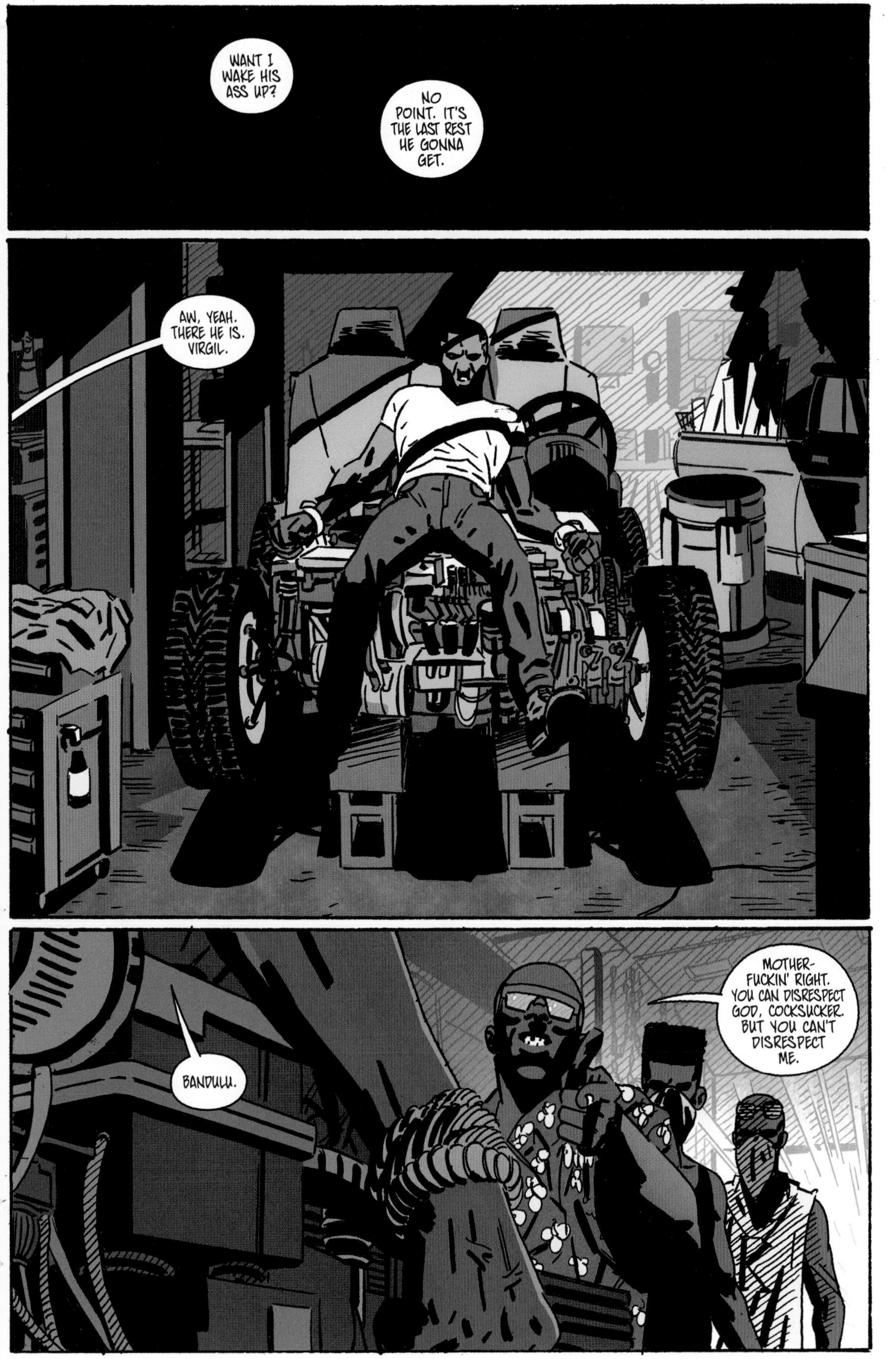
WANT I WAKE HIS ASS UP?
NO POINT. IT'S THE LAST REST HE GONNA GET.
AW, YEAH. THERE HE IS. VIRGIL.
BANDULU.
MOTHER-FUCKIN' RIGHT. YOU CAN DISRESPECT GOD, COCKSUCKER. BUT YOU CAN'T DISRESPECT ME.

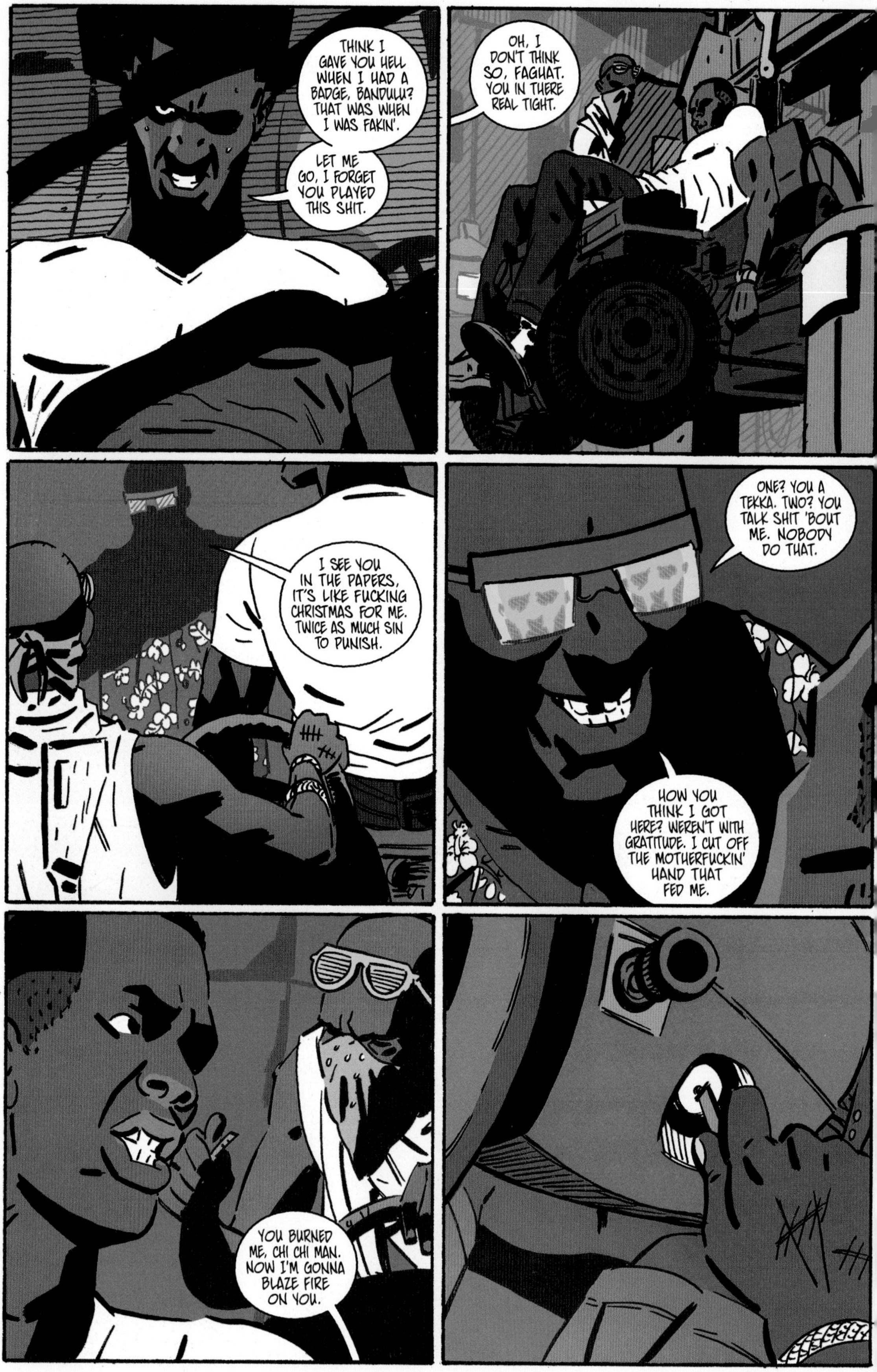
THINK I GAVE YOU HELL WHEN I HAD A BADGE, BANDULU? THAT WAS WHEN I WAS FAKIN'.
LET ME GO, I FORGET YOU PLAYED THIS SHIT.
OH, I DON'T THINK SO, FAGHAT. YOU IN THERE REAL TIGHT.
I SEE YOU IN THE PAPERS, IT'S LIKE FUCKING CHRISTMAS FOR ME. TWICE AS MUCH SIN TO PUNISH.
ONE? YOU A TEKKA. TWO? YOU TALK SHIT 'BOUT ME. NOBODY DO THAT.
HOW YOU THINK I GOT HERE? WEREN'T WITH GRATITUDE. I CUT OFF THE MOTHERFUCKIN' HAND THAT FED ME.
YOU BURNED ME, CHI CHI MAN. NOW I'M GONNA BLAZE FIRE ON YOU.

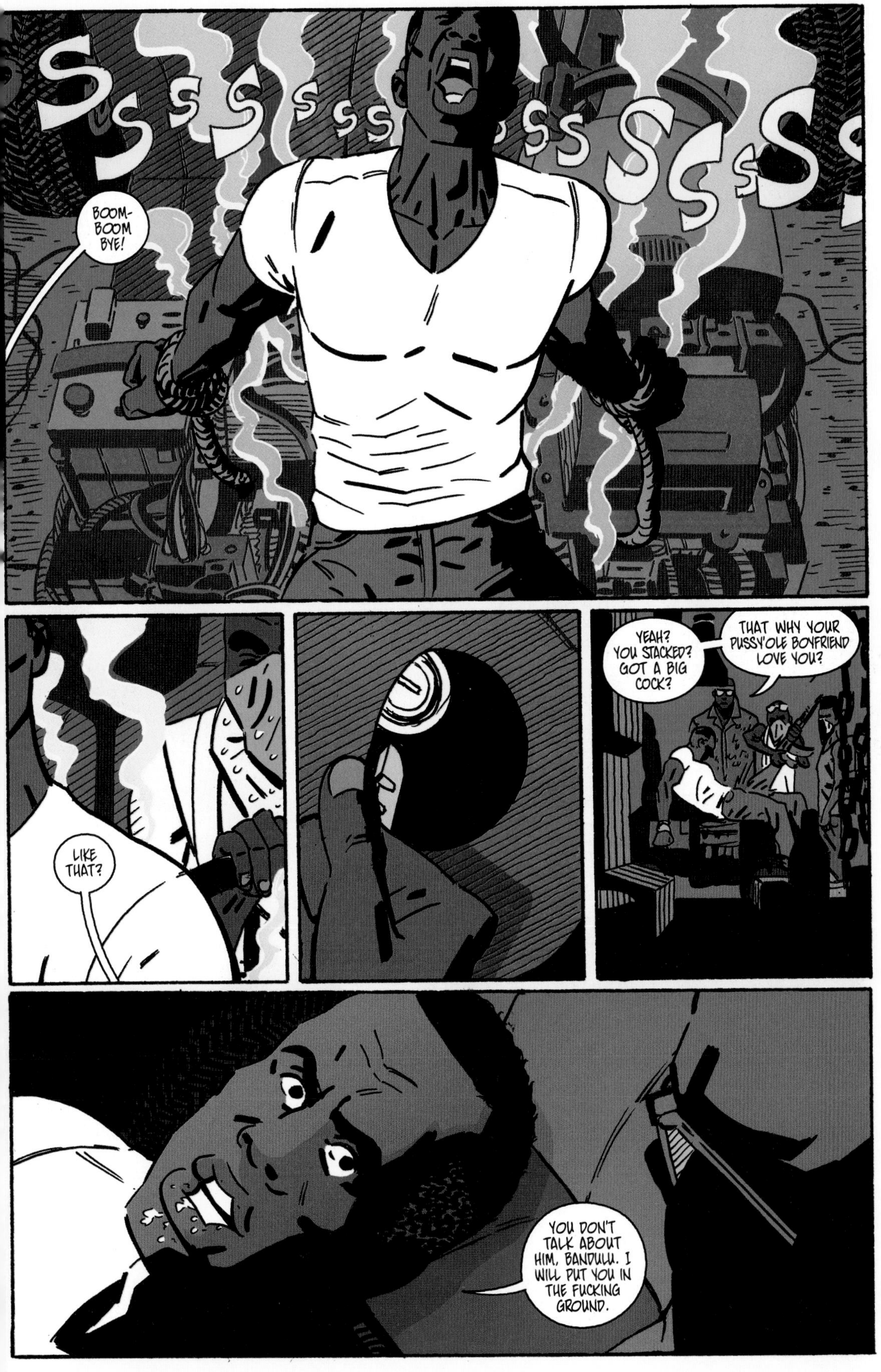
SSSSSSSSSSSSSSSSS
BOOM-BOOM BYE!
LIKE THAT?
YEAH? YOU STACKED? GOT A BIG COCK?
THAT WHY YOUR PUSSY'OLE BOYFRIEND LOVE YOU?
YOU DON'T TALK ABOUT HIM, BANDULU. I WILL PUT YOU IN THE FUCKING GROUND.

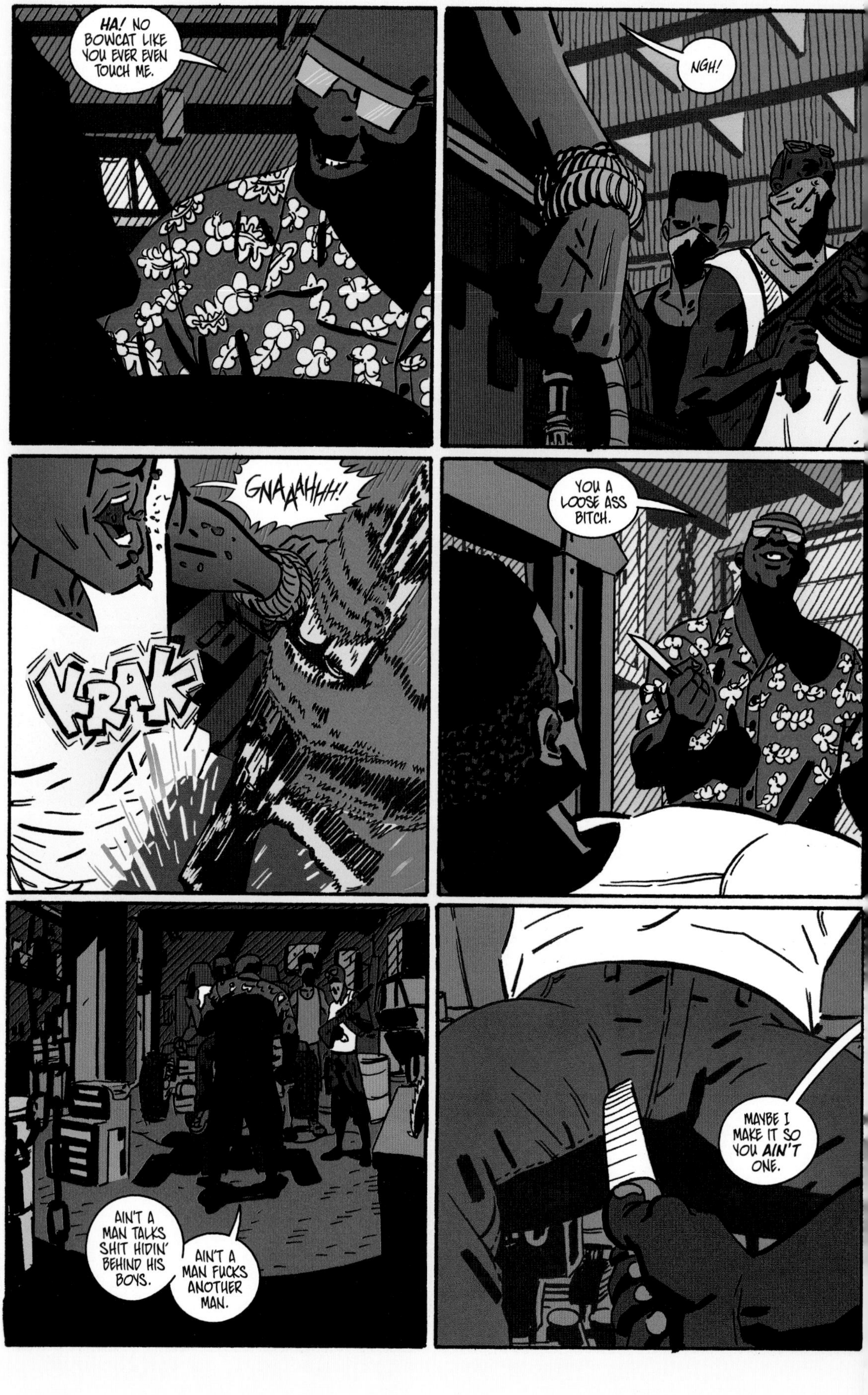
HA! NO BOWCAT LIKE YOU EVER EVEN TOUCH ME.
NGH!
GNAAAHHH!
KRAK
YOU A LOOSE ASS BITCH.
AIN'T A MAN TALKS SHIT HIDIN' BEHIND HIS BOYS.
AIN'T A MAN FUCKS ANOTHER MAN.
MAYBE I MAKE IT SO YOU AIN'T ONE.

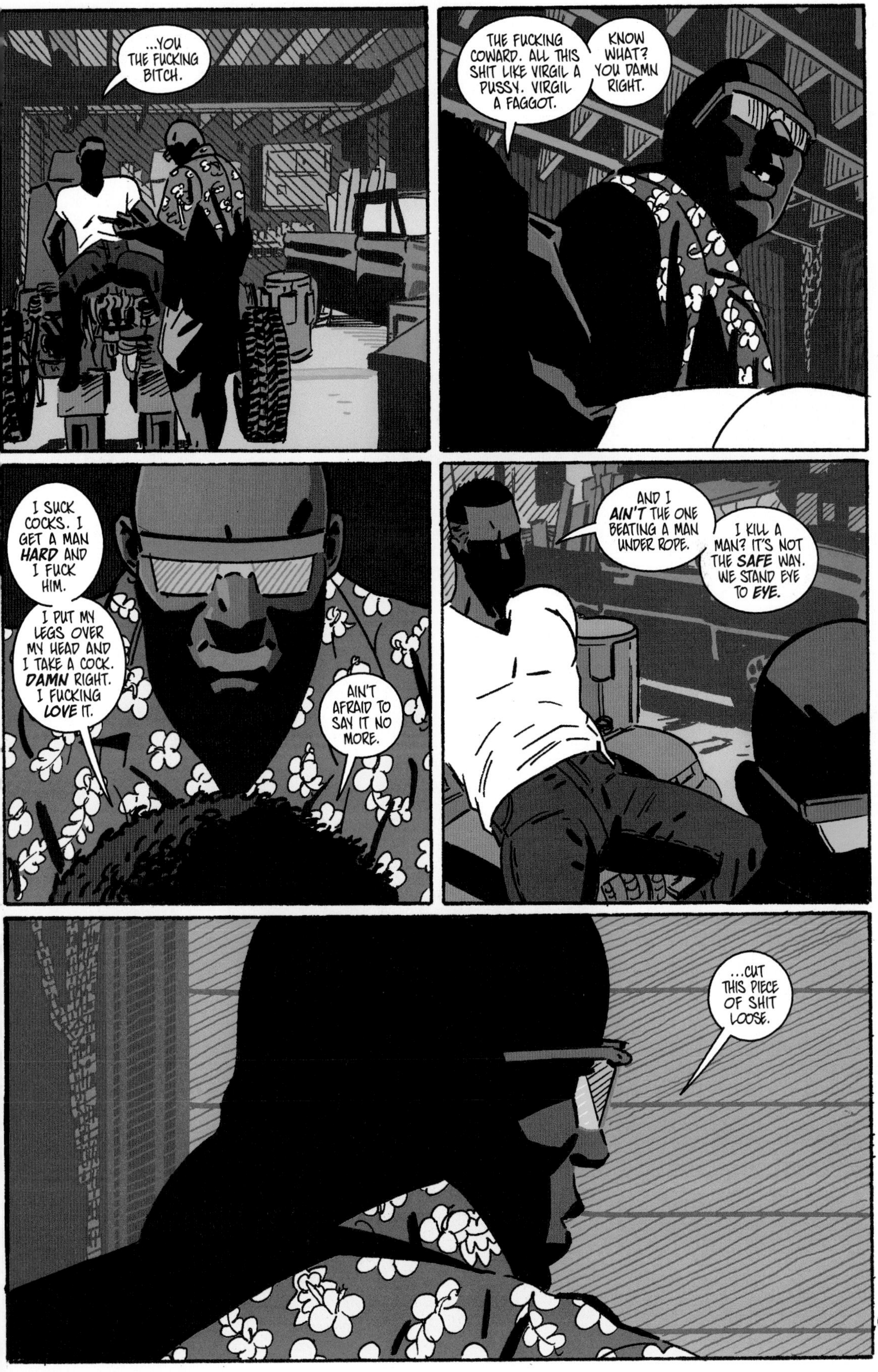
...YOU THE FUCKING BITCH.
THE FUCKING COWARD. ALL THIS SHIT LIKE VIRGIL A PUSSY. VIRGIL A FAGGOT.
KNOW WHAT? YOU DAMN RIGHT.
I SUCK COCKS. I GET A MAN HARD AND I FUCK HIM.
I PUT MY LEGS OVER MY HEAD AND I TAKE A COCK. DAMN RIGHT. I FUCKING LOVE IT.
AIN'T AFRAID TO SAY IT NO MORE.
AND I AIN'T THE ONE BEATING A MAN UNDER ROPE.
I KILL A MAN? IT'S NOT THE SAFE WAY. WE STAND EYE TO EYE.
...CUT THIS PIECE OF SHIT LOOSE.

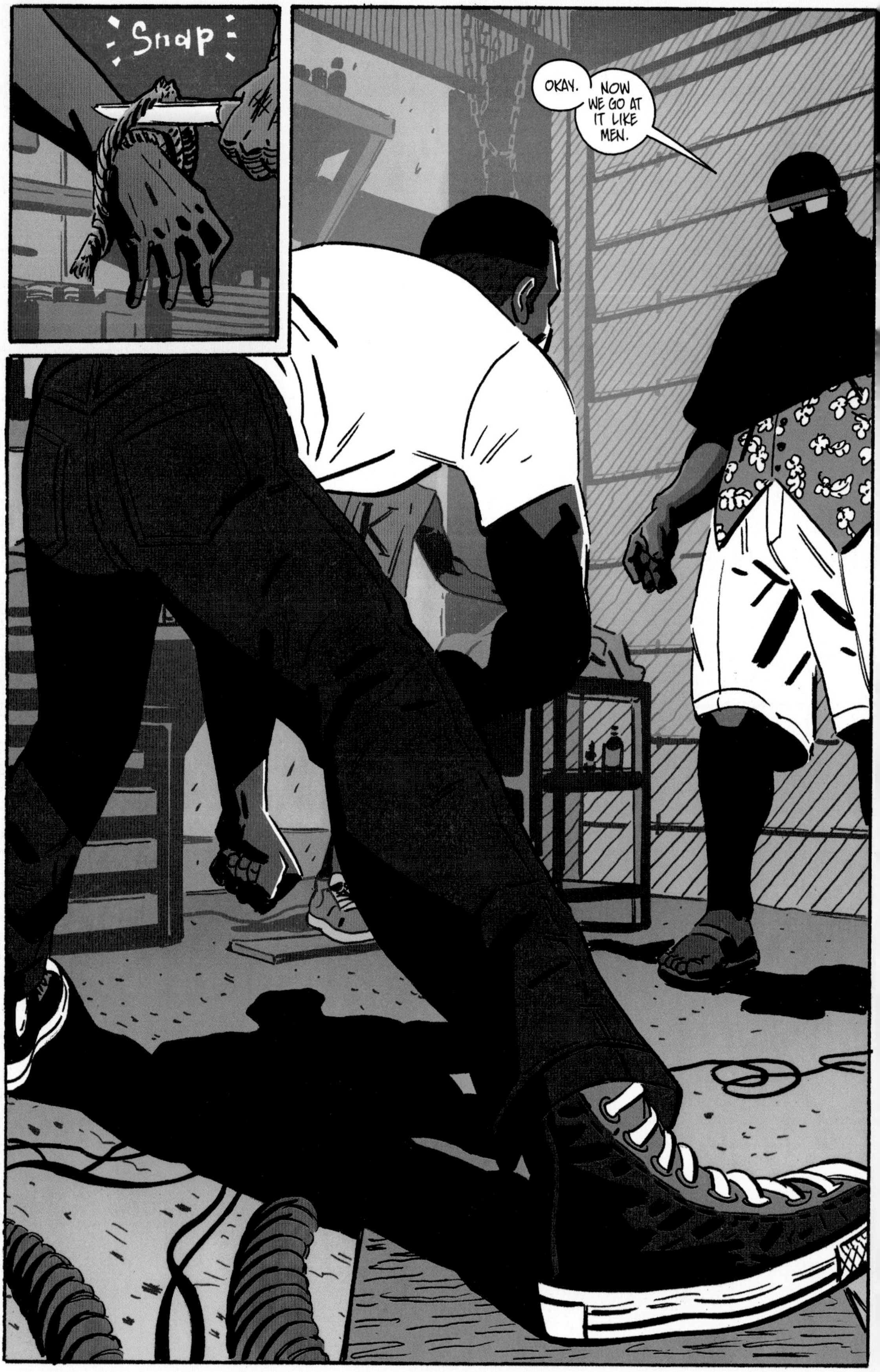
Snap
OKAY.
NOW WE GO AT IT LIKE MEN.

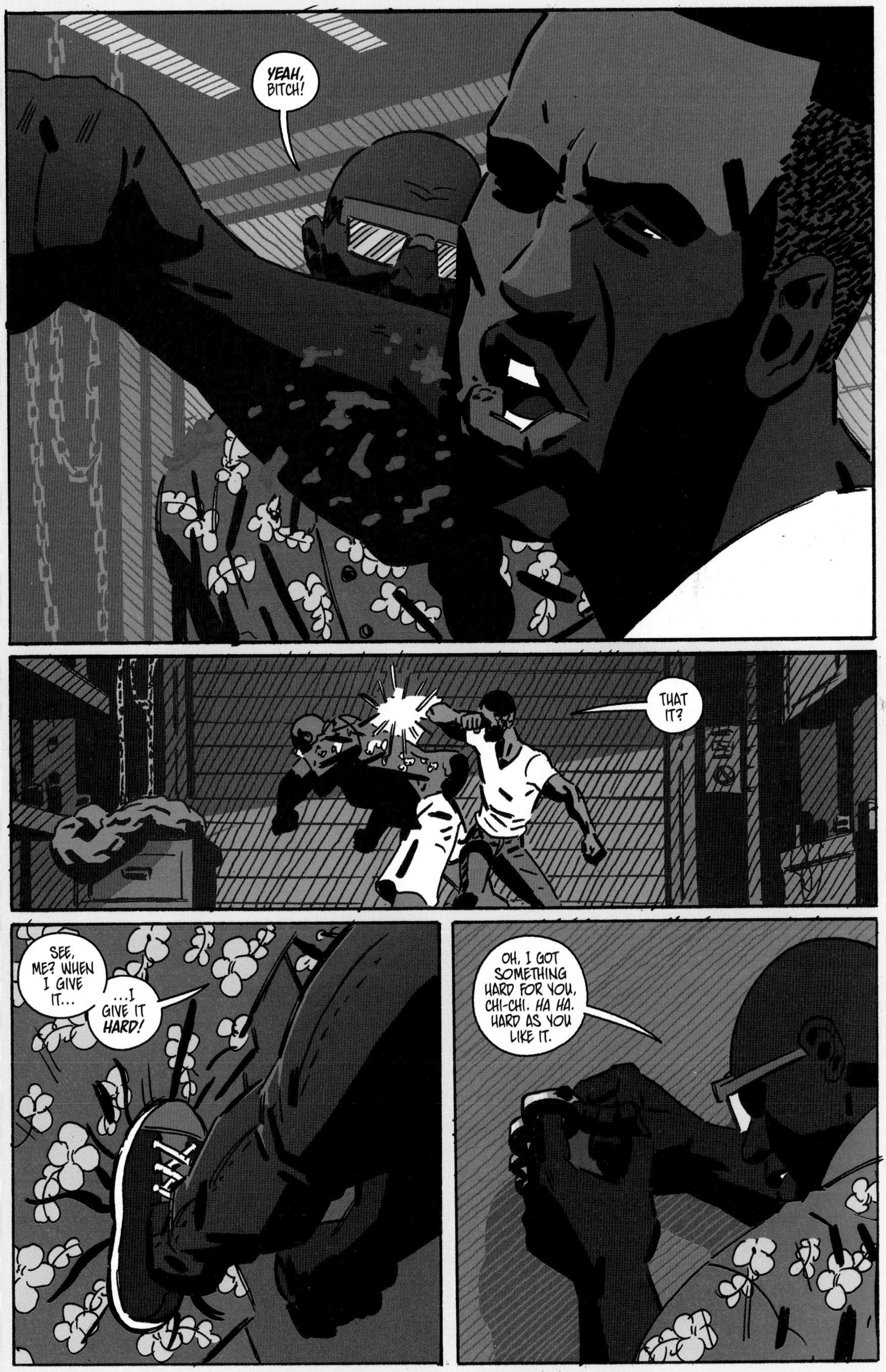
YEAH, BITCH!
THAT IT?
SEE, ME? WHEN I GIVE IT...
...I GIVE IT HARD!
OH, I GOT SOMETHING HARD FOR YOU, CHI-CHI. HA HA. HARD AS YOU LIKE IT.

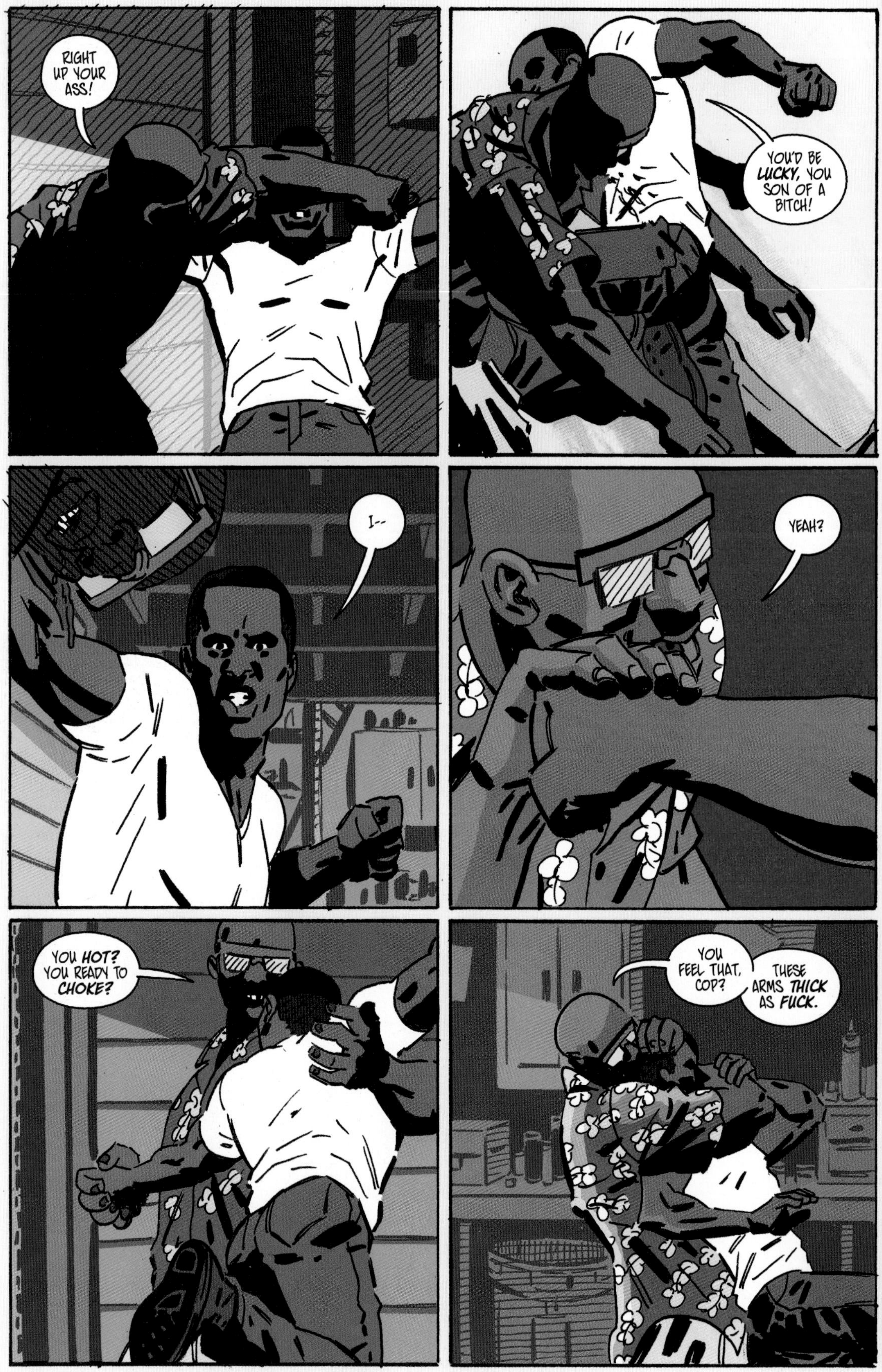
RIGHT UP YOUR ASS!
YOU'D BE LUCKY, YOU SON OF A BITCH!
I--
YEAH?
YOU HOT? YOU READY TO CHOKE?
YOU FEEL THAT, COP?
THESE ARMS THICK AS FUCK.

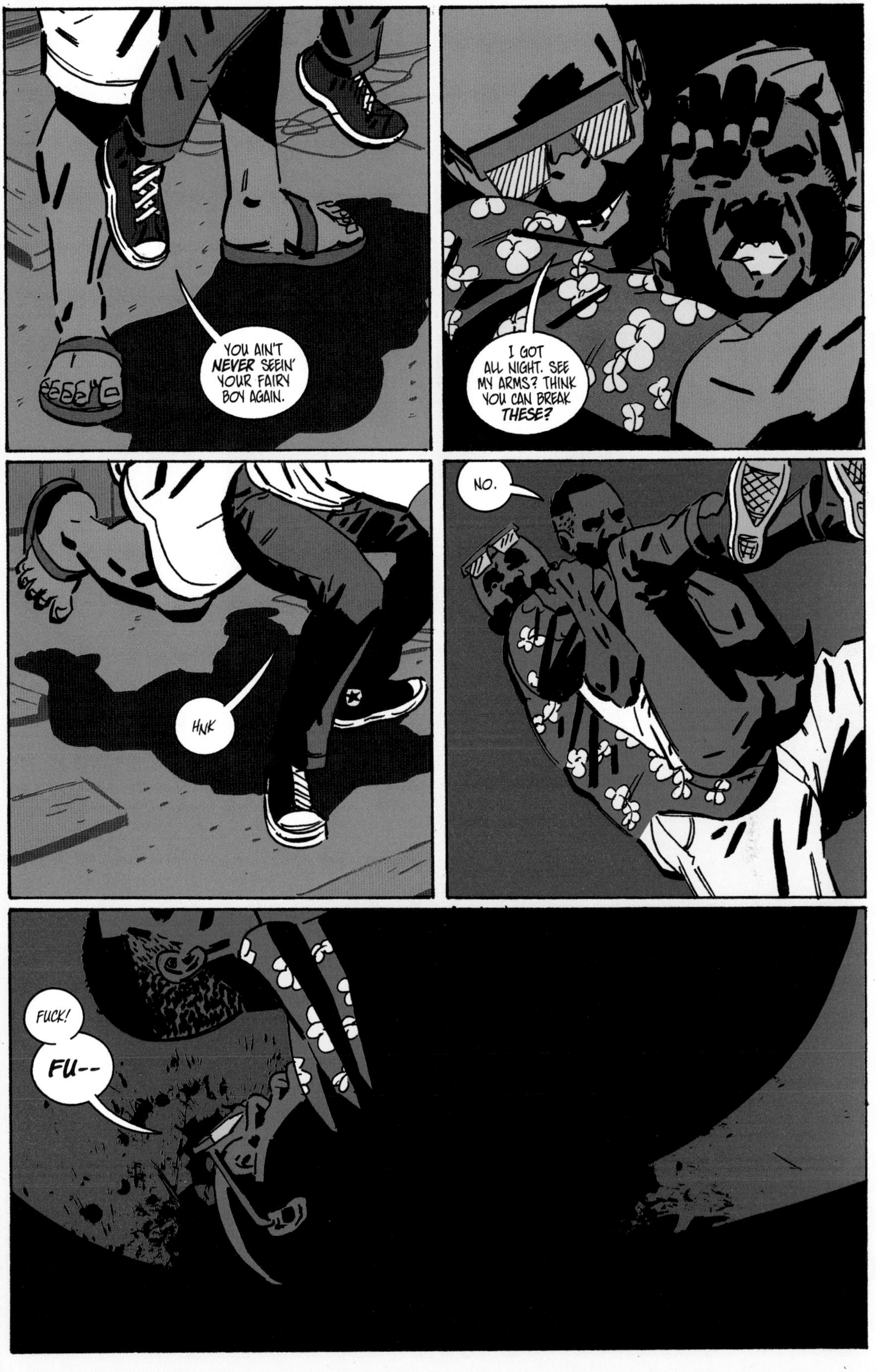
YOU AIN'T NEVER SEEIN' YOUR FAIRY BOY AGAIN.
I GOT ALL NIGHT. SEE MY ARMS? THINK YOU CAN BREAK THESE?
HNK
NO.
FUCK!
FU--

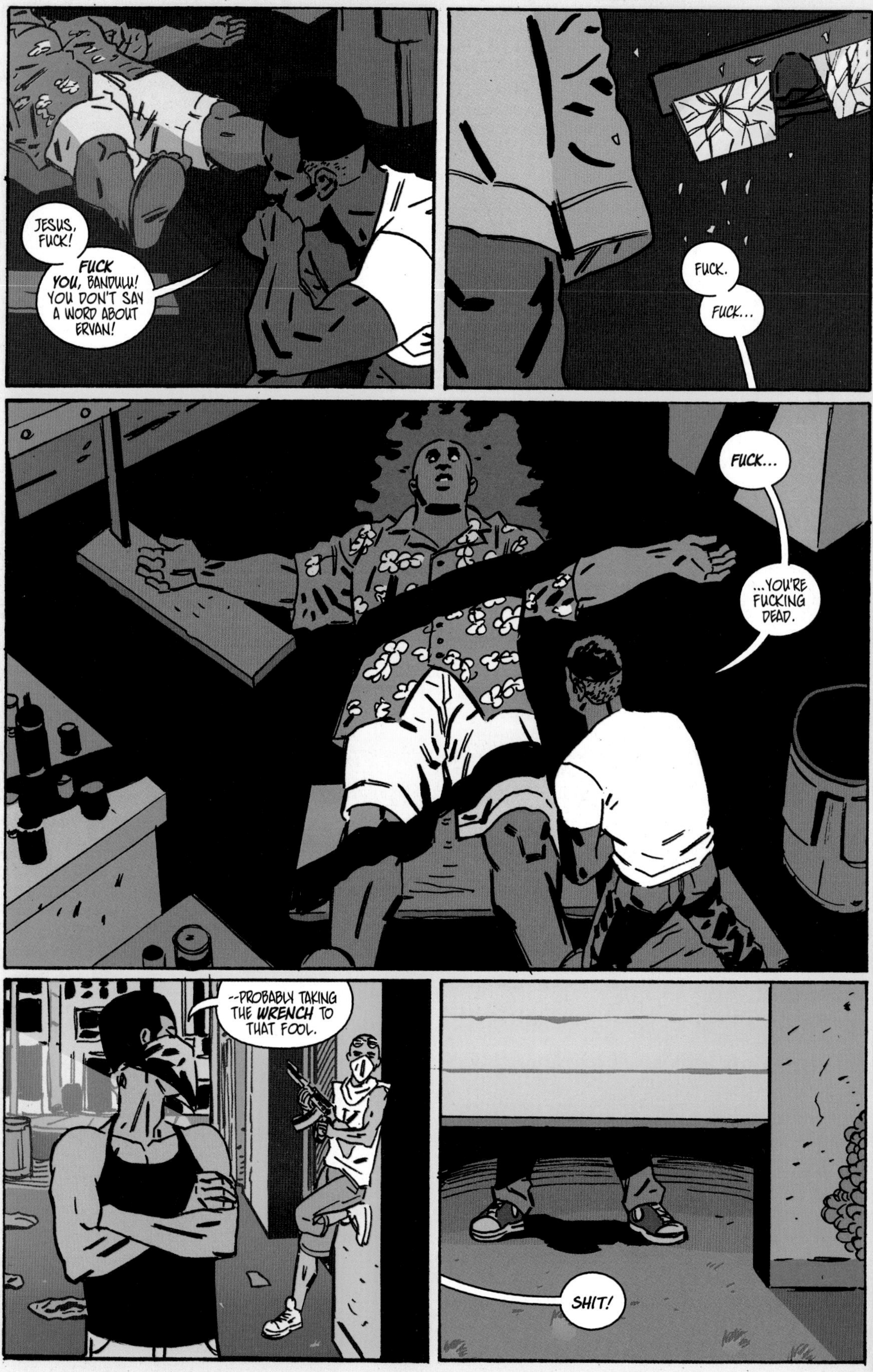
JESUS, FUCK!
FUCK YOU, BANDULU! YOU DON'T SAY A WORD ABOUT ERVAN!
FUCK.
FUCK...
FUCK...
...YOU'RE FUCKING DEAD.
--PROBABLY TAKING THE WRENCH TO THAT FOOL.
SHIT!

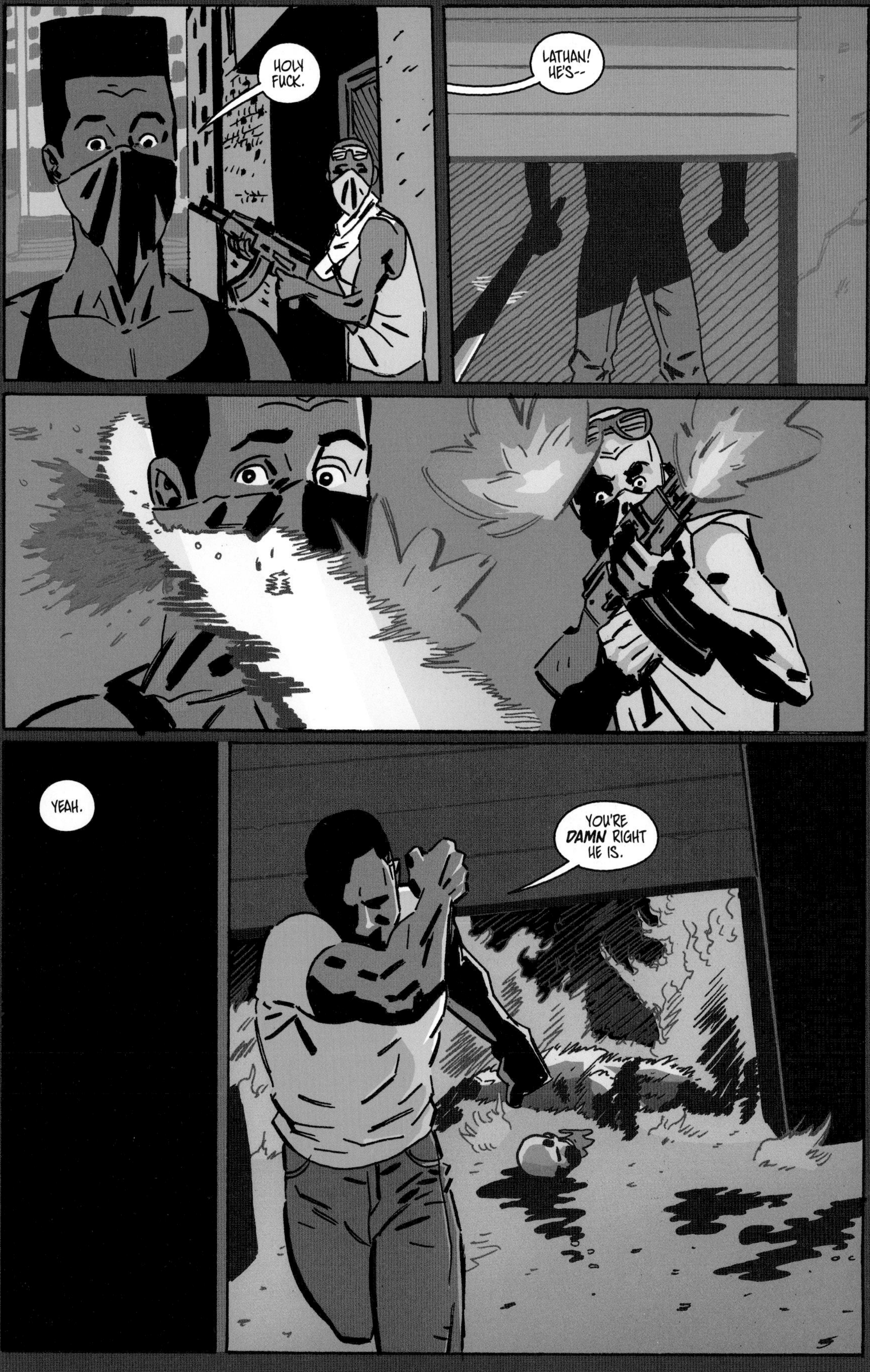
HOLY FUCK.
LATHAN! HE'S--
YEAH.
YOU'RE DAMN RIGHT HE IS.

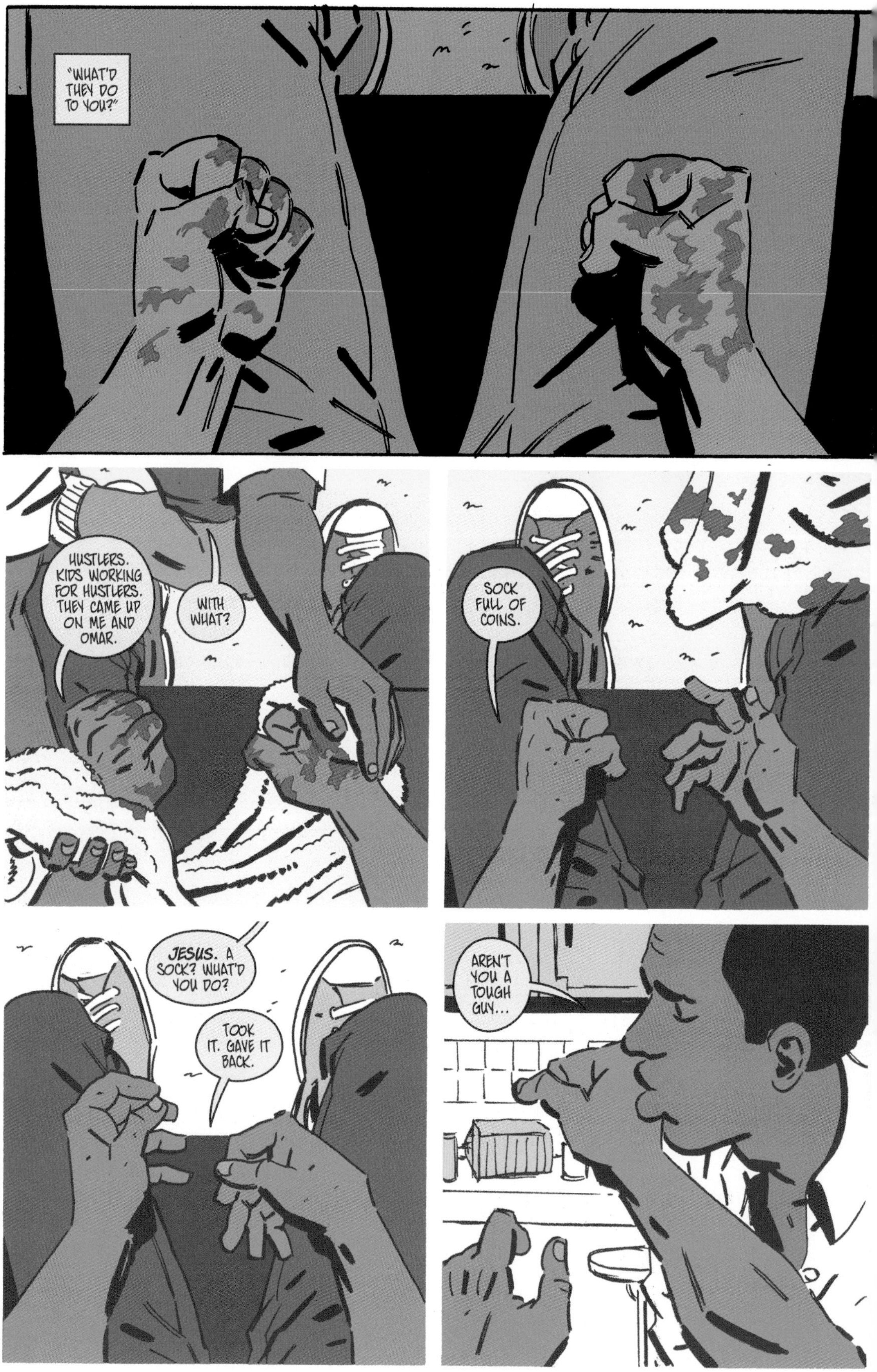
"WHAT'D THEY DO TO YOU?"
HUSTLERS. KIDS WORKING FOR HUSTLERS. THEY CAME UP ON ME AND OMAR.
WITH WHAT?
SOCK FULL OF COINS.
JESUS. A SOCK? WHAT'D YOU DO?
TOOK IT. GAVE IT BACK.
AREN'T YOU A TOUGH GUY...

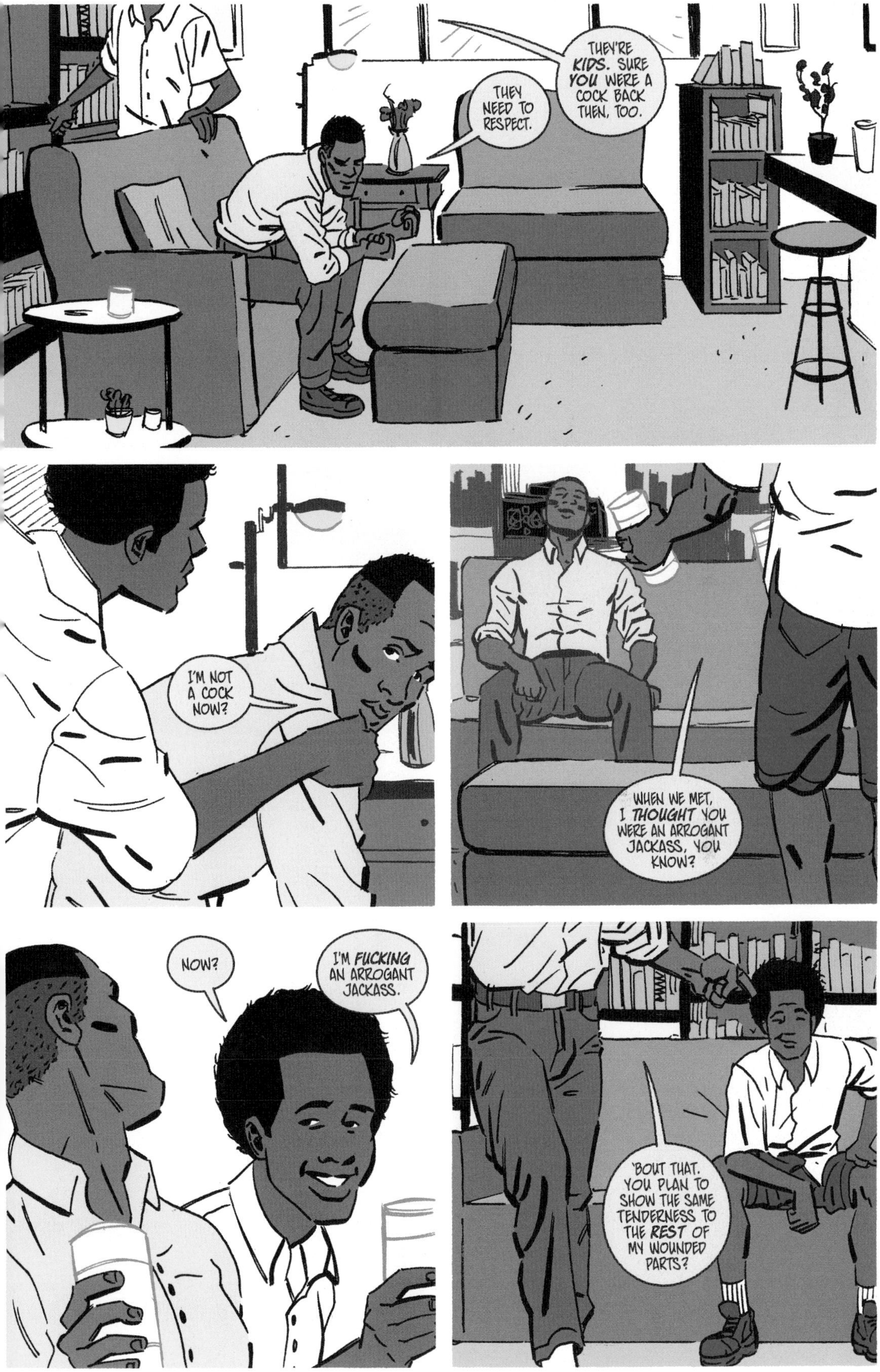
THEY NEED TO RESPECT.
THEY'RE KIDS. SURE YOU WERE A COCK BACK THEN, TOO.
I'M NOT A COCK NOW?
WHEN WE MET, I THOUGHT YOU WERE AN ARROGANT JACKASS, YOU KNOW?
NOW?
I'M FUCKING AN ARROGANT JACKASS.
'BOUT THAT. YOU PLAN TO SHOW THE SAME TENDERNESS TO THE REST OF MY WOUNDED PARTS?

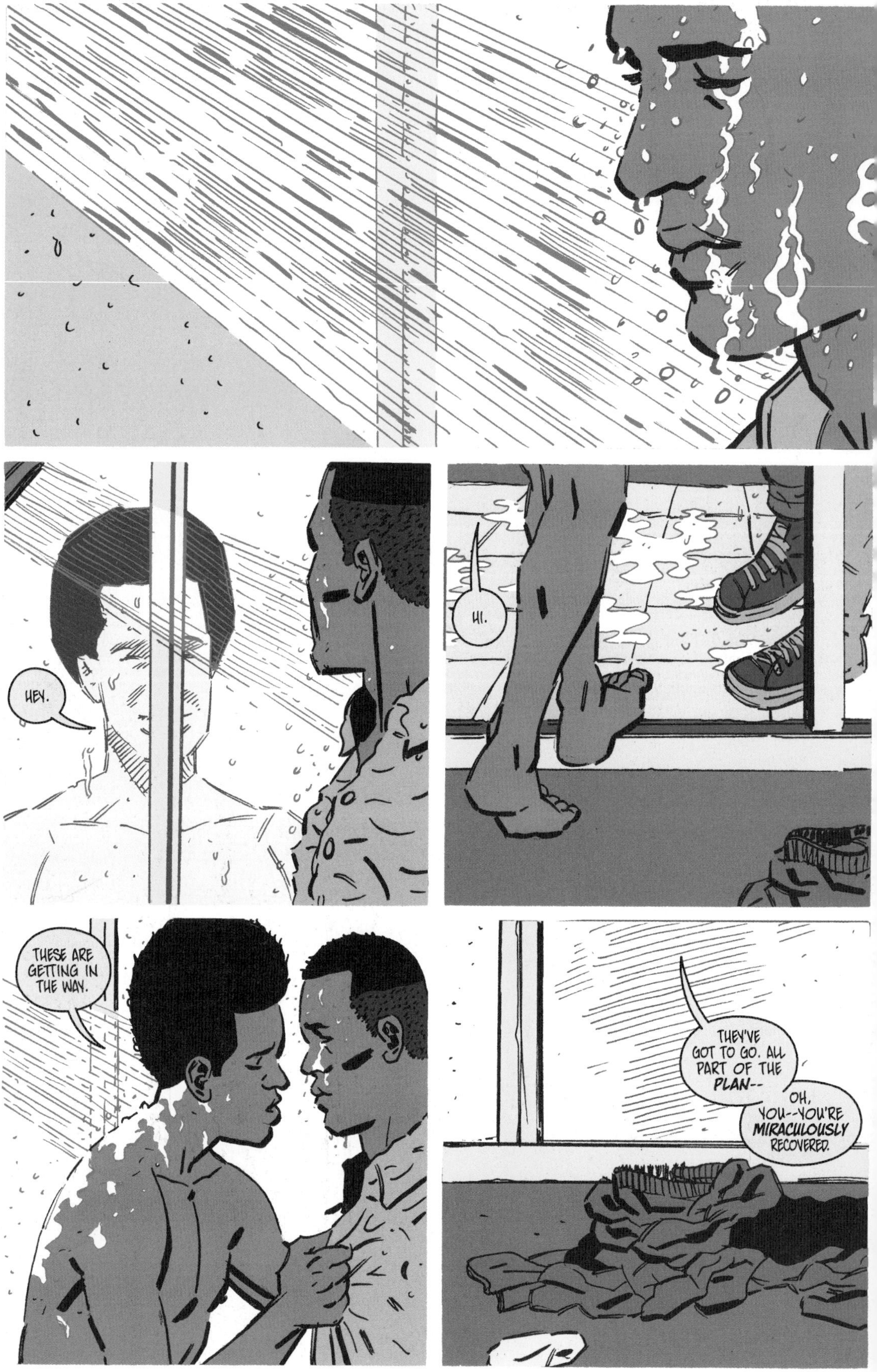
HEY.
HI.
THESE ARE GETTING IN THE WAY.
THEY'VE GOT TO GO. ALL PART OF THE *PLAN*--
OH, YOU--YOU'RE *MIRACULOUSLY* RECOVERED.

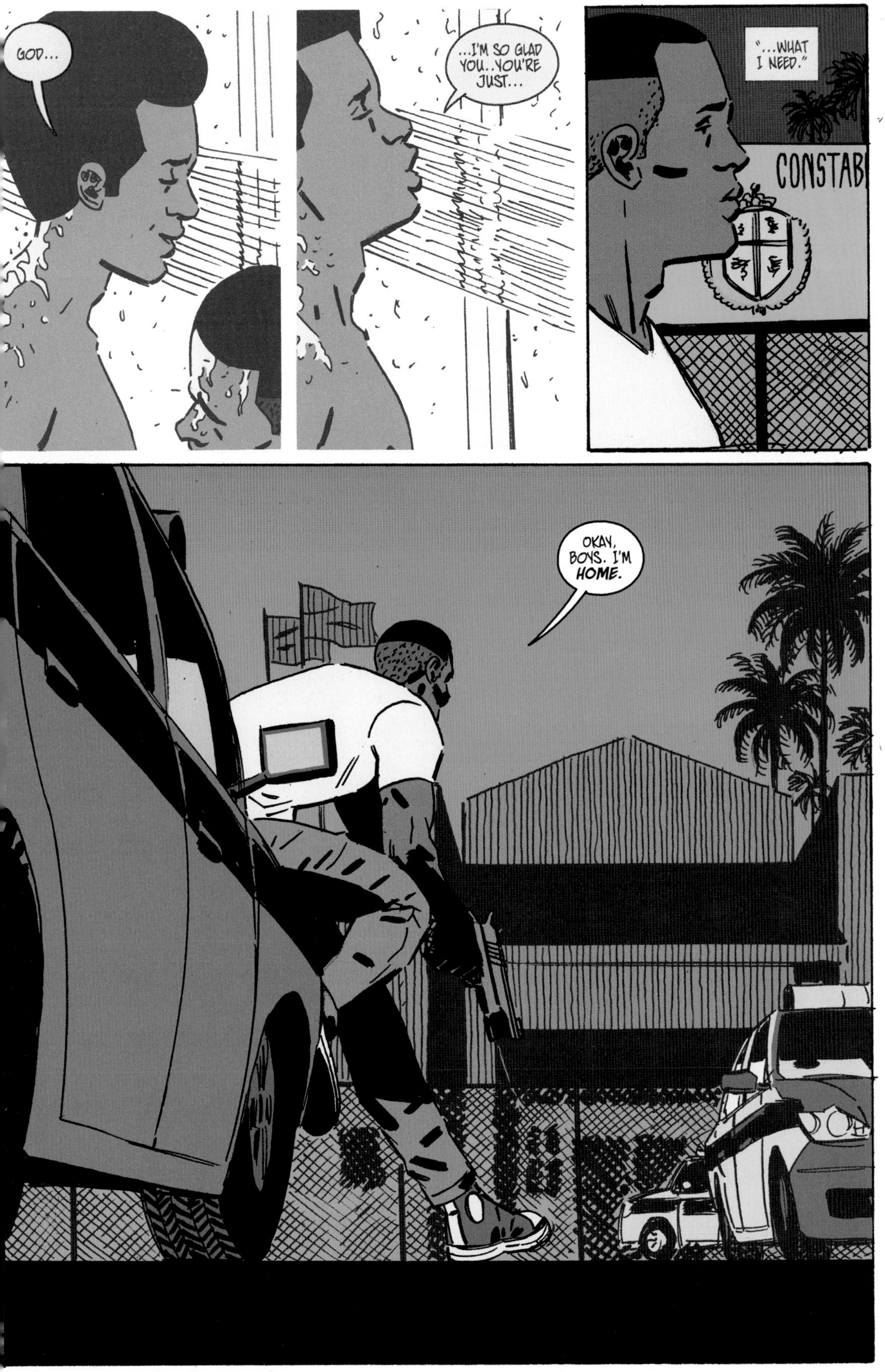
GOD...
...I'M SO GLAD YOU..YOU'RE JUST...
"...WHAT I NEED."
CONSTAB
OKAY, BOYS. I'M **HOME**.

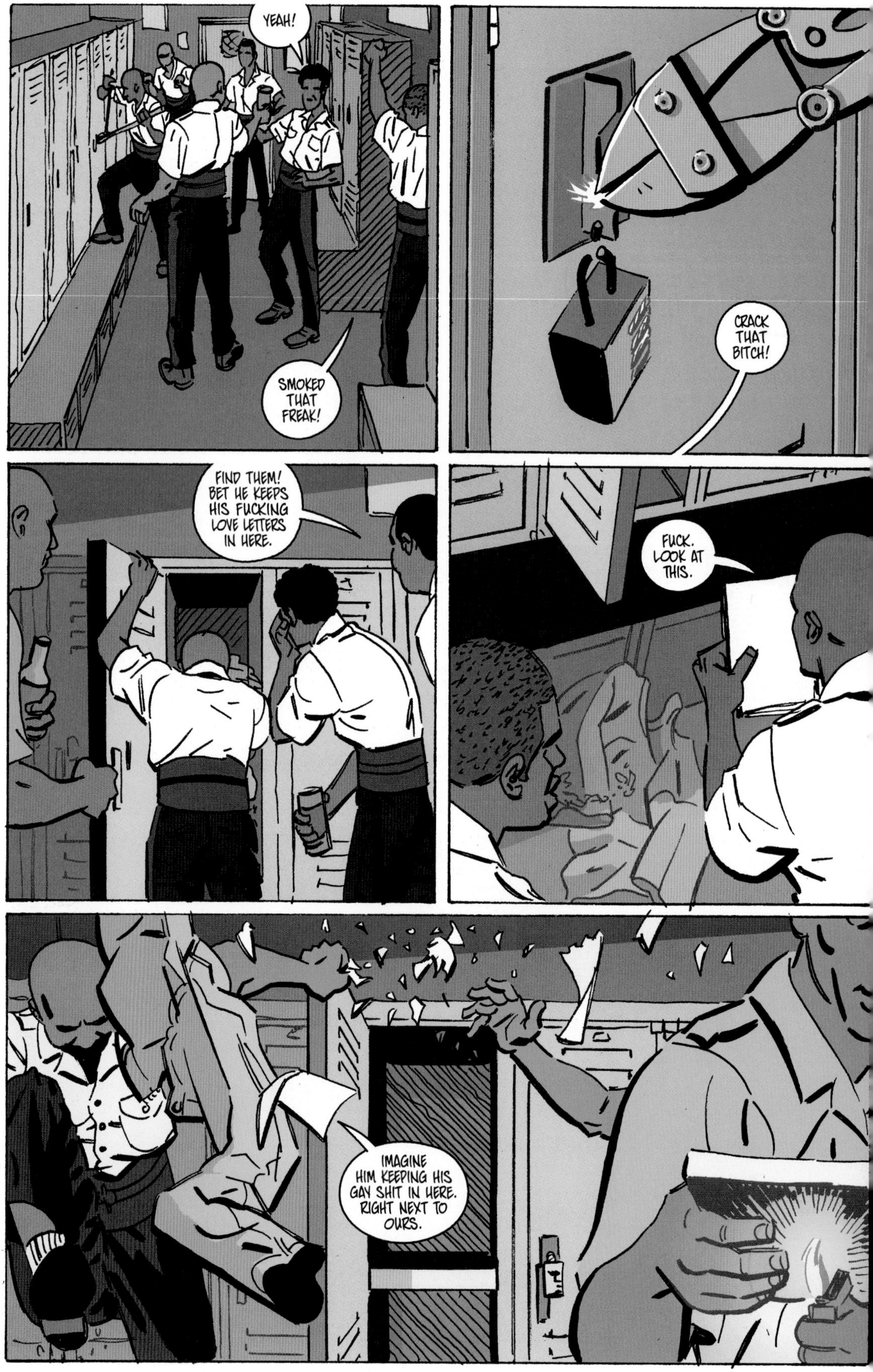
YEAH!
SMOKED THAT FREAK!
CRACK THAT BITCH!
FIND THEM! BET HE KEEPS HIS FUCKING LOVE LETTERS IN HERE.
FUCK. LOOK AT THIS.
IMAGINE HIM KEEPING HIS GAY SHIT IN HERE. RIGHT NEXT TO OURS.

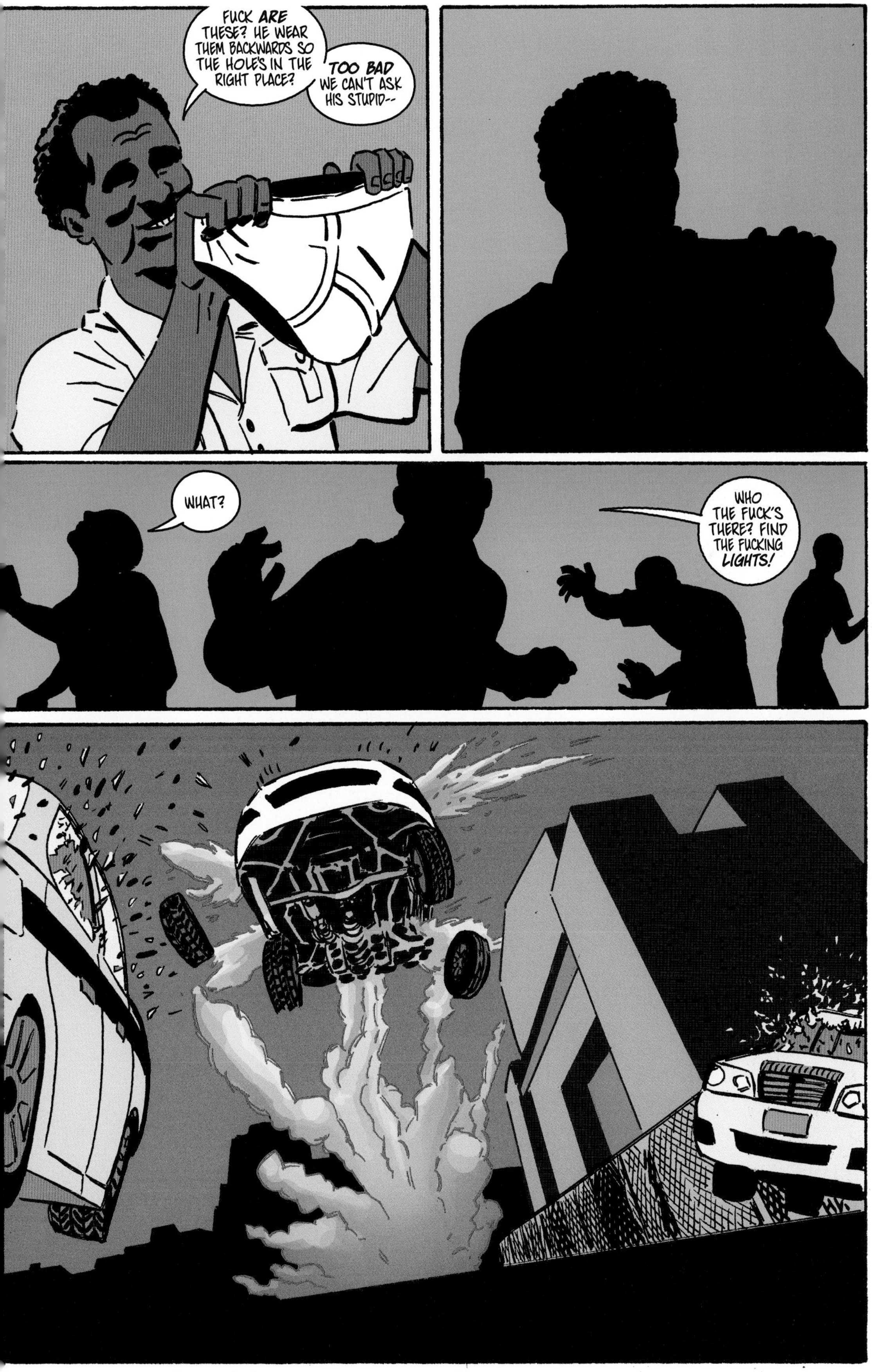
FUCK ARE THESE? HE WEAR THEM BACKWARDS SO THE HOLE'S IN THE RIGHT PLACE?
TOO BAD WE CAN'T ASK HIS STUPID--
WHAT?
WHO THE FUCK'S THERE? FIND THE FUCKING LIGHTS!

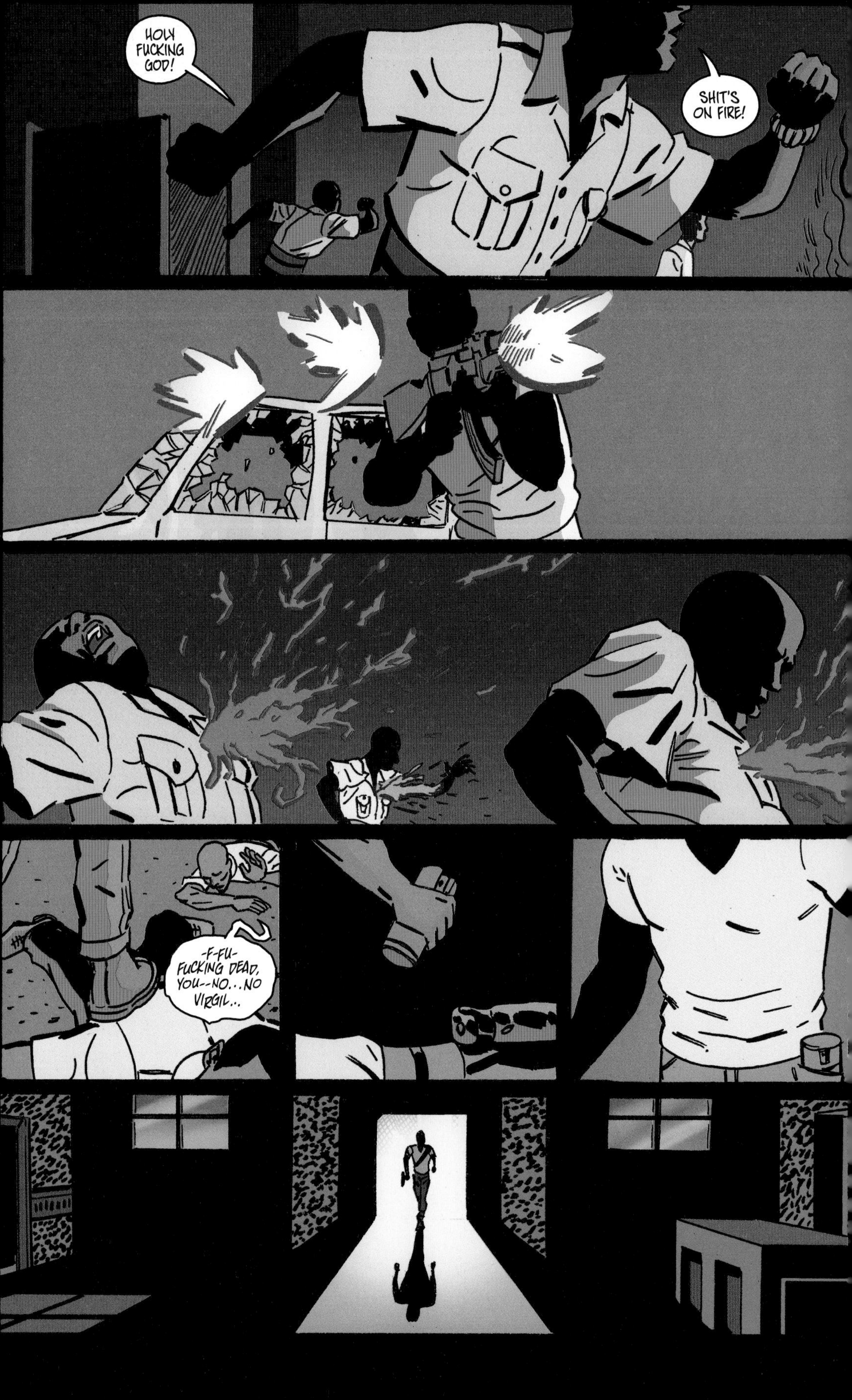
HOLY FUCKING GOD!
SHIT'S ON FIRE!
-F-FU- FUCKING DEAD, YOU--NO...NO VIRGIL...

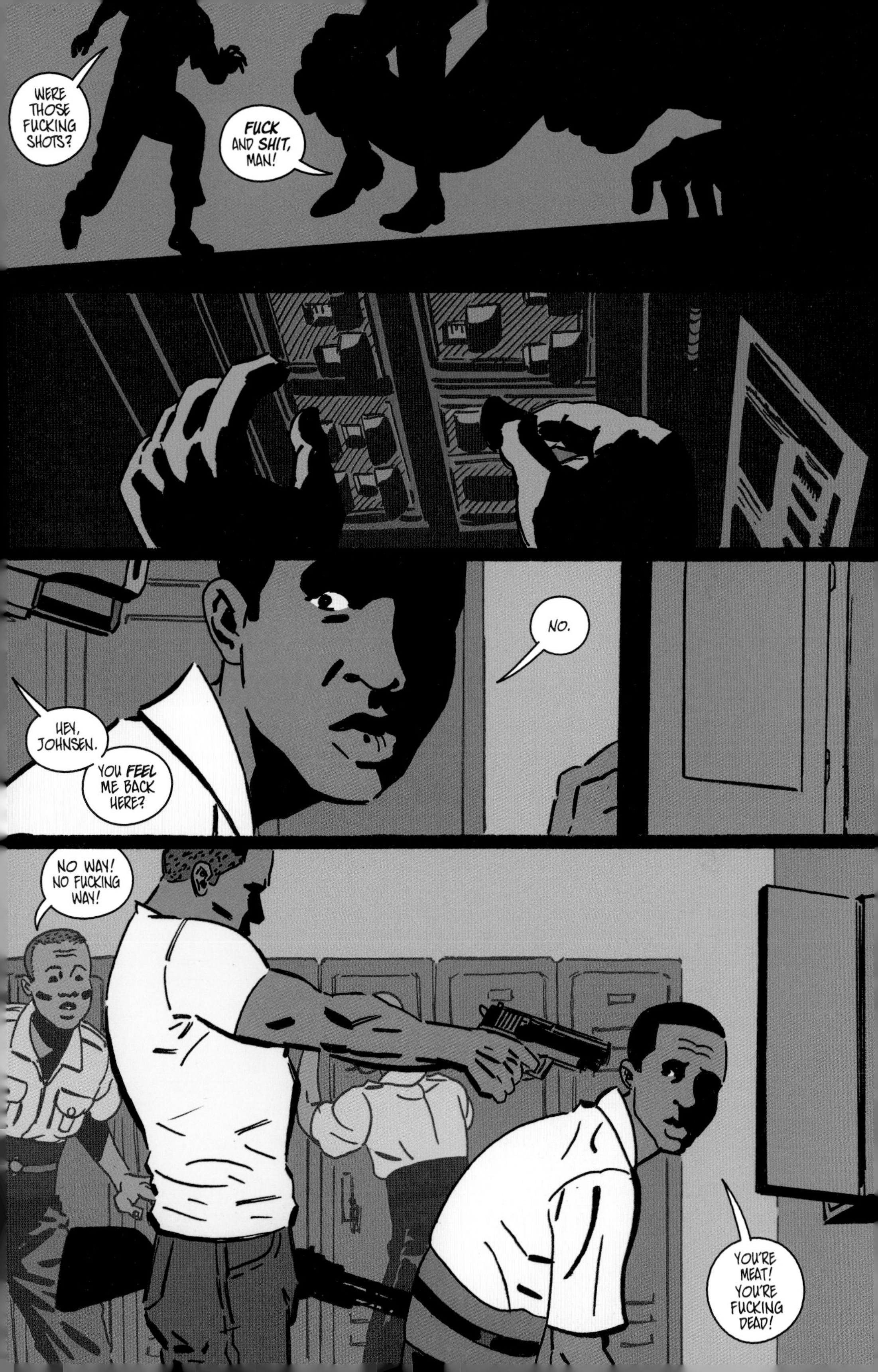
WERE THOSE FUCKING SHOTS?
FUCK AND SHIT, MAN!
NO.
HEY, JOHNSEN.
YOU FEEL ME BACK HERE?
NO WAY! NO FUCKING WAY!
YOU'RE MEAT! YOU'RE FUCKING DEAD!

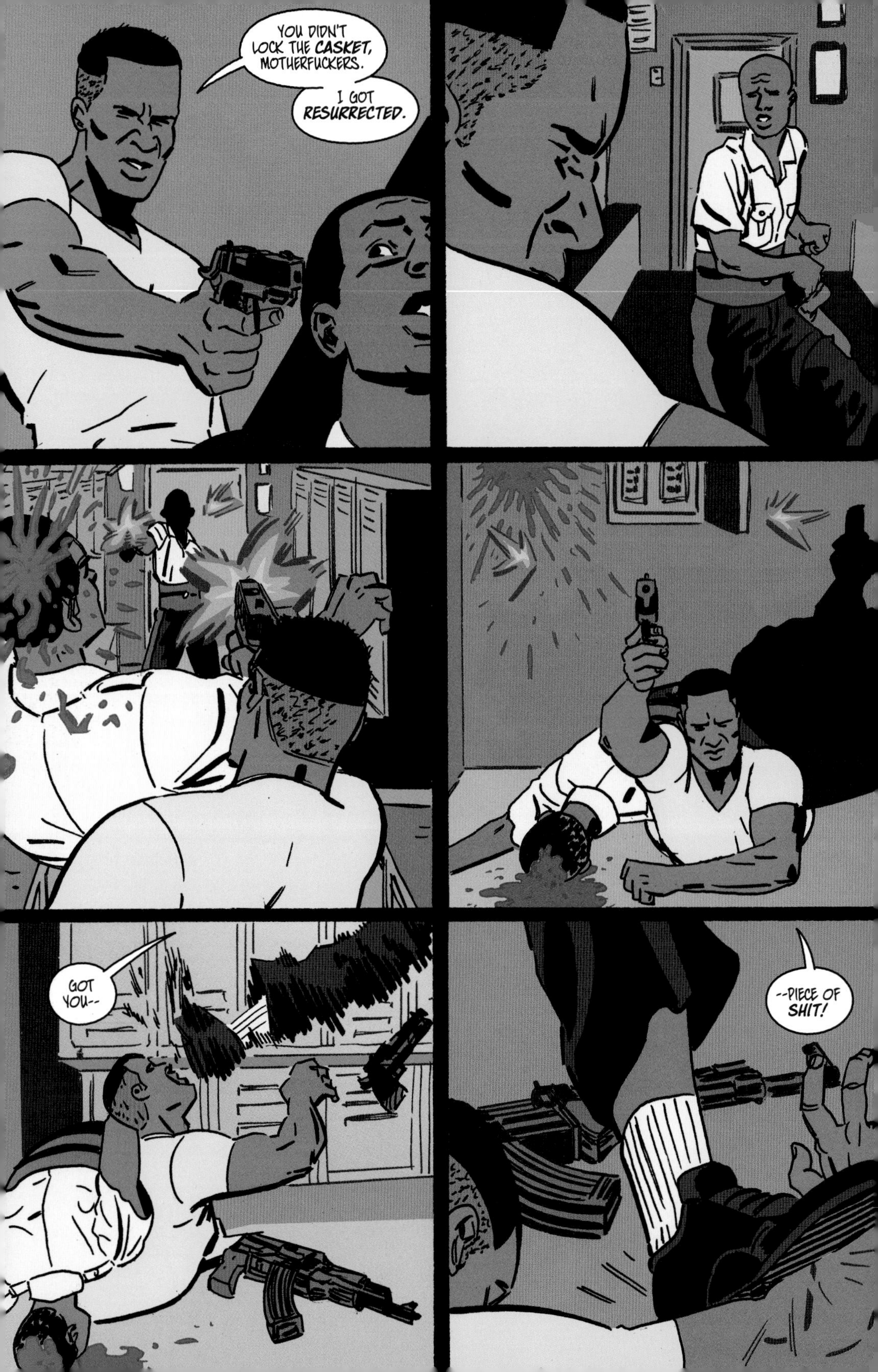
YOU DIDN'T LOCK THE CASKET, MOTHERFUCKERS.
I GOT RESURRECTED.
GOT YOU--
--PIECE OF SHIT!

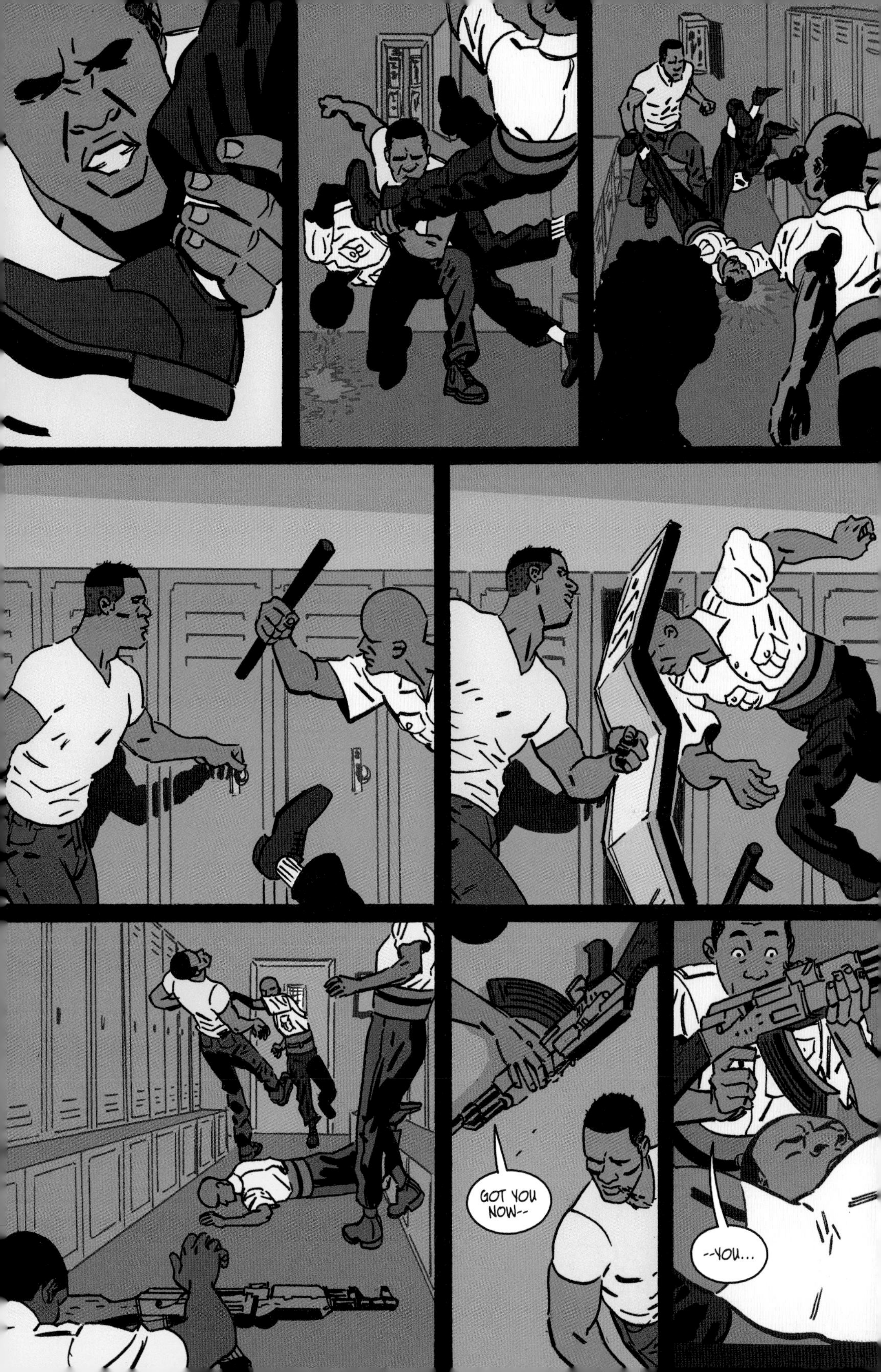
GOT YOU NOW--
--YOU...

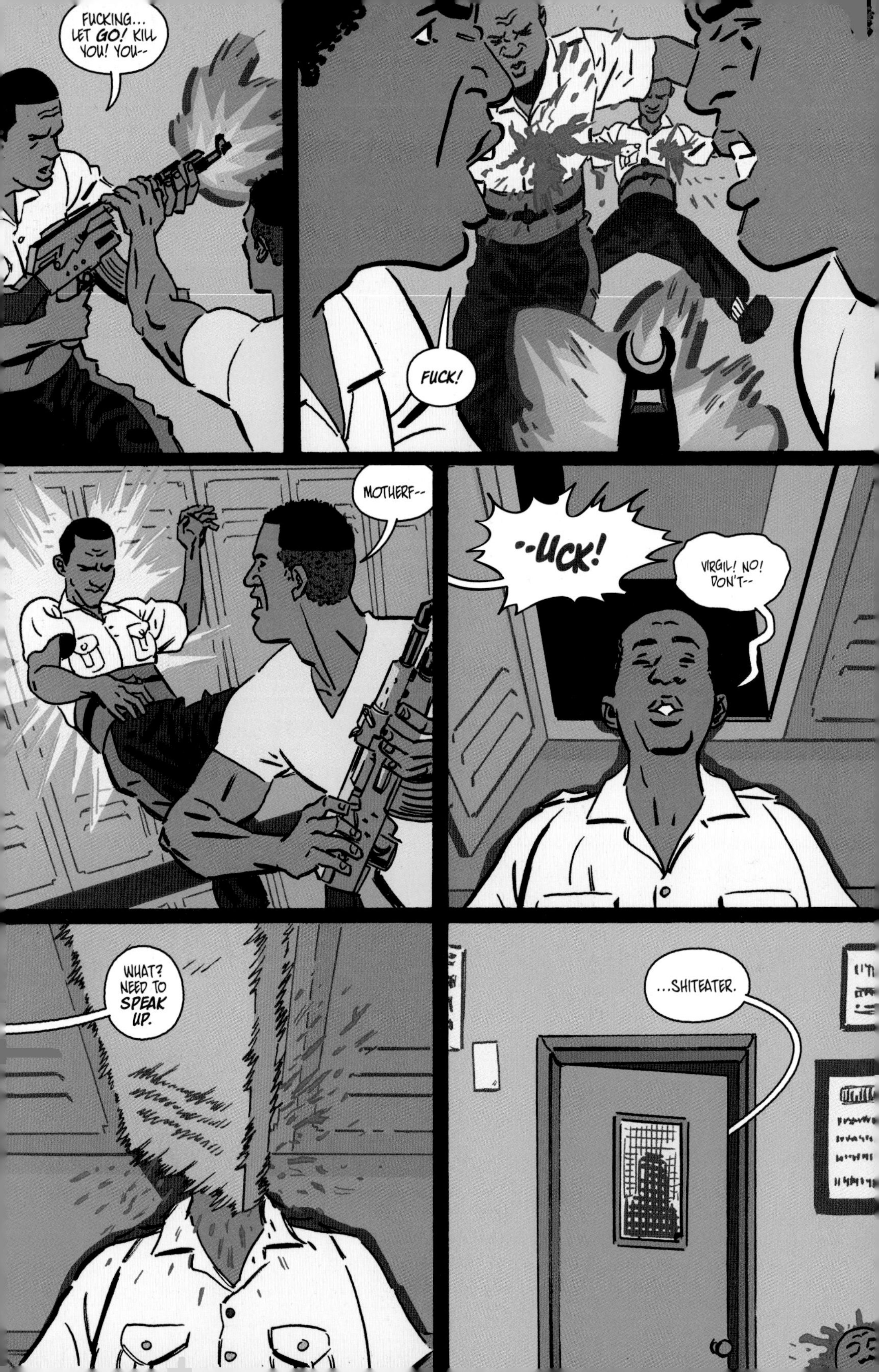
FUCKING... LET GO! KILL YOU! YOU--
FUCK!
MOTHERF--
--UCK!
VIRGIL! NO! DON'T--
WHAT? NEED TO SPEAK UP.
...SHITEATER.

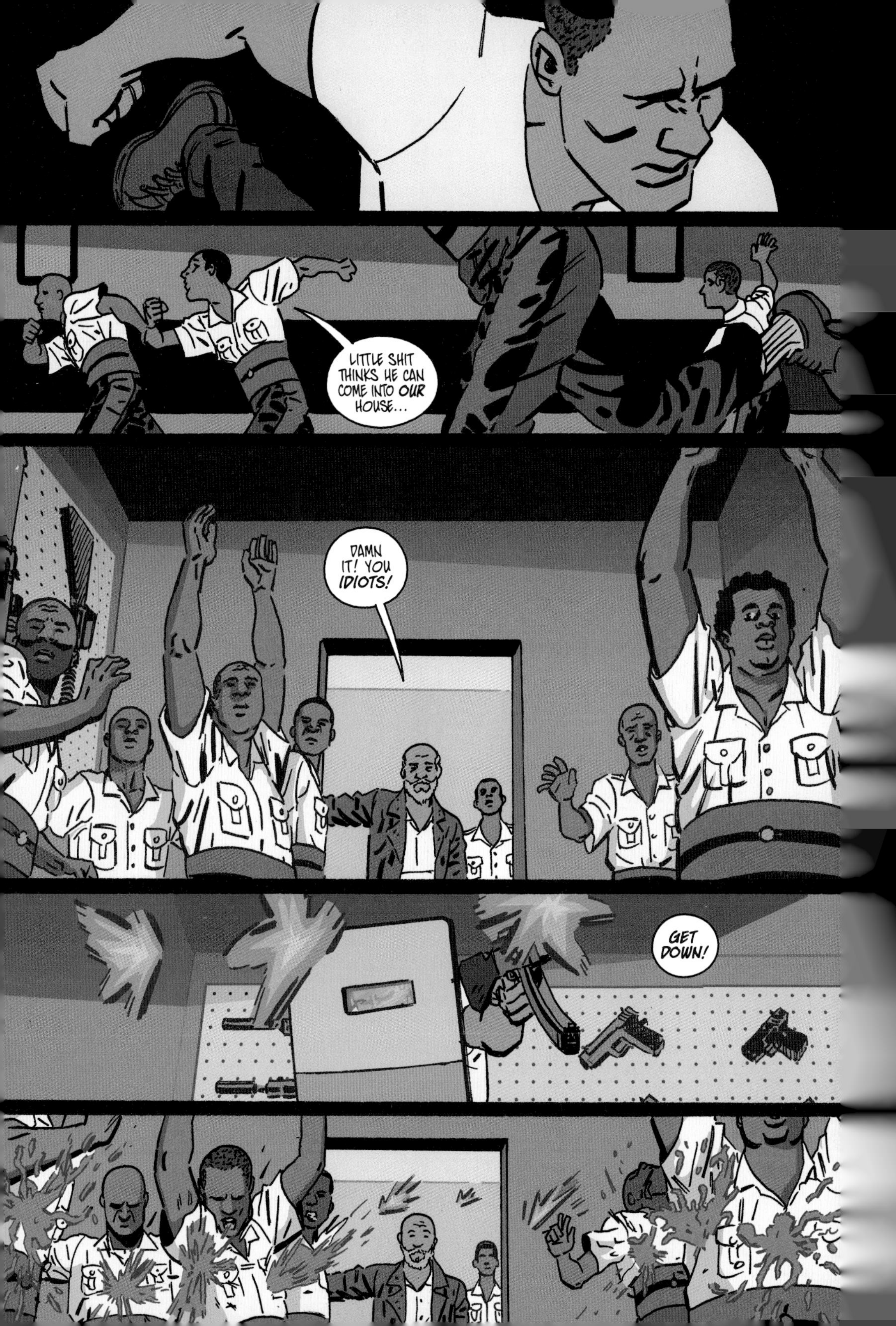
LITTLE SHIT THINKS HE CAN COME INTO OUR HOUSE...
DAMN IT! YOU IDIOTS!
GET DOWN!

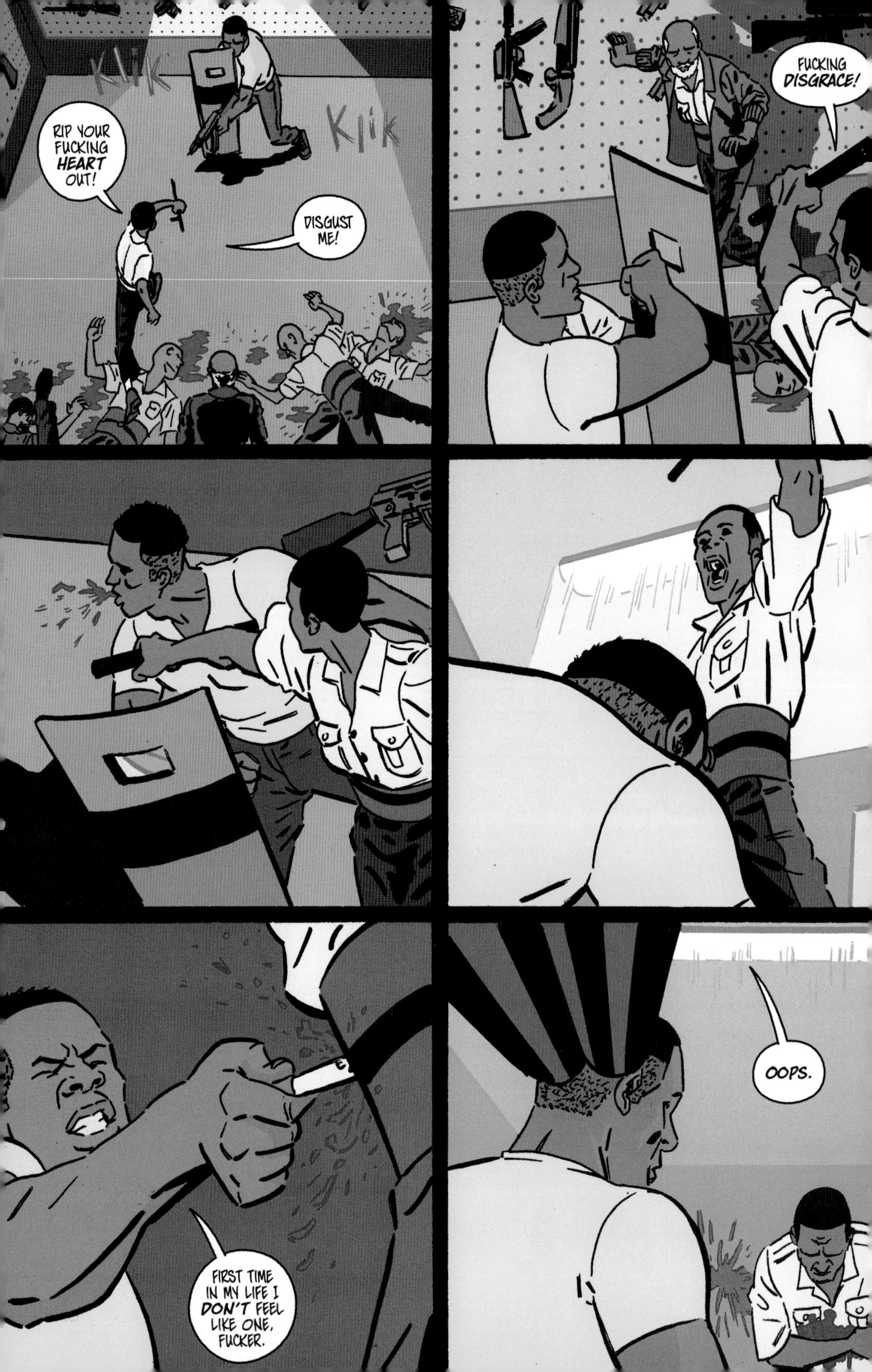
KLIK
KLIK
RIP YOUR FUCKING HEART OUT!
DISGUST ME!
FUCKING DISGRACE!
FIRST TIME IN MY LIFE I DON'T FEEL LIKE ONE, FUCKER.
OOPS.

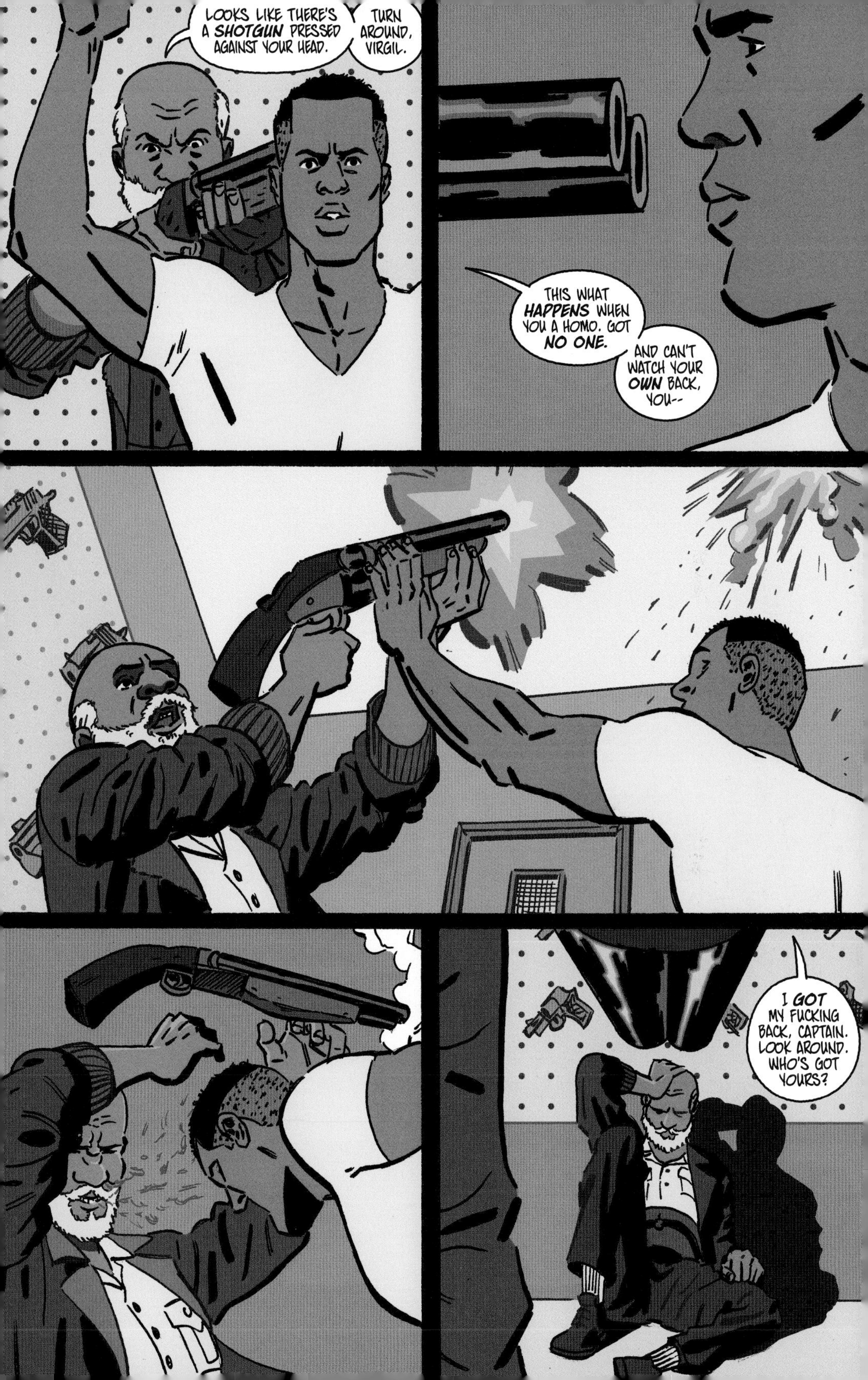
LOOKS LIKE THERE'S A SHOTGUN PRESSED AGAINST YOUR HEAD.
TURN AROUND, VIRGIL.
THIS WHAT HAPPENS WHEN YOU A HOMO. GOT NO ONE.
AND CAN'T WATCH YOUR OWN BACK, YOU--
I GOT MY FUCKING BACK, CAPTAIN. LOOK AROUND. WHO'S GOT YOURS?

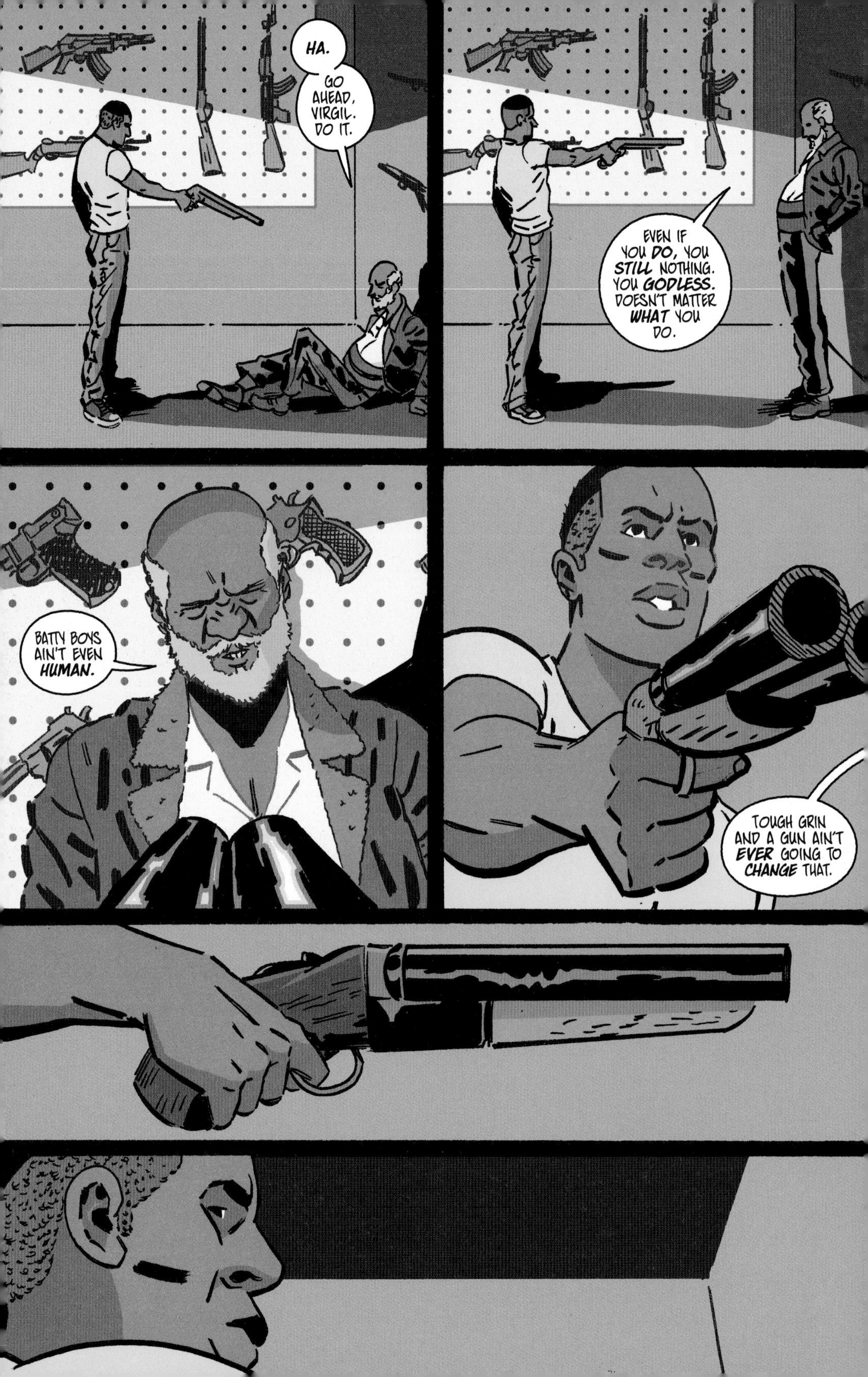
HA.
GO AHEAD, VIRGIL. DO IT.
EVEN IF YOU DO, YOU STILL NOTHING. YOU GODLESS. DOESN'T MATTER WHAT YOU DO.
BATTY BOYS AIN'T EVEN HUMAN.
TOUGH GRIN AND A GUN AIN'T EVER GOING TO CHANGE THAT.

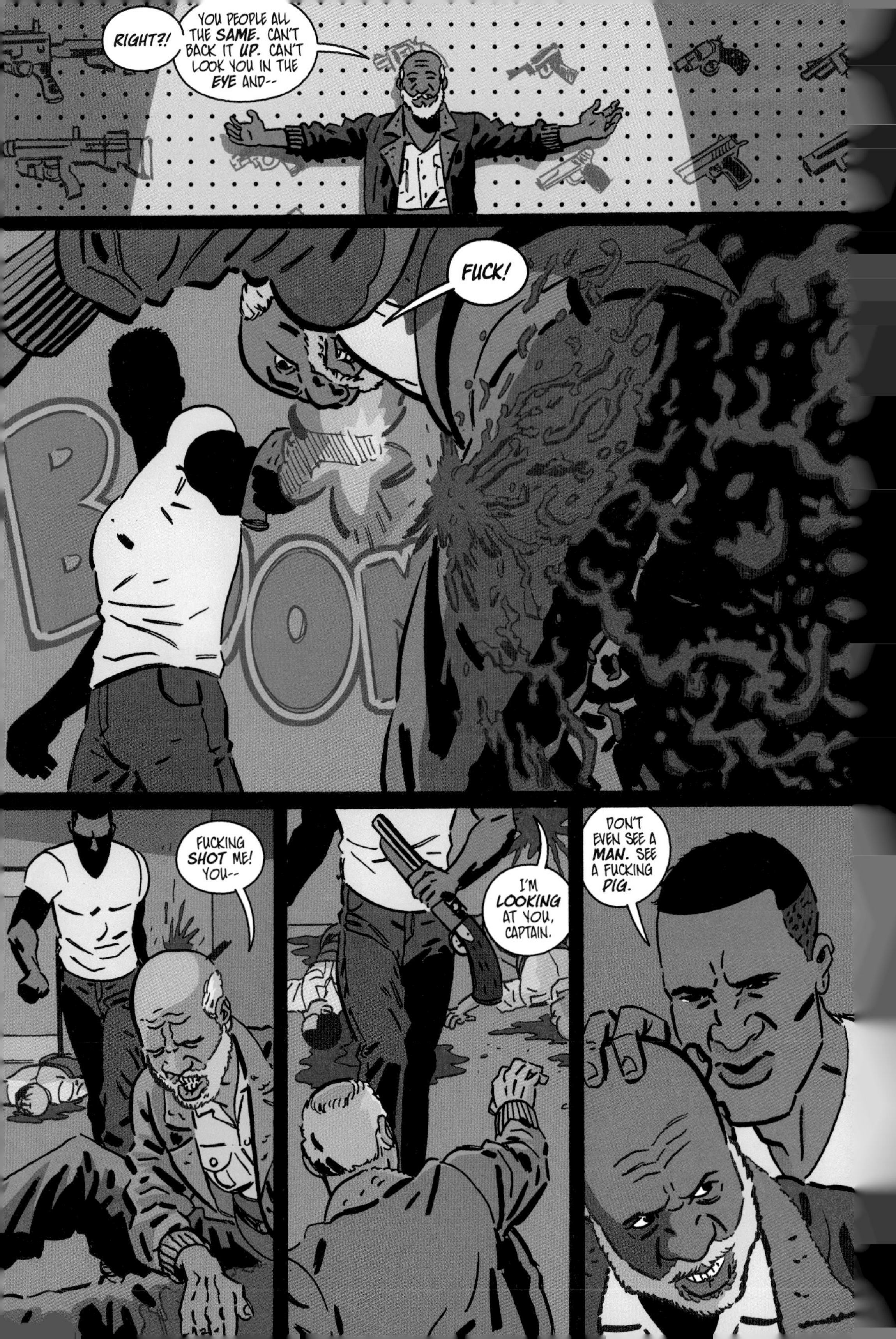
RIGHT?!
YOU PEOPLE ALL THE SAME. CAN'T BACK IT UP. CAN'T LOOK YOU IN THE EYE AND--
FUCK!
FUCKING SHOT ME! YOU--
I'M LOOKING AT YOU, CAPTAIN.
DON'T EVEN SEE A MAN. SEE A FUCKING PIG.

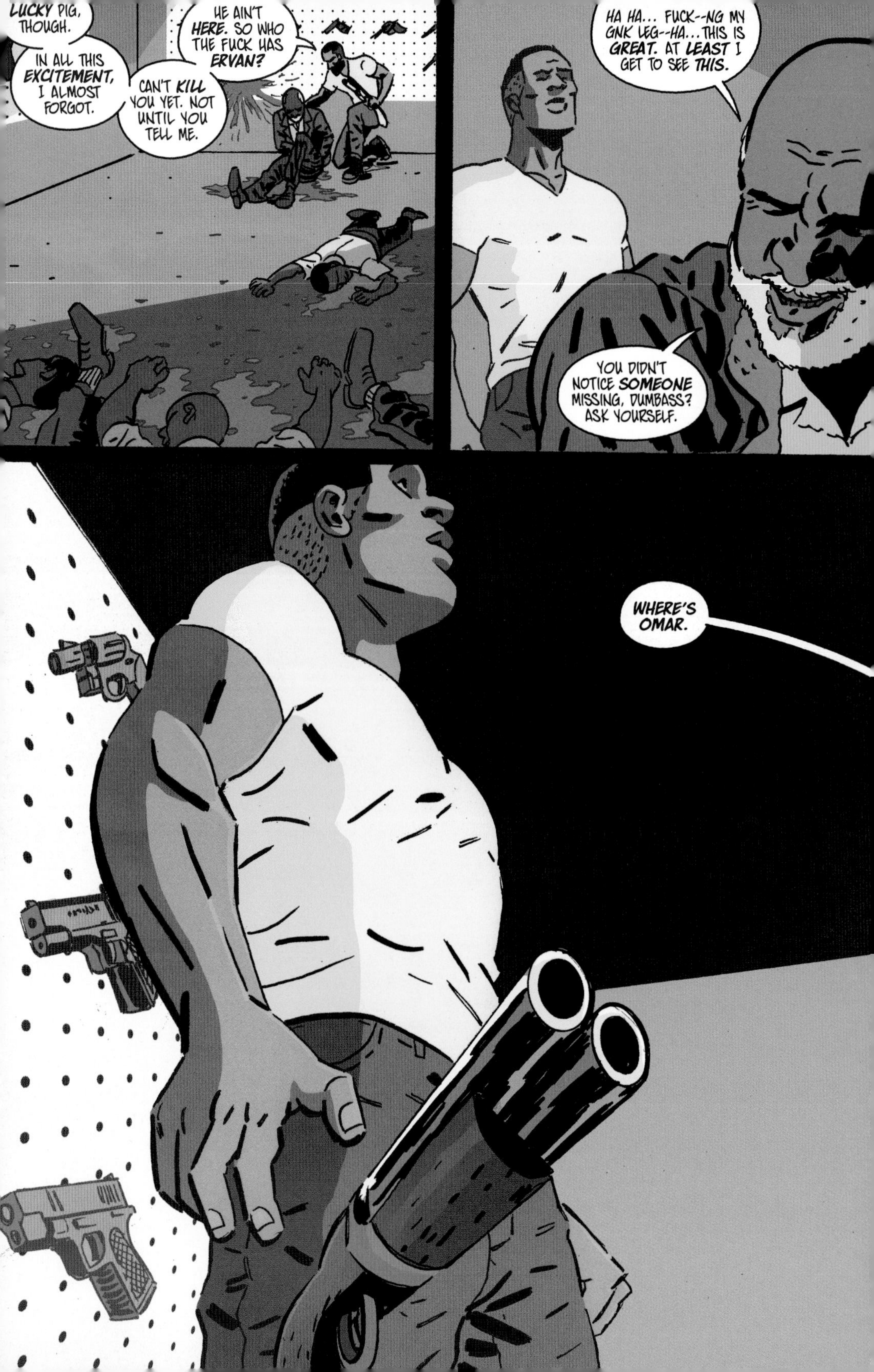
LUCKY PIG, THOUGH.
IN ALL THIS EXCITEMENT, I ALMOST FORGOT.
HE AIN'T HERE. SO WHO THE FUCK HAS ERVAN?
CAN'T KILL YOU YET. NOT UNTIL YOU TELL ME.
HA HA... FUCK--NG MY GNK LEG--HA...THIS IS GREAT. AT LEAST I GET TO SEE THIS.
YOU DIDN'T NOTICE SOMEONE MISSING, DUMBASS? ASK YOURSELF.
WHERE'S OMAR.

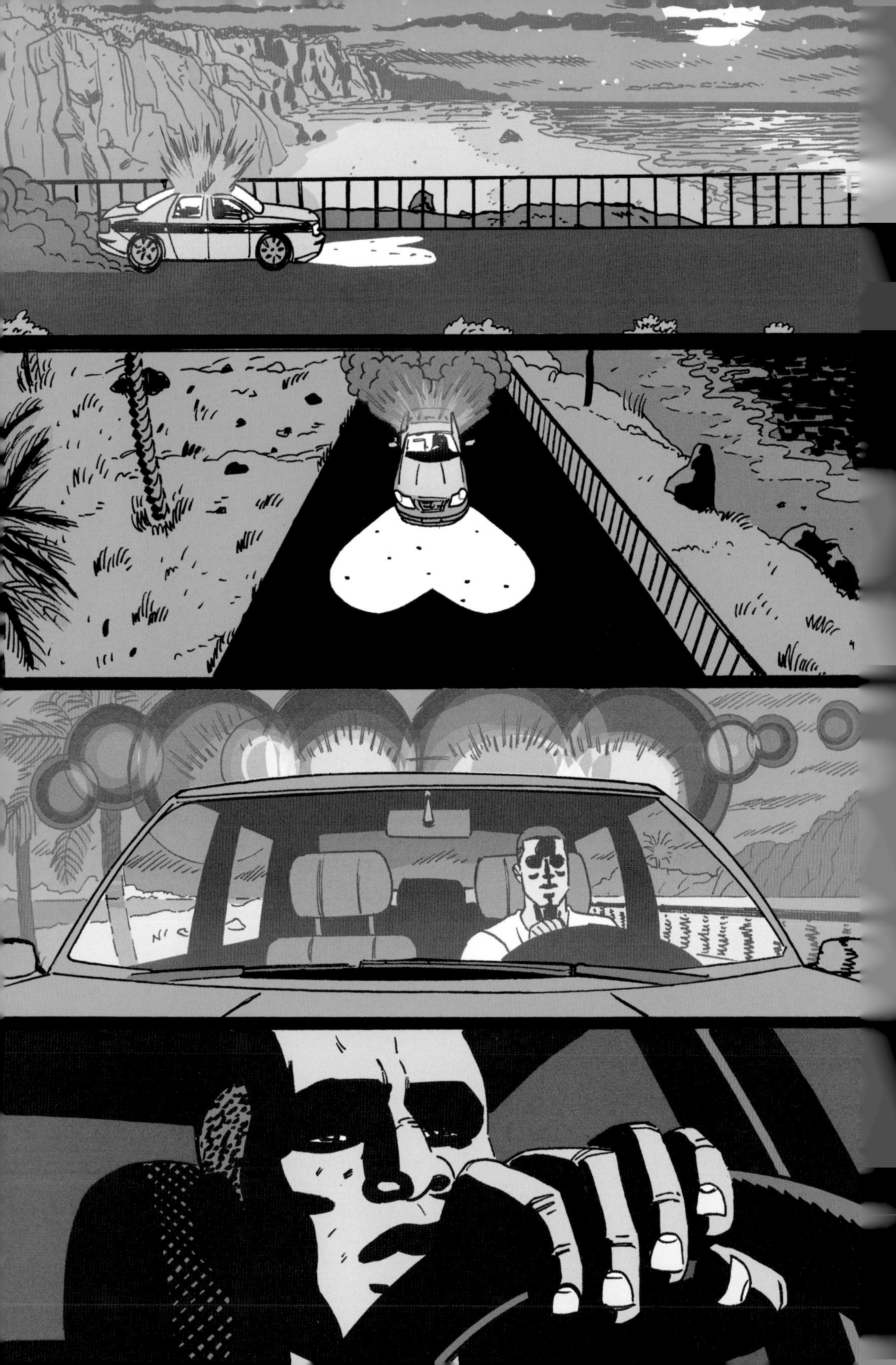

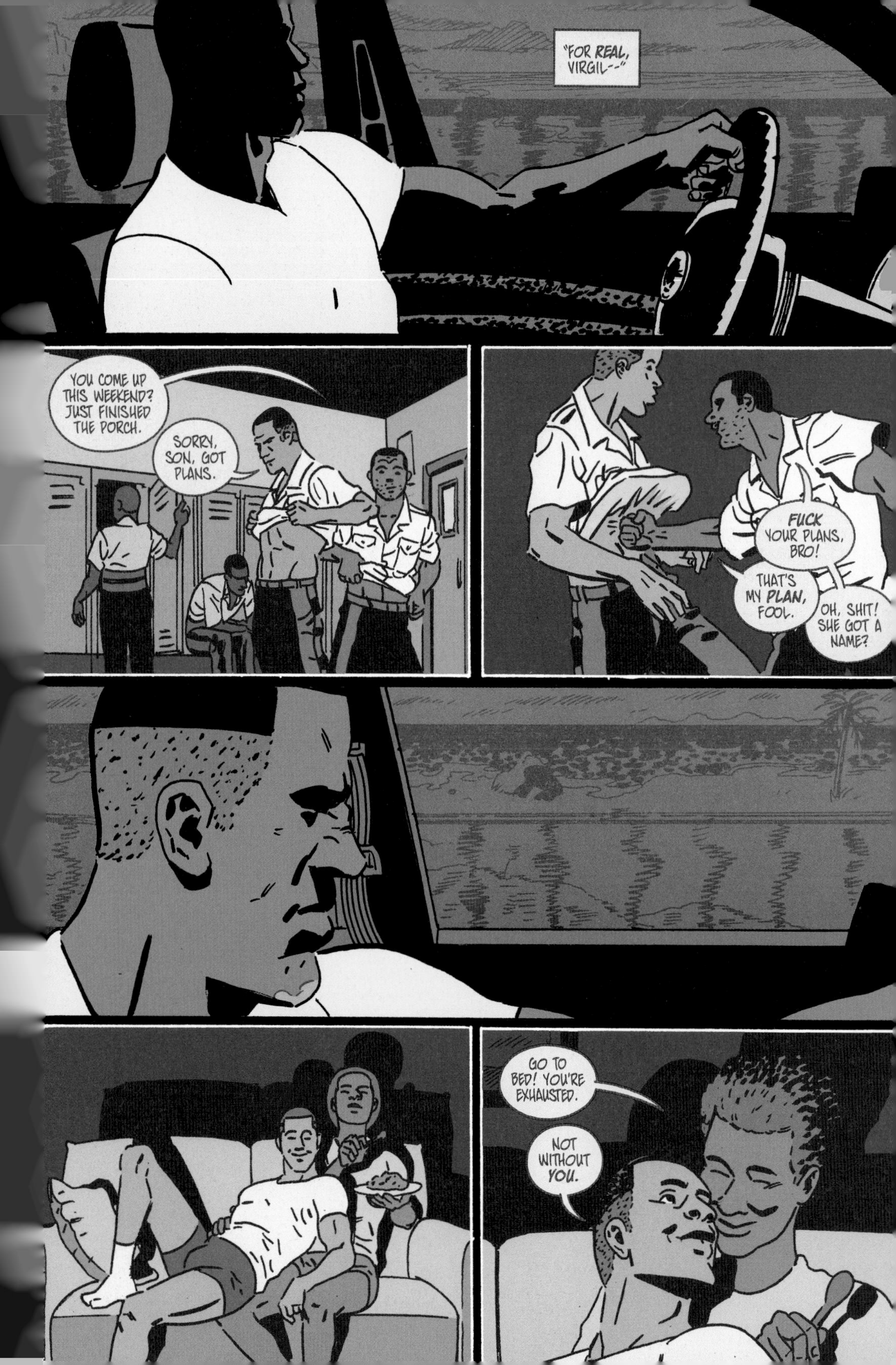
"FOR REAL, VIRGIL--"
YOU COME UP THIS WEEKEND? JUST FINISHED THE PORCH.
SORRY, SON, GOT PLANS.
FUCK YOUR PLANS, BRO!
THAT'S MY PLAN, FOOL.
OH, SHIT! SHE GOT A NAME?
GO TO BED! YOU'RE EXHAUSTED.
NOT WITHOUT YOU.

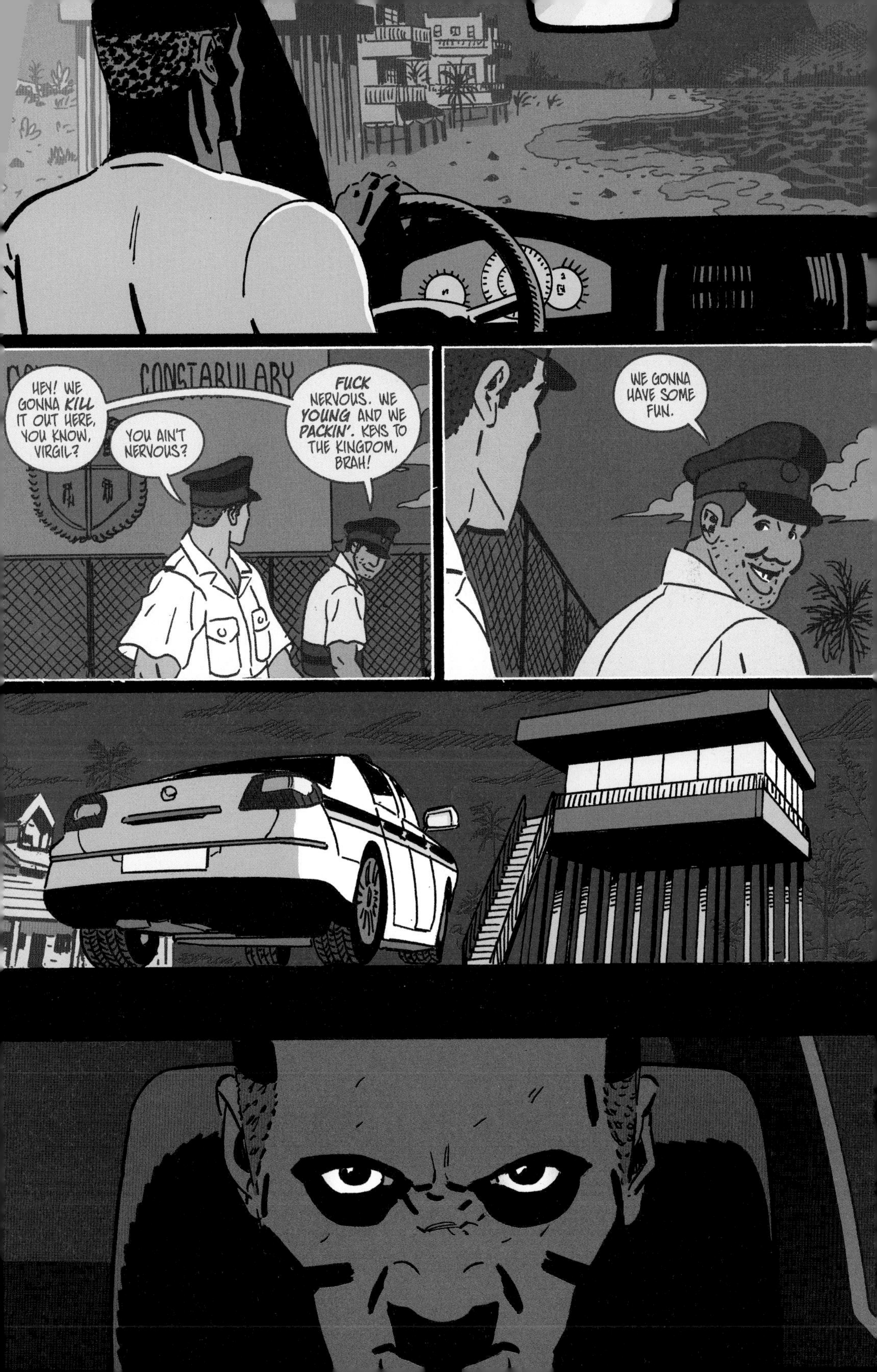
CONSTABULARY
HEY! WE GONNA KILL IT OUT HERE, YOU KNOW, VIRGIL?
YOU AIN'T NERVOUS?
FUCK NERVOUS. WE YOUNG AND WE PACKIN'. KEYS TO THE KINGDOM, BRAH!
WE GONNA HAVE SOME FUN.

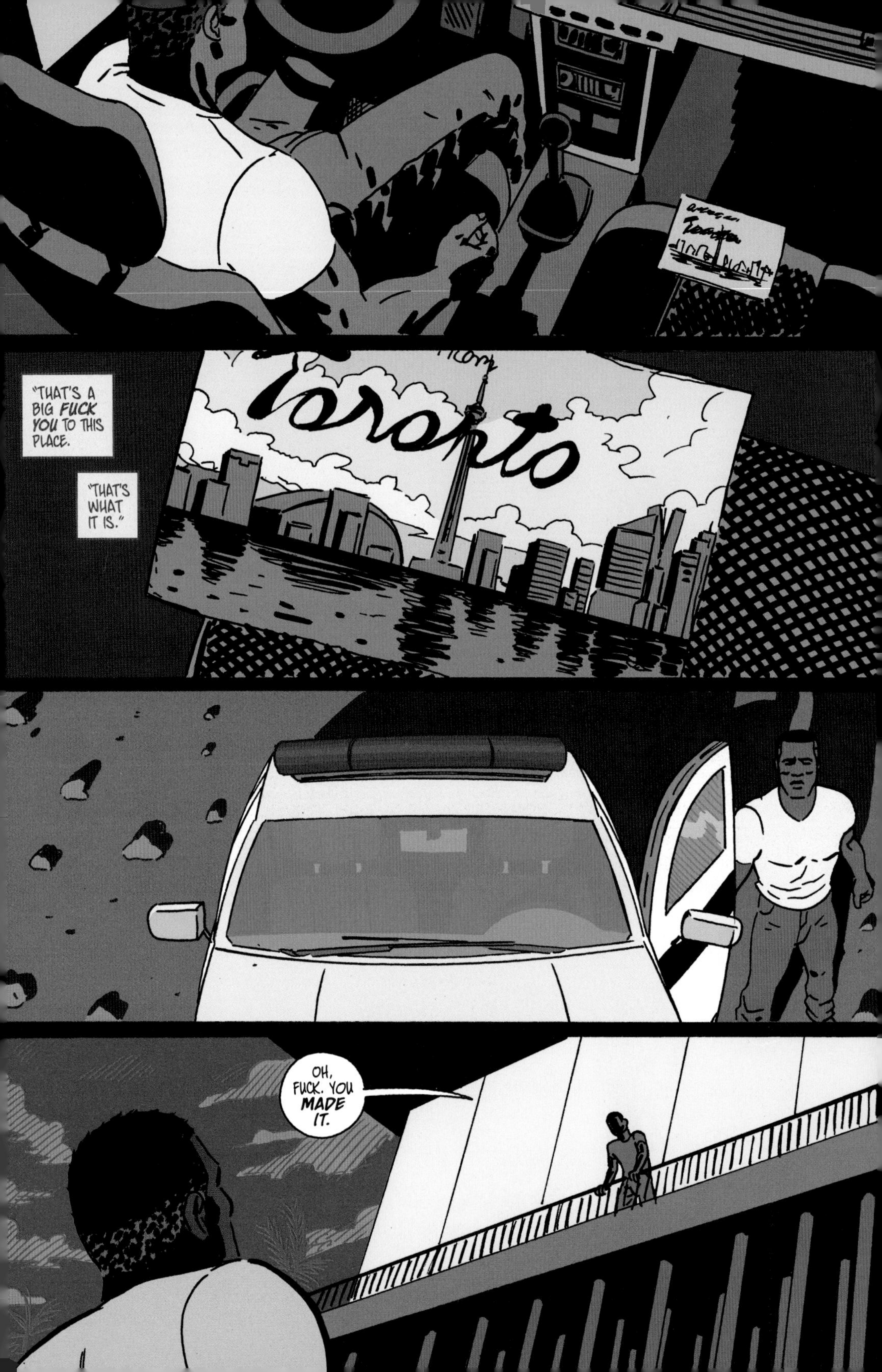
"THAT'S A BIG FUCK YOU TO THIS PLACE.
"THAT'S WHAT IT IS."
Toronto
OH, FUCK. YOU MADE IT.

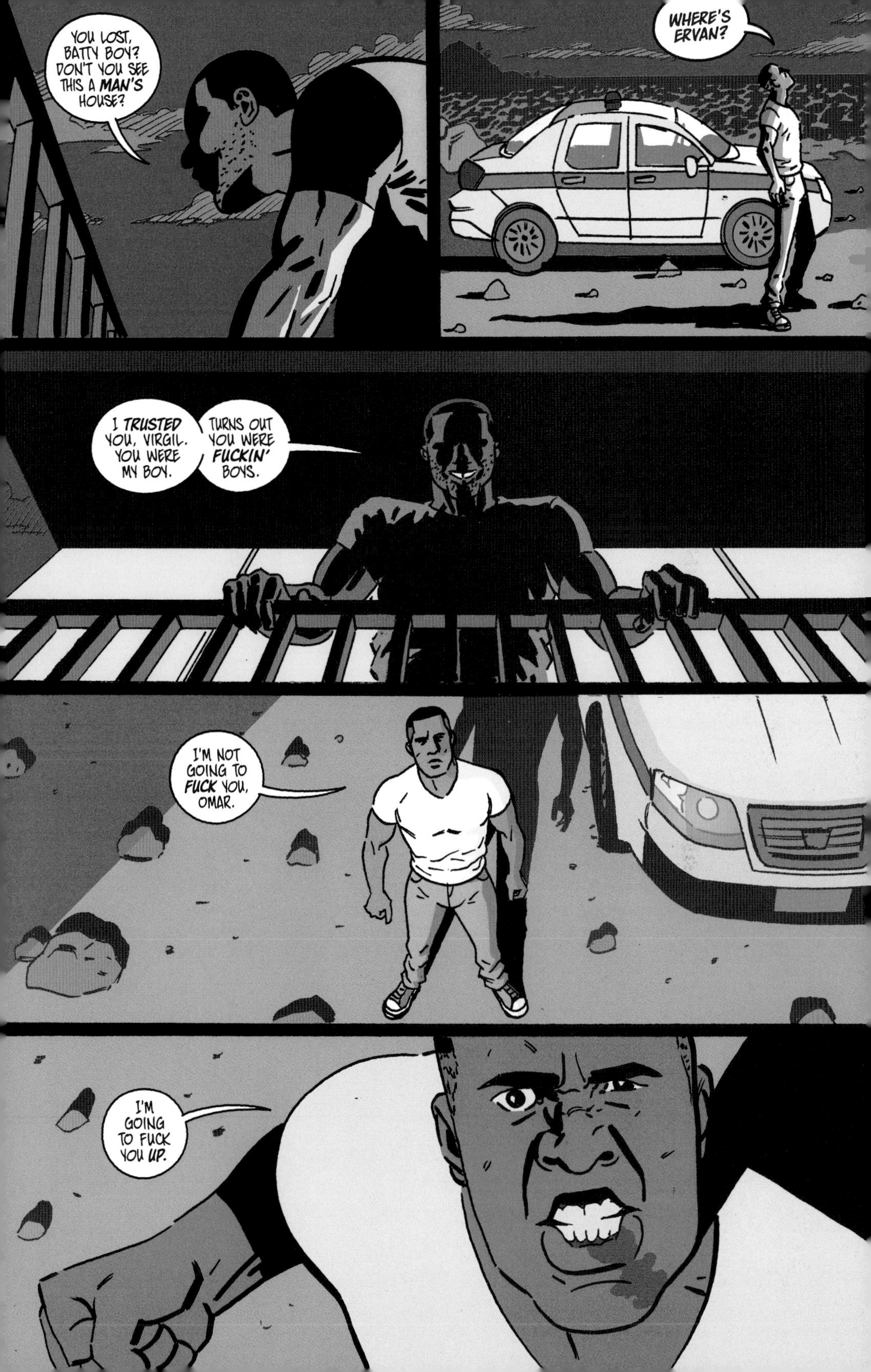
YOU LOST, BATTY BOY? DON'T YOU SEE THIS A **MAN'S** HOUSE?
WHERE'S ERVAN?
I **TRUSTED** YOU, VIRGIL. YOU WERE MY BOY.
TURNS OUT YOU WERE **FUCKIN'** BOYS.
I'M NOT GOING TO **FUCK** YOU, OMAR.
I'M GOING TO FUCK YOU **UP**.

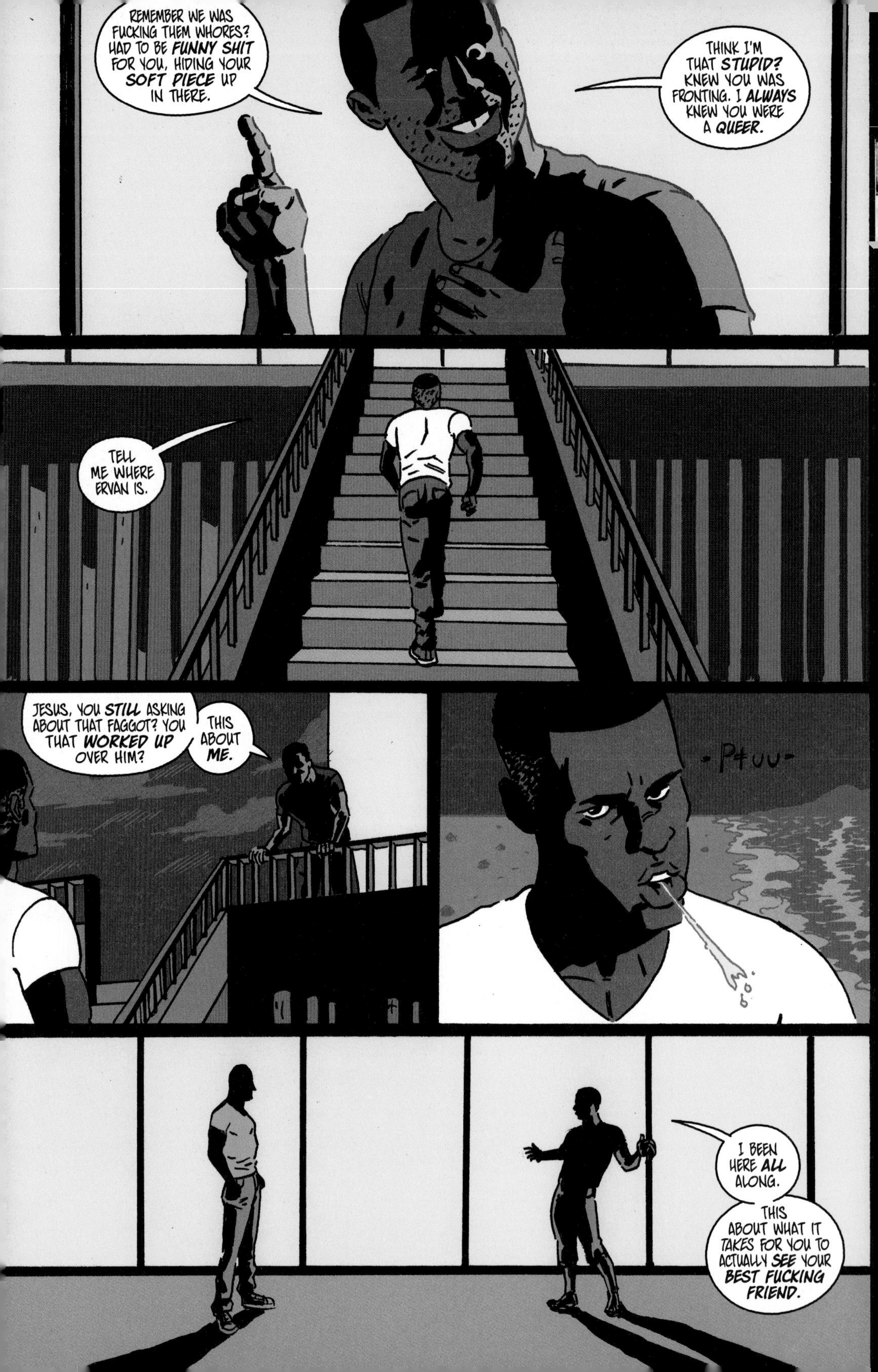
REMEMBER WE WAS FUCKING THEM WHORES? HAD TO BE FUNNY SHIT FOR YOU, HIDING YOUR SOFT PIECE UP IN THERE.
THINK I'M THAT STUPID? KNEW YOU WAS FRONTING. I ALWAYS KNEW YOU WERE A QUEER.
TELL ME WHERE ERVAN IS.
JESUS, YOU STILL ASKING ABOUT THAT FAGGOT? YOU THAT WORKED UP OVER HIM?
THIS ABOUT ME.
-PTUU-
I BEEN HERE ALL ALONG.
THIS ABOUT WHAT IT TAKES FOR YOU TO ACTUALLY SEE YOUR BEST FUCKING FRIEND.

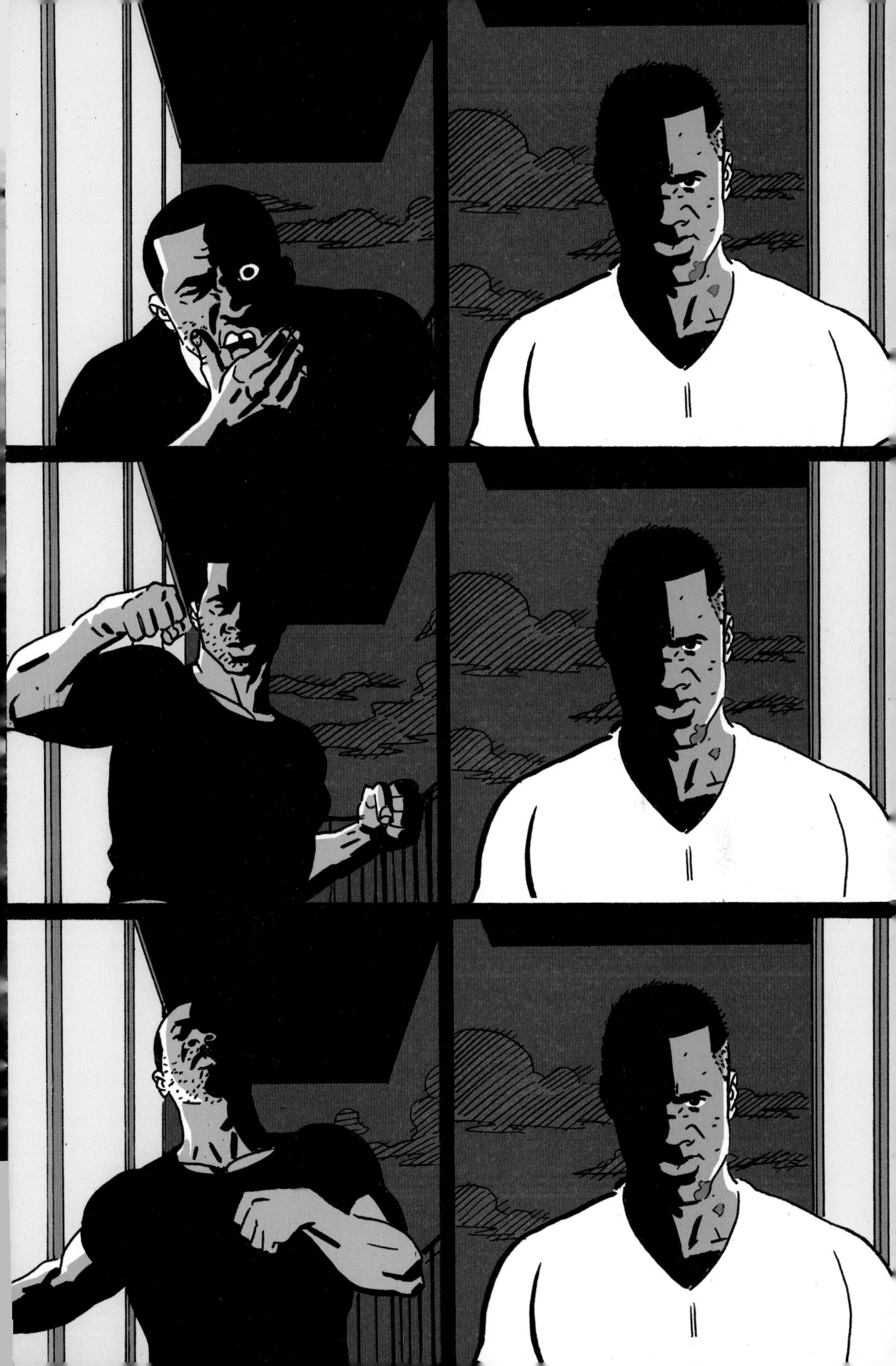

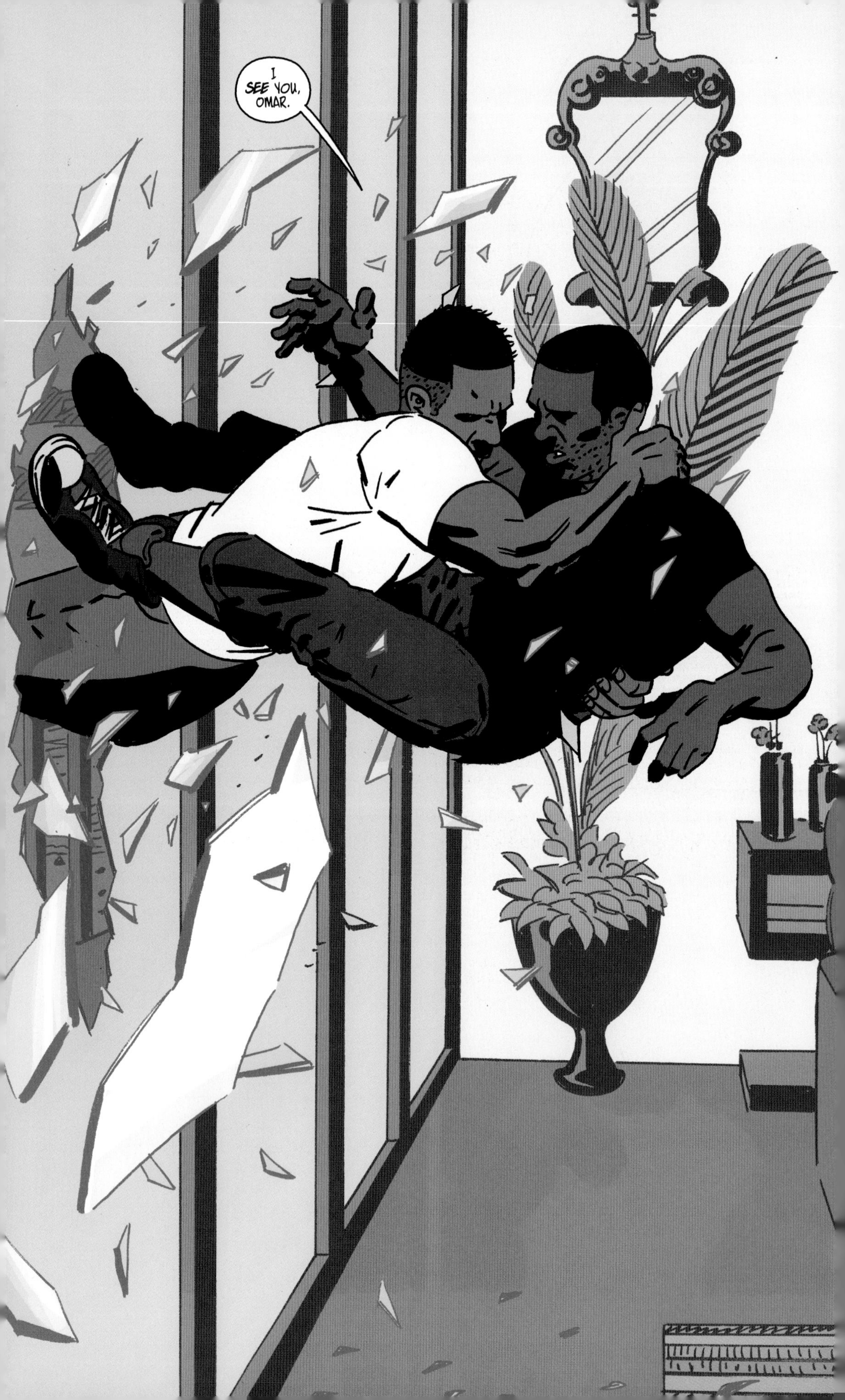
I SEE YOU, OMAR.

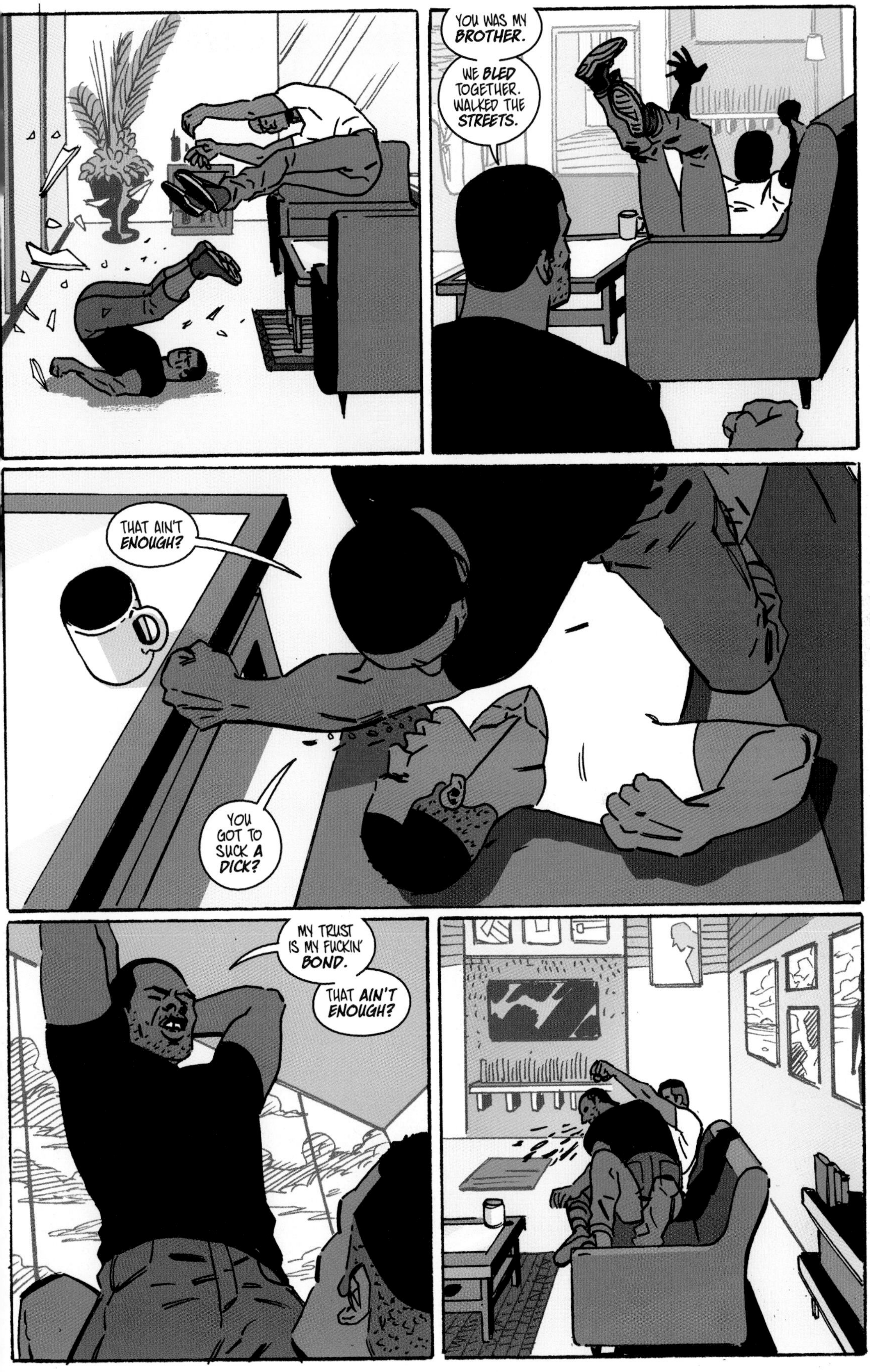
YOU WAS MY BROTHER.
WE BLED TOGETHER. WALKED THE STREETS.
THAT AIN'T ENOUGH?
YOU GOT TO SUCK A DICK?
MY TRUST IS MY FUCKIN' BOND.
THAT AIN'T ENOUGH?

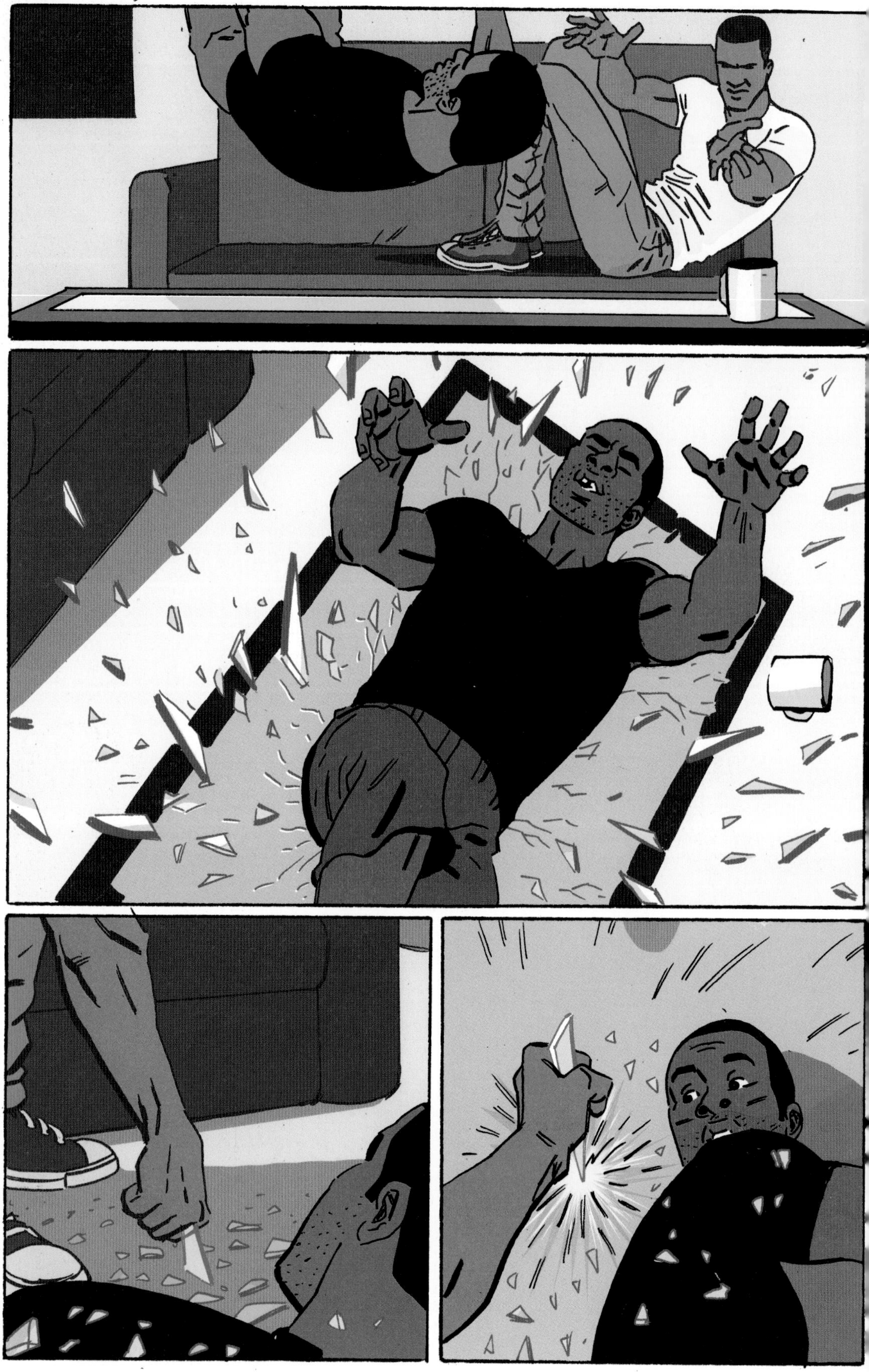

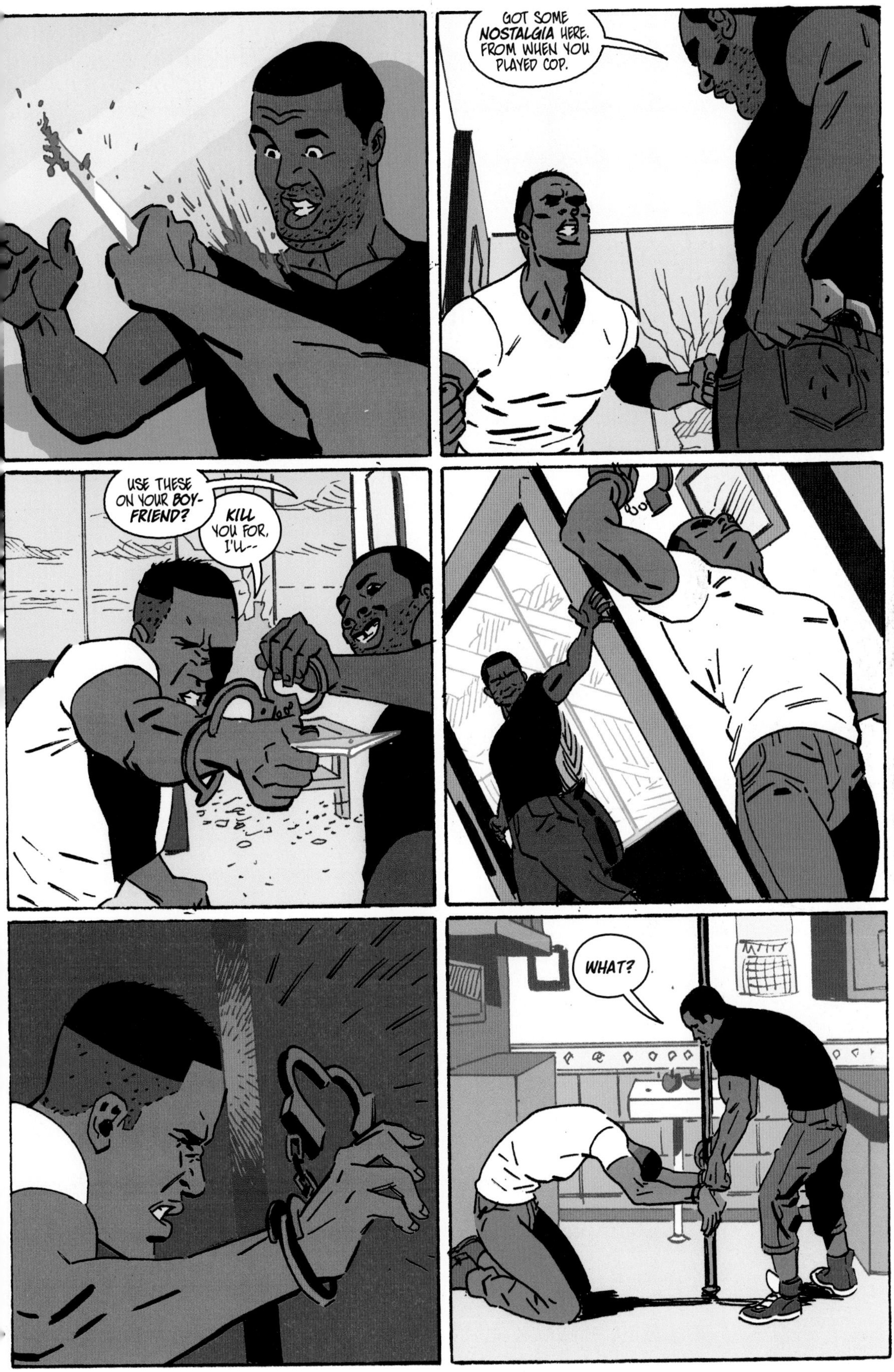
GOT SOME NOSTALGIA HERE. FROM WHEN YOU PLAYED COP.
USE THESE ON YOUR BOY-FRIEND?
KILL YOU FOR, I'LL--
WHAT?

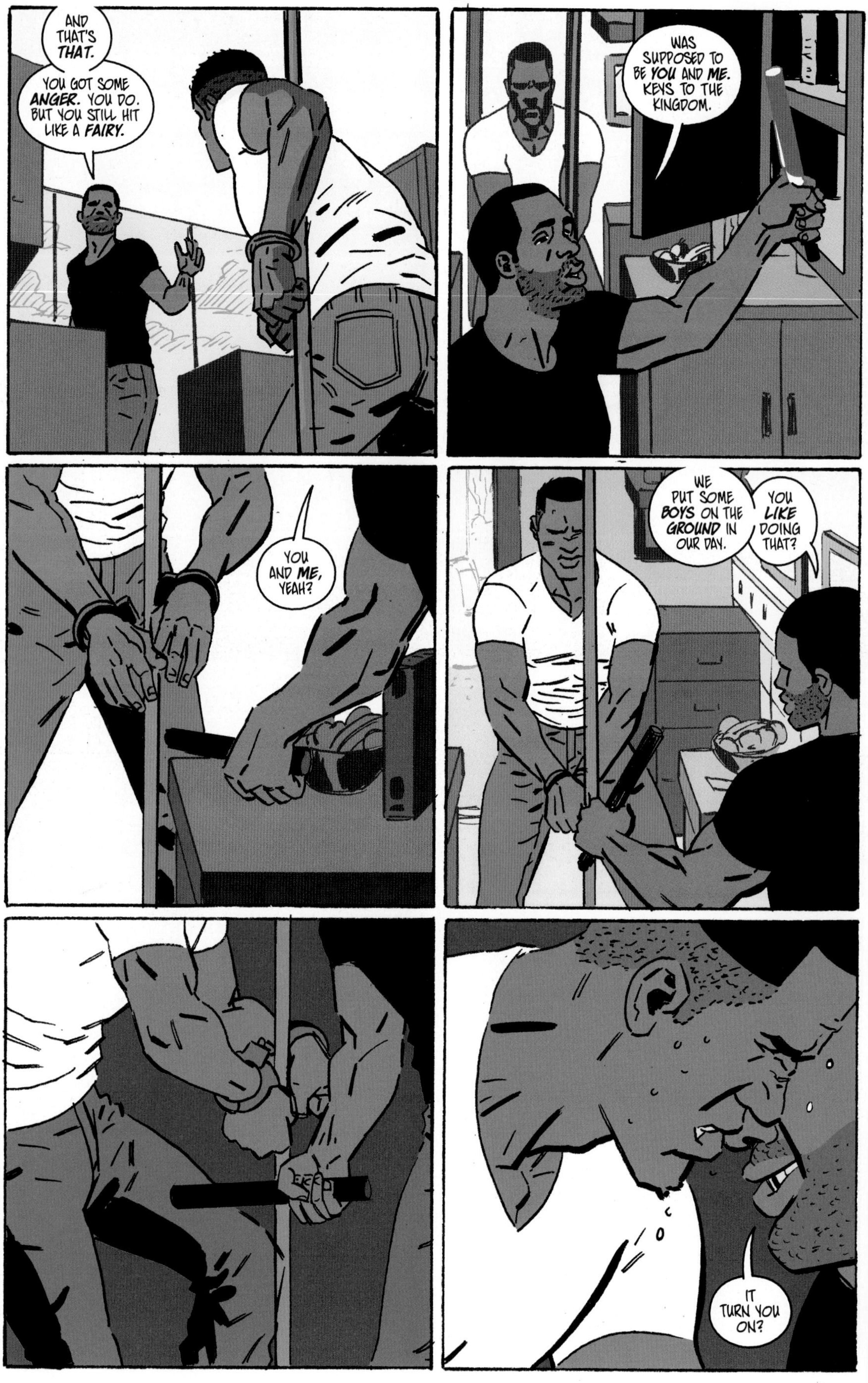
AND THAT'S THAT.
YOU GOT SOME ANGER. YOU DO. BUT YOU STILL HIT LIKE A FAIRY.
WAS SUPPOSED TO BE YOU AND ME. KEYS TO THE KINGDOM.
YOU AND ME, YEAH?
WE PUT SOME BOYS ON THE GROUND IN OUR DAY.
YOU LIKE DOING THAT?
IT TURN YOU ON?

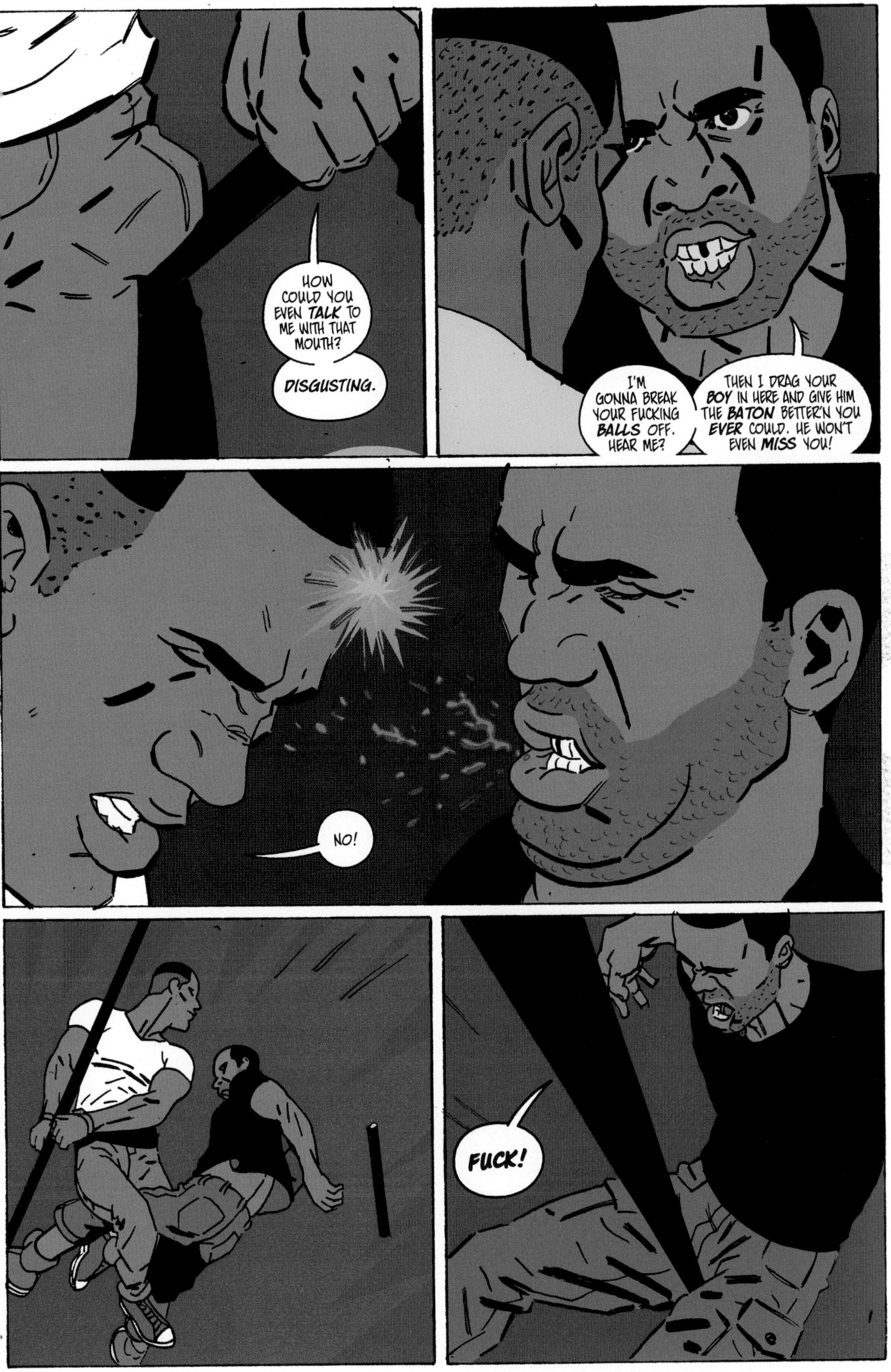
HOW COULD YOU EVEN TALK TO ME WITH THAT MOUTH?
DISGUSTING.
I'M GONNA BREAK YOUR FUCKING BALLS OFF. HEAR ME?
THEN I DRAG YOUR BOY IN HERE AND GIVE HIM THE BATON BETTER'N YOU EVER COULD. HE WON'T EVEN MISS YOU!
NO!
FUCK!

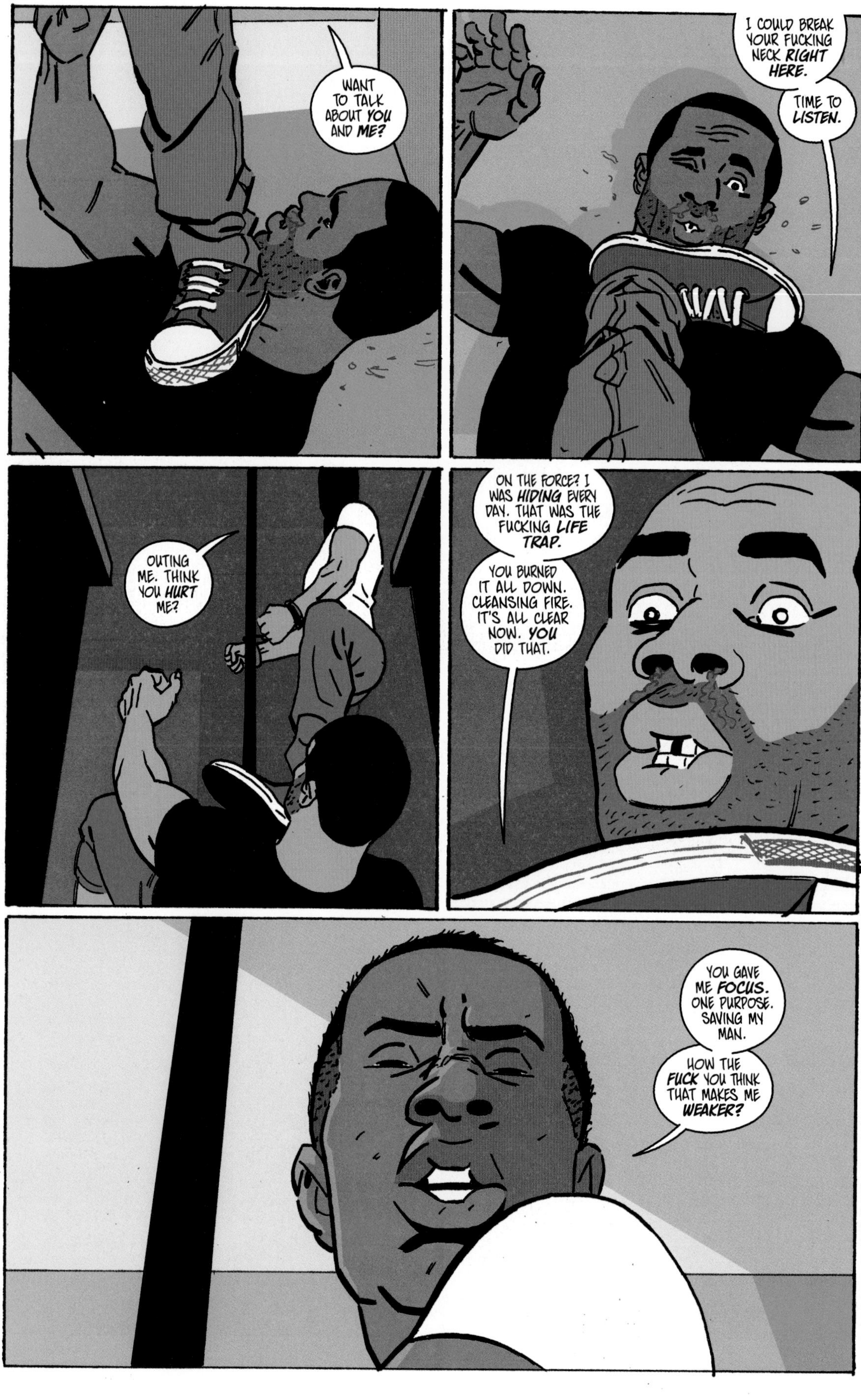
WANT TO TALK ABOUT YOU AND ME?
I COULD BREAK YOUR FUCKING NECK RIGHT HERE.
TIME TO LISTEN.
OUTING ME. THINK YOU HURT ME?
ON THE FORCE? I WAS HIDING EVERY DAY. THAT WAS THE FUCKING LIFE TRAP.
YOU BURNED IT ALL DOWN. CLEANSING FIRE. IT'S ALL CLEAR NOW. YOU DID THAT.
YOU GAVE ME FOCUS. ONE PURPOSE. SAVING MY MAN.
HOW THE FUCK YOU THINK THAT MAKES ME WEAKER?

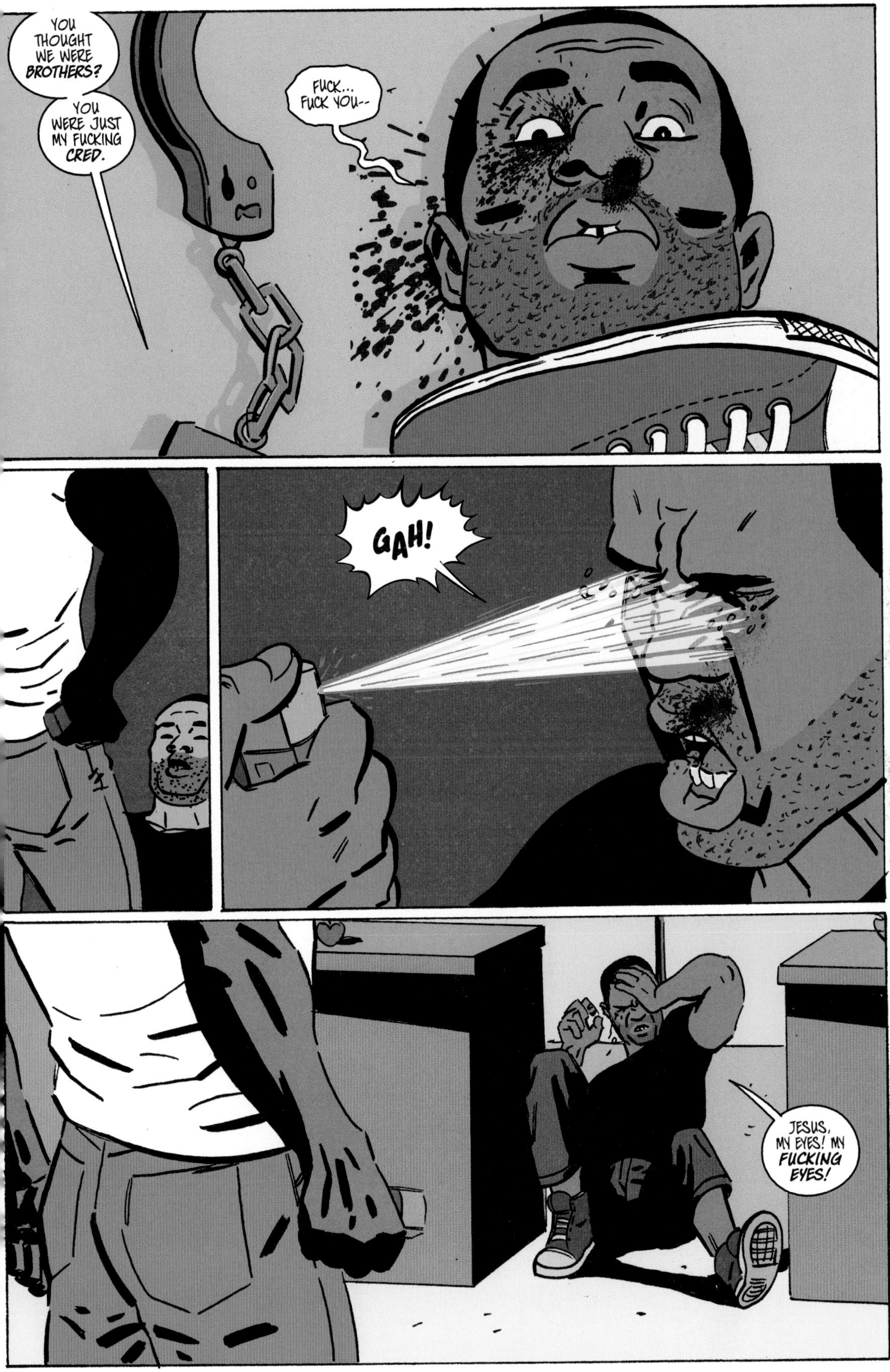
YOU THOUGHT WE WERE BROTHERS?
YOU WERE JUST MY FUCKING CRED.
FUCK... FUCK YOU--
GAH!
JESUS, MY EYES! MY FUCKING EYES!

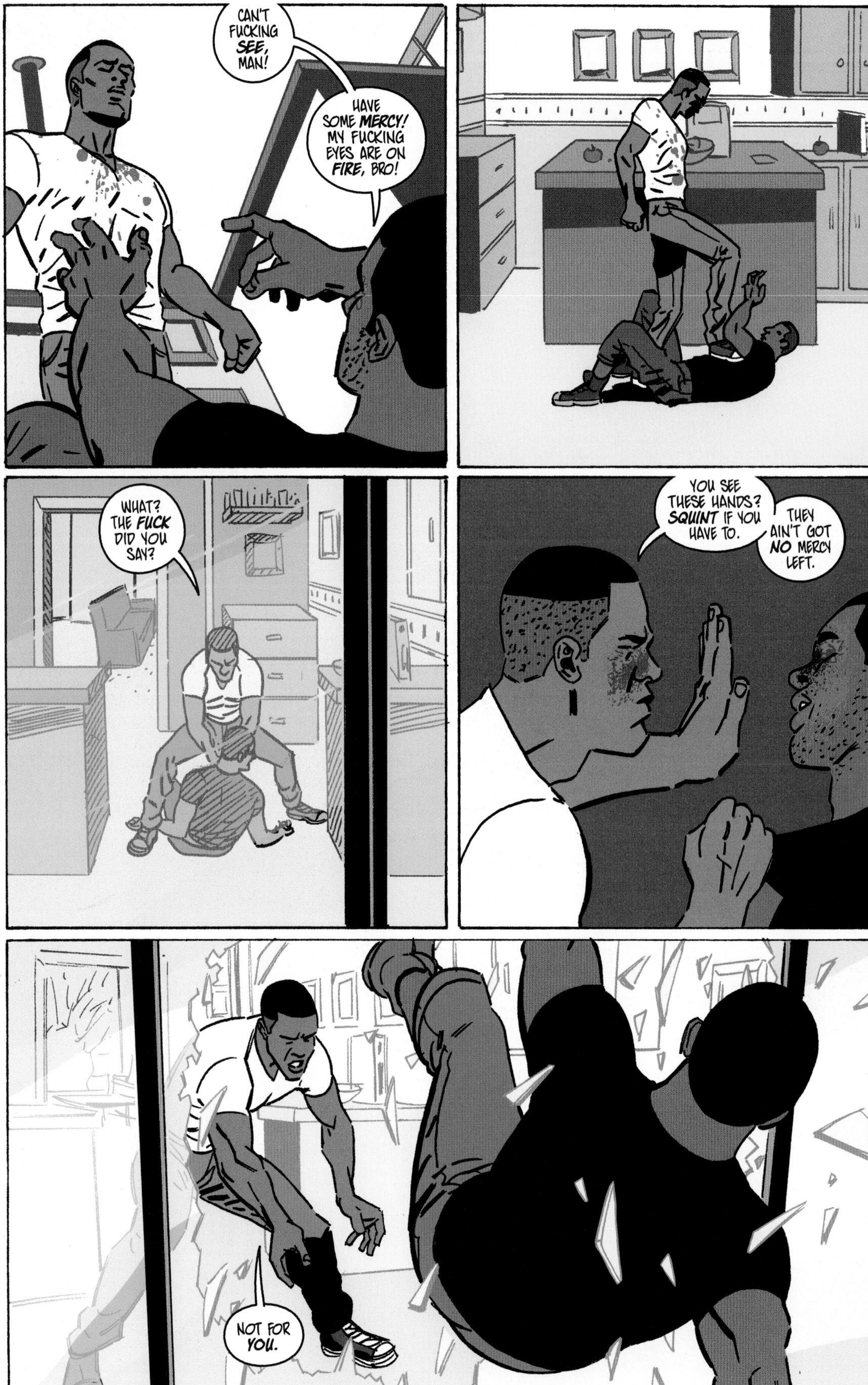
CAN'T FUCKING SEE, MAN!
HAVE SOME MERCY! MY FUCKING EYES ARE ON FIRE, BRO!
WHAT? THE FUCK DID YOU SAY?
YOU SEE THESE HANDS? SQUINT IF YOU HAVE TO.
THEY AIN'T GOT NO MERCY LEFT.
NOT FOR YOU.

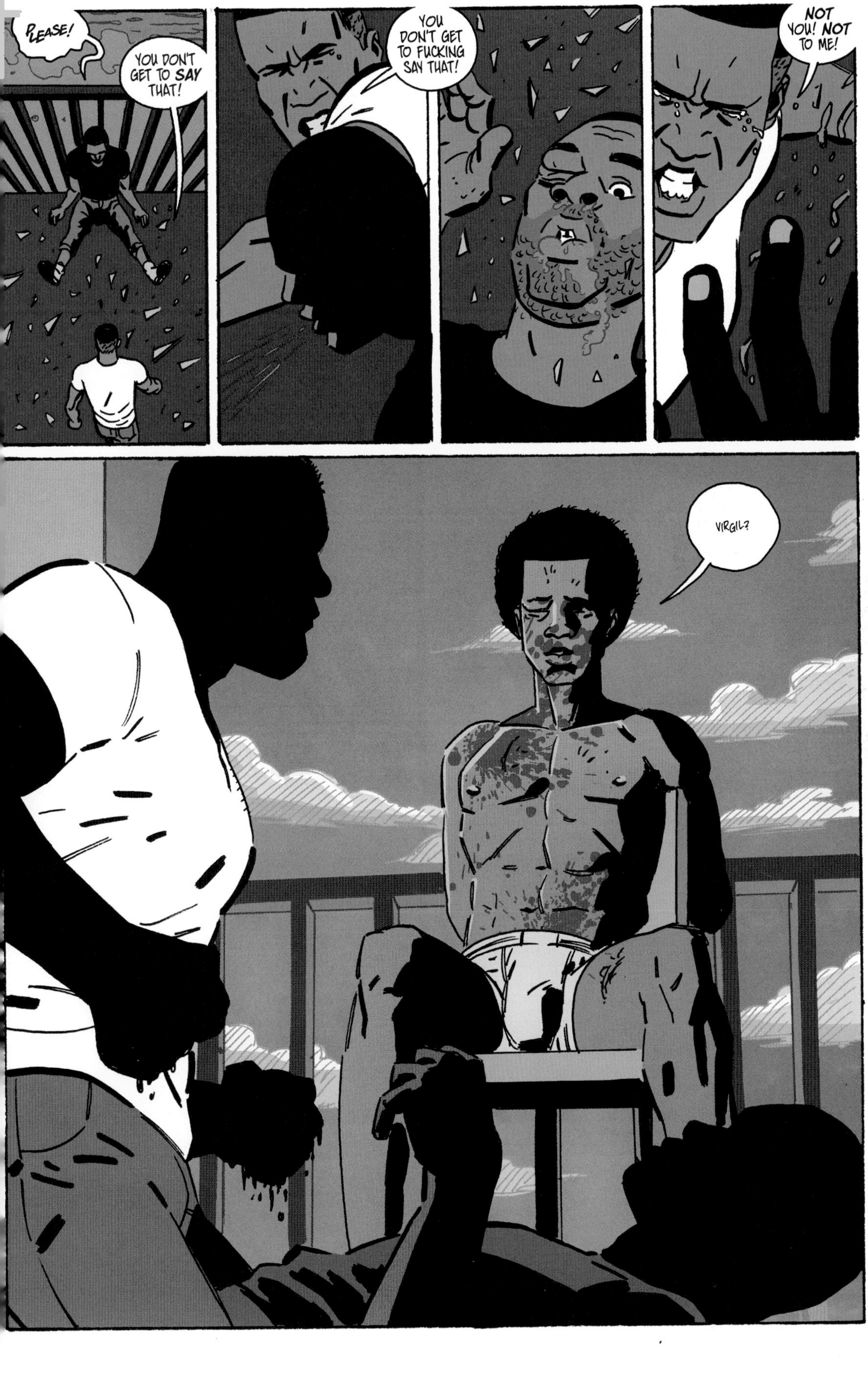
PLEASE!
YOU DON'T GET TO SAY THAT!
YOU DON'T GET TO FUCKING SAY THAT!
NOT YOU! NOT TO ME!
VIRGIL?

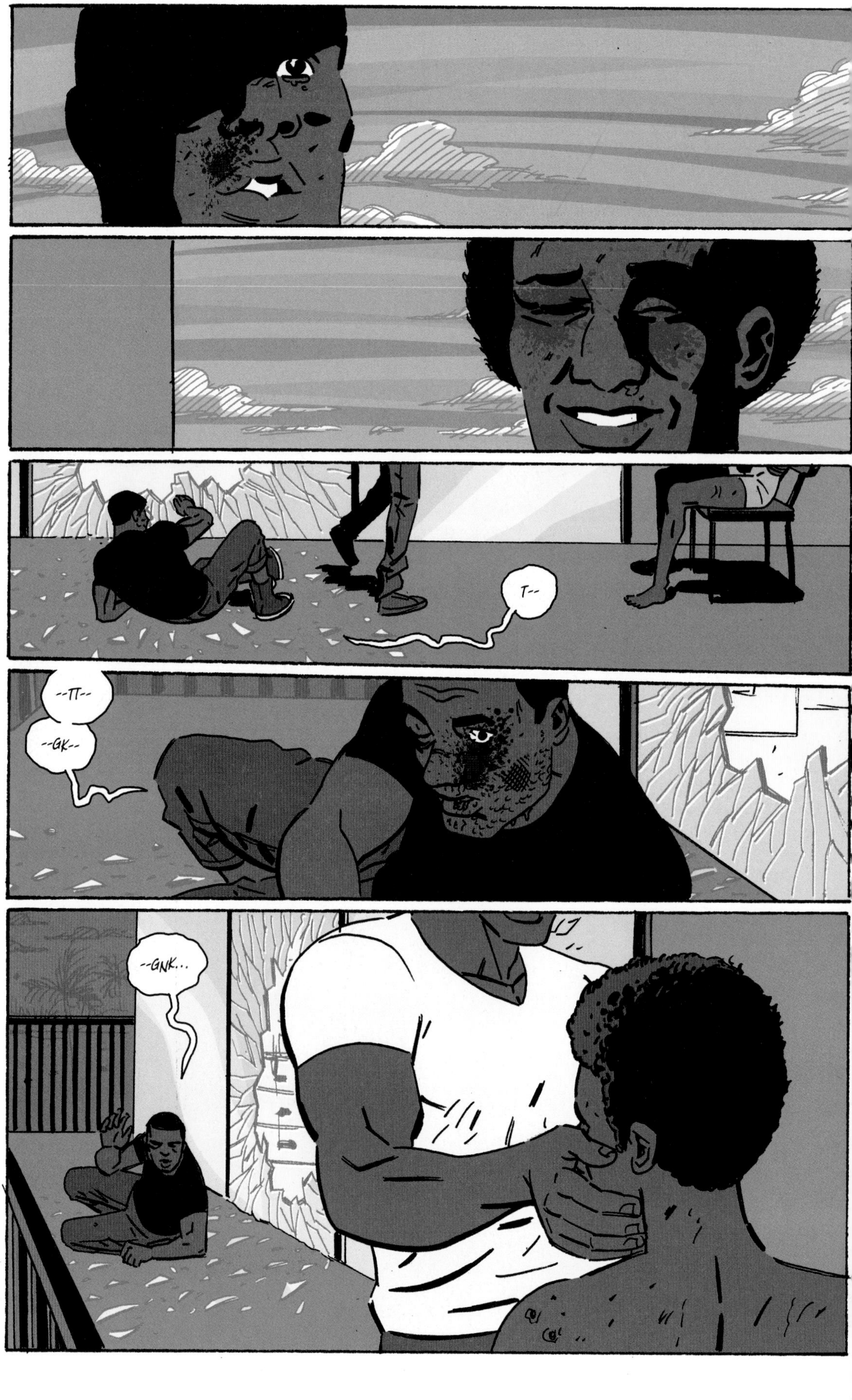
T--
--TT--
--GK--
--GNK...

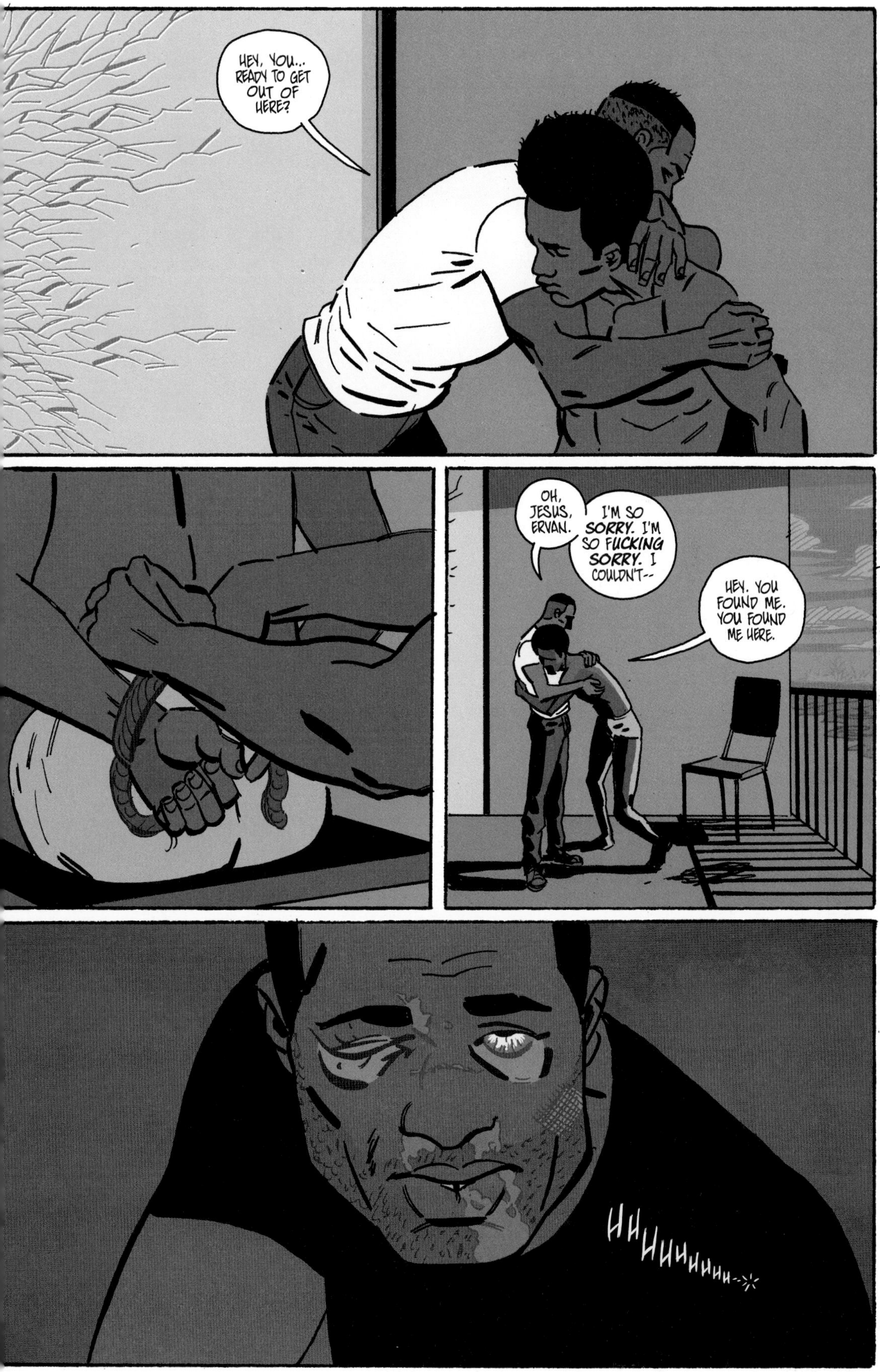
HEY, YOU... READY TO GET OUT OF HERE?
OH, JESUS, ERVAN.
I'M SO SORRY. I'M SO FUCKING SORRY. I COULDN'T--
HEY. YOU FOUND ME. YOU FOUND ME HERE.
HHHHHHHH--

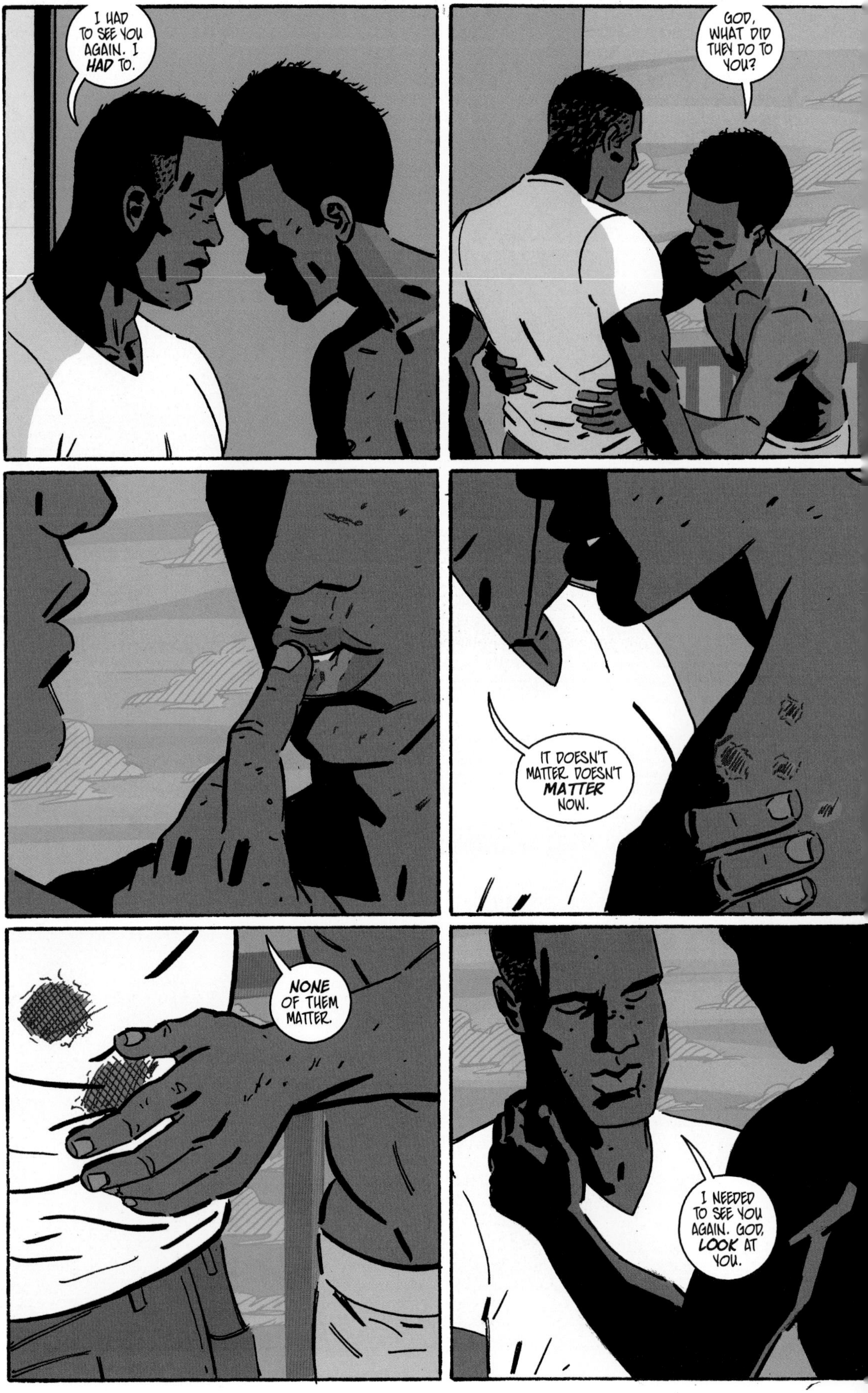
I HAD TO SEE YOU AGAIN. I HAD TO.
GOD, WHAT DID THEY DO TO YOU?
IT DOESN'T MATTER. DOESN'T MATTER NOW.
NONE OF THEM MATTER.
I NEEDED TO SEE YOU AGAIN. GOD, LOOK AT YOU.

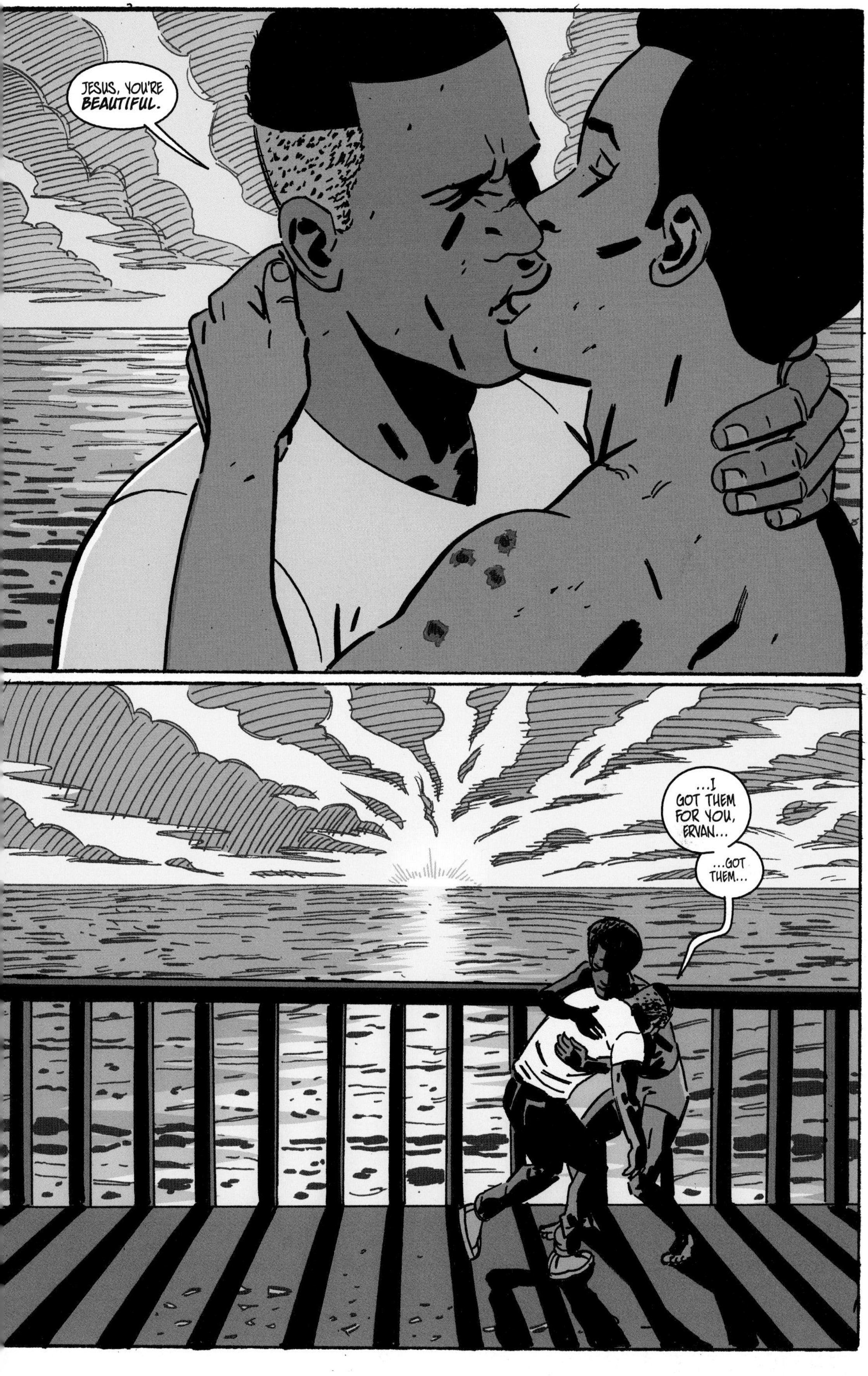
JESUS, YOU'RE BEAUTIFUL.
...I GOT THEM FOR YOU, ERVAN...
...GOT THEM...

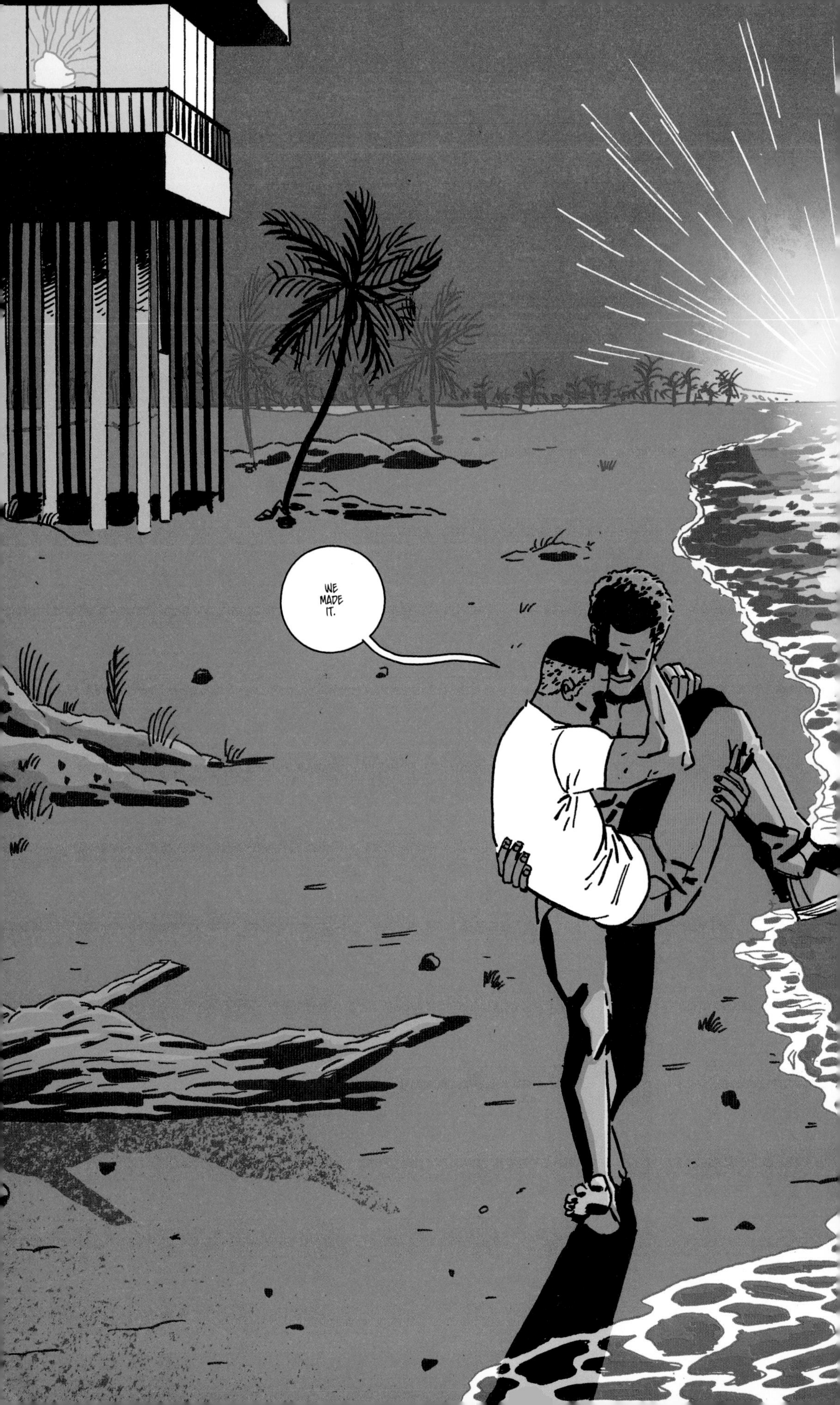
WE MADE IT.

Greetings From
Toronto

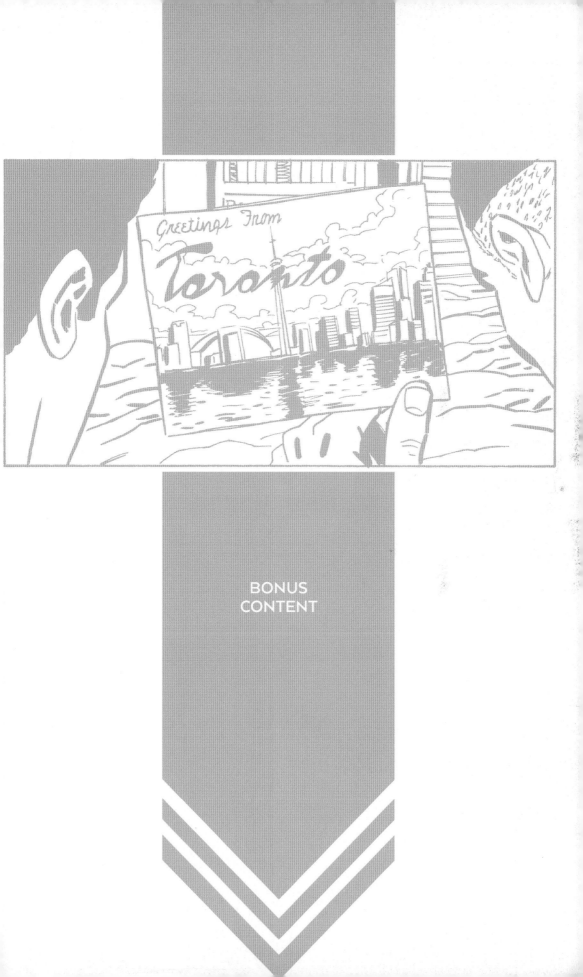

BONUS
CONTENT

TOUGH. RIGHTEOUS.

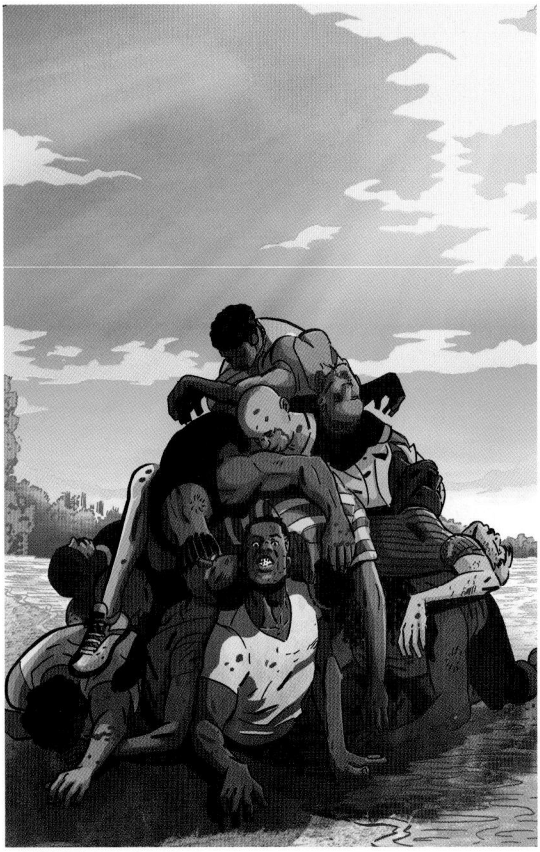

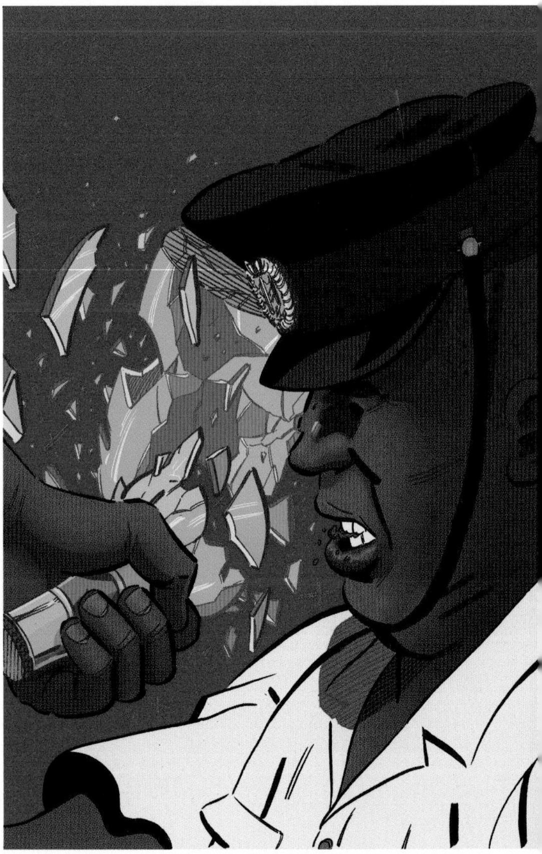

VIRGIL began with Kevin Keller from *Archie Comics.* Here was a formerly dogmatic title, infused with a confident queer character. The nonchalance of its approach was powerful. This wasn't a fetishized "issues" book, it was daring in its normalcy, unwilling to treat queerness as a taboo.

That notion fueled a growing storm, as I had been surrounding myself with exploitation cinema new and old; *Django Unchained, Cleopatra Jones, Across 110th Street.* I was hungry to create a similar narrative for the contemporary struggles of the queer community, to follow the blaxploitation tradition and create queersploitation.

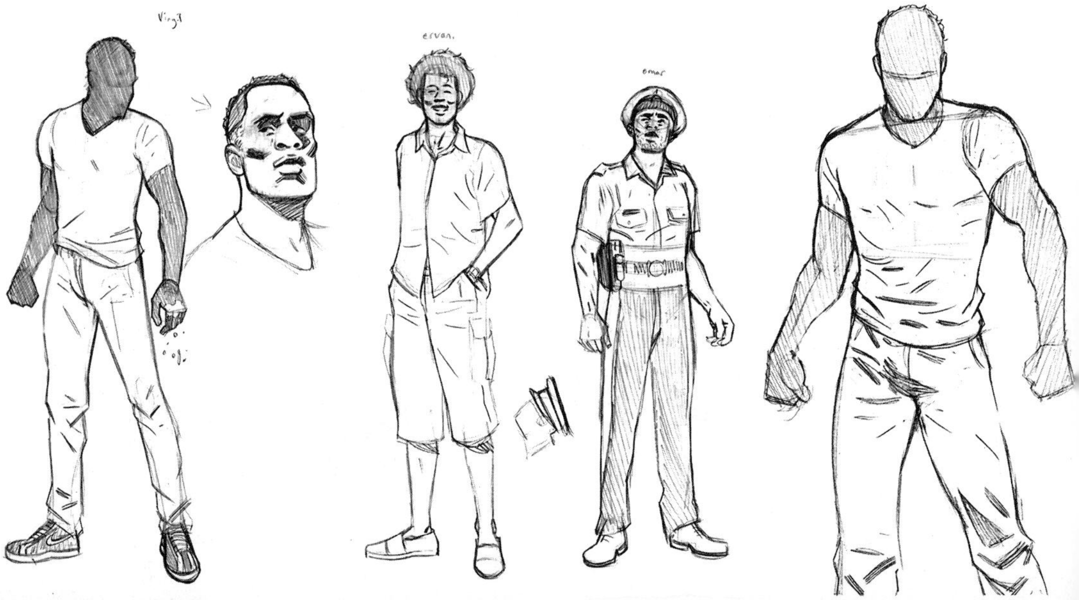

FIGHTING FOR HIS MAN.

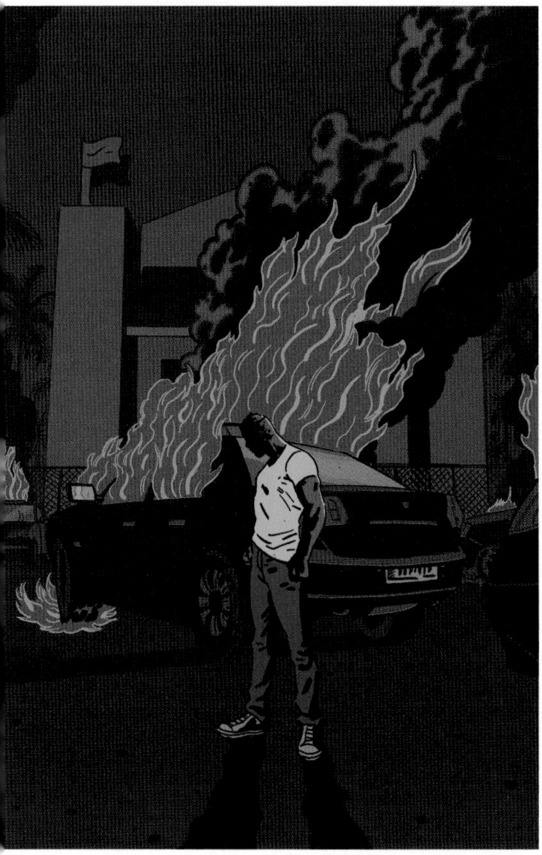

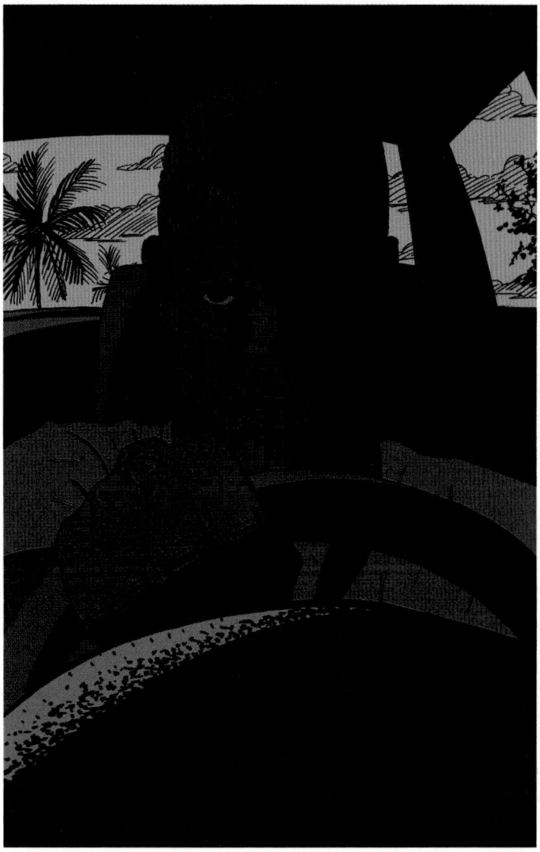

Foxy Brown showed us an assertive female hero unashamed of who she was. *VIRGIL* offers this in a gay man. A hero with the grit of John Shaft, of Jackie Brown, out for blood and fighting for his man. A hero who takes on the system, kicking against oppressors within and without. He's not perfect. But he breaks conceptions of gay masculinity, traveling a road so many do, from conflict, to anger, to acceptance, to righteous passion.

And he doesn't give a damn who gets in his way.

—Steve Orlando

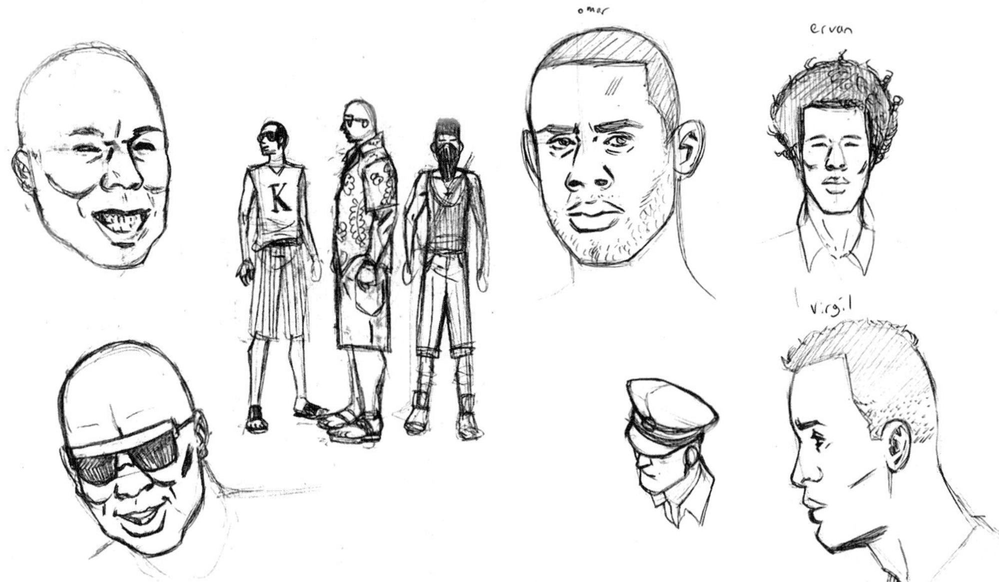

omar
ervan
K
virgil

BIOGRAPHIES

Writer STEVE ORLANDO lives in Albany, NY. He has contributed to the Eisner Award nominated *Outlaw Territory*, and with artist Artyom Trakhanov co-created the miniseries *Undertow*—both at Image Comics. He has contributed to DC Comics/Vertigo's *Mystery in Space* and *CMYK: Yellow* anthologies, and writes the ongoing *Midnighter* series for DC Entertainment. His small press work includes his own newsprint independent release *Octobriana*, and has otherwise been published by 215 Ink and Poseur Ink.

Artist J.D. FAITH is based in Portland, OR. He's drawn an installment of Ed Brisson's *Murder Book* for Dark Horse, *Just Another Sheep* for Action Lab, and an issue of *San Hannibal* for Pop! Goes The Icon. He wants a cat.

Colorist CHRIS BECKETT has worked on DC Comics' *Smallville*, BOOM!'s *Stan Lee Presents The Traveler*, and Cartoon Network's *Ben 10 & Generator Rex*. Besides coloring, Chris also edits a number of queer publications for publishers *Queer Young Cowboys* and *Greetings, From Queer Mountain*. He lives in Austin, TX with his two boyfriends and his two pups.

Letterer and designer THOMAS MAUER has worked on Harvey and Eisner Award nominated and winning titles, such as *The Guns Of Shadow Valley* and the *Outlaw Territory* and *Popgun* anthologies. Among his recent work are Image Comics' *Bang!Tango, Copperhead, Four Eyes, Rasputin,* and *Umbral* as well as Black Mask Studios' *The Disciples* and Legendary's *LL-3* for the United Nations' World Food Programme.